HORSES
in
HEAVEN

Douglas Knick

www.ten16press.com - Waukesha, WI

"*The wind of heaven is that which blows between a horse's ears.*"

Arabian Proverb

To my wife, Tammie, who offers her hand as we journey through life and steps into the saddle as we ride off into the sunset.

CHAPTER 1
JUNE 12, 1975

The moment he rambled through her line of vision he seized her attention and piqued her curiosity. The degree of distress associated with each step he took was entertaining, provocative even. If he had taken a seat on one of the blue plastic chairs she probably would have diverted her attention to another, she was a people watcher, but he continued to roam the gate terminal. Like the metal shavings from a Wooly Willy sketch pad dragged by the magnetized wand, she tracked his every move. As a professional people watcher she mastered the skill of surveillance without detection but, unwitting, her gaze lingered longer than she realized, which by social standards fit the definition of staring. As his eyes joined with hers she shook her head ever so slightly, unrecognizable to others and probably even to him, but sufficient to restore her level of decorum connected with people watching.

With his backside towards her and the distance between them expanding, she broke another cardinal rule of people watching, she questioned. She pondered if their moment of optical bonding actually registered for him. A single question quickly exploded into a host of other questions. Why should that matter? Why should she care if he bonded with her? She was, after all, simply using him for her entertainment, a means of passing time. A second subtle shake of her head yielded no greater clarity than the first.

The arrival of flight 427 from Dallas at gate 11 intensified the congestion in the terminal as passengers deplaned and loved ones impatiently pressed forward to get a first glimpse. By the time she aligned her eyes to contend with the increased number of bodies pressing tightly against one another he had disappeared from her line of sight. The crack in the plastic seat pinched her bottom as she shifted her weight left and right in an effort to scan the crowd thoroughly. The additional movement and even irritation to her backside was to no avail. Positioning her butt in the center of the seat to avoid any further discomfort she concluded that he was probably among those meeting a passenger from the Dallas flight and under the camouflage of the crowd she missed his departure from the gate area.

As the concourse cleared of Dallas passengers she surveyed the bodies that remained at gate 11 and at her gate, gate 12, where passengers would eventually board a flight for Seattle. She was into her third hour of a five-hour layover in Denver; one can't be picky when booking a flight at the last minute. It had been a long, taxing day and it was far from completion. The distraction of watching people, the more eccentric the better, aided in the passing of time.

She had crawled out of bed in the darkness of 4am leaving her husband undisturbed. The previous four hours in bed had not been restful as her mind refused to stop replaying the phone call from earlier in the evening. Compounding her inability to reach REM was her refusal to set the alarm on their newly purchased digital clock radio. Consequently, every twenty minutes she forced her eyes open to read the green numbers for fear she would over sleep. While showering and dressing in the dark she stubbed a toe that still throbbed eight hours later. Before she left the comforts of her suburban home to make the hour-plus commute to the Atlanta airport, she whispered a sweet "I love you" to her husband and carefully opened both her children's bedroom doors in order to blow them a kiss. At ages 10 and 8 she knew the kids would miss her even though her son, Scott, would never admit to such a thing publicly. Emily, on the other hand, who was never far from her "apron string" could possibly benefit from the separation.

She needed someone whom she could monitor for the next hour in order to blanket the chaos that awaited her arrival in Seattle. At the far end of gate 12 two bodies entwined and became one. Their affection caused the elderly woman seated next to her to comment how such a public display was disgusting. Upon examination she couldn't determine if there were two bodies or simply one deformed individual. Slight movement from the smaller of the two figures brought clarity. A jumpsuit-clad hippy, probably a commune living woman, was breastfeeding her child. The young mother made no effort to hide her left breast that was supplying the infant with nourishment and comfort. Unlike the woman next to her who did not attempt to conceal her disgust, she carefully crafted each passing glance. Scanning the pair for a fourth time, she saw how the infant kneed the fleshy breast to ensure consistent flow of milk. Even though it had been seven years since she experienced such intimacy with her daughter she felt a surge of warmth spreading across her chest. Wearing a smile of approval and understanding she no longer felt the need to disguise her gaze. She decided that if the mother looked up she would nod approval and motherhood would bond the two for a moment in time. She also decided that if the white haired woman next to her uttered another judgmental remark she would respond, "You need to be a mother to understand."

With the elderly woman once again more interested in wrapping the purple yarn around her knitting needle, solitude engulfed her space and secretly she bonded with the hippy mother whose only concern was nurturing her baby. When the infant was effortlessly shifted to the mother's right side she allowed herself to follow the flow of movement and not become embarrassed when the woman's nipple was momentarily exposed before disappearing in the baby's mouth. When her vision finally left the baby's head and floated upward over the mother's shoulder something, or someone, snagged her attention. It had to be someone since the object continued to move closer, but even then it, he or she, was forty maybe even fifty yards away.

At thirty yards there was no mistaking who seized her attention a second time. He lumbered with every step he took as he moved away from the restroom and back to the gate. He had not departed from the terminal after all but merely left to use the bathroom. Unfortunately for him an empty bladder did little to alleviate the tension that riddled his form.

She had never personally experienced walking in a blizzard but she had seen pictures and his walk, rigid, stiff, inflexible with shoulders rolled in towards his chest, made him appear as though he was moving into the head winds of a raging blizzard.

Passing directly in front of her, nearly stepping on her toes, she noticed the fancy cowboy boots. The two-tone boots had two and a half, possibly even three inch, heels and she wondered if the height of his footwear had something to do with his less than graceful movement. She had watched The Duke, John Wayne, in plenty of westerns and remembered that he too sort of lumbered and waddled with each step. The return passage revealed that his boots, unlike the current popular style, were not square toed, but narrow and pointy. Perhaps the combination of higher heels and narrow toes made his walk unnatural. Therefore, even though she was glad for his return to the gate area she wished he would take a seat and rest. As someone who experienced tension headaches she surmised that with his shoulders arching forward his neck must be screaming out beneath the stabbing pain.

Fixated on the blood that pulsed through the arteries of his swollen temples, she did not mentally process that on his third trip into her territory he stopped and leaned against the round pillar and looked directly at her. When her mind finally took control of her eyes she was caught staring a second time. Rather than being humiliated she was angry with herself that she permitted herself to be exposed as one who violated another person's personal space by watching.

Over the years of people watching she observed people performing private acts in public. The sharing of an intimate moment such as a kiss, or the causal brush across another's privates. The not so causal squeeze of the privates, or the other extreme of a bodily function; the picking of one's nose, adjusting the elastic band of underwear pinching or crawling into spaces not meant for elastic, a bra strap needing to be moved as it dug into the shoulder, or the best one of all, a roll onto one butt cheek in order to pass gas. Now she had become the object of other's eyes. And for that, she was angry. Or was she?

She diverted her eyes only after permitting herself a long lingering gaze. Long in that she searched the soul behind his eyes for four, maybe five seconds. She then nodded slightly, offered a smile, and quickly lowered her head as though turning her attention to the paperback book on her lap. The true motivation for not waiting for a response was driven by fear that her gesture of friendliness may not be reciprocated.

Monitoring his presence she noted the instant his foot moved from the pillar. In response she elevated her eyes while keeping her head down. She wanted, no, she needed to keep track of his whereabouts. This was so uncharacteristic of her, she found herself behaving and feeling like an adolescent schoolgirl. But she really didn't care at that moment for there was something about this gentleman that drew her to him. As she labored to put words to her feelings she heard the announcement, "Passengers flying to Seattle, we will begin boarding in five minutes starting with passengers holding first class tickets."

Moving with the crowd towards the entrance to the jetway, she started to sweat. *"Gentleman? What was I thinking? Why did I refer to him as a gentleman? What was it about this guy that was so magnetic? Was it his unusual behavior?"* It had to be, she told herself because it wasn't his physical appearance; he was average at best. Other than the sleeves of his shirt being filled to capacity and the gap that appeared between the second and third button, the direct result of the fabric being stretched tight, he was just another muscular guy. A guy she convinced herself she would forget about once they were airborne.

CHAPTER 2

The last thing he wanted was to book a flight that required a layover or, even worse yet, demanded changing planes, but when making arrangements at the figurative eleventh hour one did not have many options. The woman at the travel agency was extremely patient and tried every option available, or so she said. She continued to remind him that at this late date, one day prior to departure, he was lucky to even secure a seat. She ended the conversation with, "This is the last available seat on any airline leaving Minneapolis-St. Paul International Airport for your point of destination."

The early June storm created an unstable weather pattern across the central plains that made the flight from Minneapolis to Denver rougher than normal. Being squished between two oversized women, who apparently had decided that bathing was a male conspiracy concocted to manipulate females into conforming to macho expectations, was exasperated as the plane struck a turbulent pocket and dropped several feet causing the women's flabby arms to leave their sides and emit a nauseous odor. The combination of the overweight women, the seat being too small, the seatbelt light never extinguishing so he could use the restroom, his seat rocketing forward each time the toddler behind him kicked his seat, and a stewardess who spilled coffee on his thigh and refused to get him a pillow tested his patience and his ability to empathize. The triple bounce of the tires on the tarmac upon landing was the exclamation point to a horrible flight. With the seatbelt light finally turned off he meticulously elevated his body from the seat, as though he was an Olympic weightlifter driving upward from a squatting position until the weight of reality, an hour layover in a smoked filled terminal followed by a three hour plane flight, nearly hammered him back down.

An airline attendant with big, soft, loose curls, a wannabe fashion statement replicating Olivia Newton-John from *Grease*, stood at the terminal door armed with a clipboard to assist in directing passengers to connecting flights. Her slender fingers swayed from one edge of the clipboard to the other as they progressed down the page to locate his connecting flight number. When the motion finally ceased with less than a quarter of the page remaining she looked up flashing her pearly whites and said, "Good news, your gate is on this concourse only four gates down."

Any other trip, that would have been welcomed news, but today, standing erect and moving was less taxing than sitting. He secretly hoped the flight to Seattle would depart from the other side of the terminal. What he required even more than the number of his gate was a restroom. Unfortunately, before he could ask the attendant for directions to the closest restroom he was forced away from her by his two seat mates who feared their legs would never carry them with speed and agility if they needed to crisscross the terminal.

In a laborious effort to located the restroom to empty his bursting bladder, he wandered the concourse the better part of ten minutes before recognizing that he had passed the same seats several times. His sixth sense alerted him that he was being watched. An additional pass solely for the purpose of confirming his suspicion narrowed his focus to an elderly woman unconsciously pulling long strands of purple yarn from a small knitting basket and an attractive woman seated at her elbow. His next lap confirmed that his every step was under scrutiny and the culprit was the sensual woman. Even though he was literally about to feel a warm flow of liquid down his leg if he didn't get to the restroom, his boots didn't move. It was as if they were anchored to the carpet. He couldn't help but stare at her lovely facial features. A slight toss of her head enabled the light to capture the streaks of frosting layered perfectly through her brunette hair. He aspired to inquire if she was a Clairol model, but the pressure of pee had reached the tip of release plus, even if he attempted to speak his words would have been drowned by the intercom announcing the arrival of flight 427 from Dallas.

Returning from having bonded with the porcelain urinal, pleased with himself that his briefs were dry, he set out to investigate why such an attractive woman monitored his movement. He assumed that her presence in the airport was not for the purpose of meeting someone arriving from Dallas. Moving down the long corridor toward the assigned gate, he passed a large advertisement screen where he caught a side glimpse of himself. The shadow in the glass startled him to the point where he stopped and turned to face himself. He realized for the first time that he probably appeared comical and quite possibly even threatening, as though suffering the affects of alcohol or an overdose of drugs. Sadly, he convinced himself, the best scenario would be if people simply assumed some debilitating disease plagued him. Since his movement was stilted and rough it wasn't difficult to reach such a conclusion. With his shoulders cast forward to propel the rest of his body, each step became a clumsy hobble with a momentary pause to expel a bit of air as though releasing the sharp stabbing pain.

Once the majority of the passengers from flight 427 vacated gates 11 and 12, he took a quick survey of the landscape to determine if she was still seated in the gate area. Her presence next to the elderly woman still pulling strands of purple yarn increased the speed of his footwork, which was pure foolishness for it resulted in a spike of pain. Numbness like tentacles from a flooded river shot down both legs. To keep from dropping to the floor he reached for the nearest thing to stabilize himself. His right palm felt the coldness of a pillar and he knew he would regain control of his body before ending up on the floor like a toddler in the early stages of walking.

With his boots a foot away from the base of the pillar he carefully stabilized his torso against it and proceeded to move milliliters at a time in order to locate the position that decreased the pain. As feeling began to warm his legs he glanced up to discover that he was eye to eye with her and, strangely, there was a warming in his eyes. He allowed himself to search her eyes longer than permissible for a stranger. The corners of her eyes rose slightly and he realized she was smiling. Without moving his head his eyes meandered down the sides of her nose and, as he came to her soft full lips, her smile took his breath away. By the time he recovered from gasping for air she had tilted her head down and her hair covered her graceful face.

Without moving from the pillar he could feel the soft texture of hair as he imagined himself combing his fingers through it. He knew he had a preoccupation with hair, the longer the better. He came by it quite naturally through all the time his fingers worked the mane and hide of a horse. He didn't share this with others because, well, they would never understand how his love for the horse translated into his love for life itself. It was also his love for the horse that was the cause of his current pain.

A middle-aged woman, who had recently purchased a horse with the guarantee that the mare was dead broke, had delivered the horse to his farm a week earlier. The phrase *dead broke*, always made him laugh, as the only dead broke horse was a dead horse. Unfortunately for this woman, she purchased the horse at an auction and there was little chance of tracking down the previous owner to collect on the guarantee. Even though he had five other horses in varying stages of learning, he agreed to spend time with the creature in an attempt to discover the source of her disruptive (bucking) behavior. If the cause were something other than physical, other than lameness, an alignment issue, or tack that didn't fit properly, he would work with the horse to help her solve the problem and in the process increase her level of confidence.

The first three days on the bay colored mare went smoothly. Every ride was calm and the horse performed every task requested to perfection. It was on the fourth day, as he introduced a new environment, that the mare exploded. Fifteen minutes into a trail ride and she bolted at a full pace gallop, when he brought her down from the headlong race she started bucking. Her leaps would have qualified her for Oklahoma City and the finals of the National Rodeo. Still unable to cast her rider from her back she spun right and headed for the closest and lowest branch that would just clear her back. Five minutes later, staring up at stars in the light of day, his brain throbbed against the lining of his skull. The stinging pain on the base of his rib cage originated from the bark of a tree limb that stood firm and left deep scratches oozing with a mixture of blood and clear fluid. Lifting his right arm while remaining flat on his back to check out the damage to his chest produced a pain far greater than either in his head or chest. The slightest twist of his torso drove what felt like a railroad spike into his lower back. Raising his head slowly to avoid passing out from the combined pain of his head, chest and back he noticed that the bay mare stood three feet beyond his boots. Hoping she wasn't too spooked he called out for her to come closer. With her head held low she cautiously worked her way closer until she stood beside him. Grabbing a firm hand full of her long black tail he weaved his fingers between the strands so as not to lose his grip. As he began to pull the mare slowly moved forward and hoisted him up. With his right hand still buried in her tail the mare pulled him on an hour long journey back to the barn.

Five days since such a disastrous fall was hardly adequate time to heal. At least he could put one foot in front of the other without being pulled and, from time to time he was able to situate his body in a way that lessened the pain. The pillar was providing such a moment of relief. Even though she was no longer sharing the moment with him, he returned her smile and tipped the brim of his cowboy hat, as any gentleman would do when acknowledging another. Allowing the hat to ride low covering his eyes he pushed himself away from the pillar. Less than fifteen feet from her the intercom interrupted his thoughts, "Passengers flying to Seattle, we will begin boarding in five minutes starting with passengers holding first class tickets."

CHAPTER 3

"We will now begin boarding coach. Rows five through twelve may board."

The mob approaching the door and ticket attendant certainly appeared to be greater than the 48 people with tickets for rows five through twelve. Unlike the predawn flight from Atlanta that had nearly every B and E seat empty she feared that the 727 Airliner would be filled to capacity. She never could quite figure out what the rush was to get on the plane, getting off was another issue entirely. It wasn't like they would run out of seats, if one possessed a ticket one owned a seat on the plane. Rather than joining the throng of people waiting to board, she assisted the elderly woman next to her scoop up her belongings.

Quite unpredictably her row was summoned to board the plane. Rather than continuing to load from the front to the back of the plane, the attendant with the handheld microphone invited people seated in rows twenty to twenty-eight to proceed to the plane. The elderly woman thanked her for assisting in the collection of her knitting tools and said she would stay put since holding a ticket for row thirteen she apparently would be among the last to load.

While collecting her belongings and speaking words of comfort to the elderly woman who had never flown, she secretly scrutinized the mob, similar to a witness viewing a police lineup, to determine if he was amongst them. Her analysis generated the conclusion that he was not among those who pressed forward to board the plane before their row was called. And although she had told herself that once the plane was in the air she would forget about him, she was still attached to the earth so as she moved toward the door she surveyed the terminal one last time to determine if he was still lumbering about. Again her efforts to locate him yielded nothing.

Moving down the aisle in a traffic jam stop and go motion she had plenty of time to examine the faces seated from first class through row twelve and then those who sprinkled the seats between rows thirteen and nineteen, and finally those seated in the last rows of the plane before the restrooms. If an individual's face was not immediately visible, as the person was folded over to stow an item under the seat, she paused momentarily until the party returned to the proper sitting position. No one came close to possessing the same intriguing persona.

The bold print on her ticket stub read, **ROW 27 SEAT A**. She didn't have a lot of options for seat selection when booking the flight on such short notice. Late in the afternoon when King County Human Services called and reported that her brother was living on the streets she knew she needed to leave immediately. The noise and vibrations were greater at the rear of the plane but she was thankful that she had been able to select a window seat. The location was not necessarily for the view, she usually pulled the shade, but from pervious experiences of flying alone she wanted to be able to seclude herself by curling up against the wall of the plane. It enabled her to shut out everyone and everything, which was the plan once the plane stabilized at 30,000 feet.

Buried in the book resting on her lap and feeling the breeze jettisoning from the air nasal overhead she slowly lowered her shoulders and relaxed. Enjoying the sweet refreshing flavor of a mint in preparation for takeoff the words on the page blurred and she smiled reflecting on how the fetish of watching people yet again served her well. The five plus hours of being stuck in an airport evaporated more quickly than she could have predicted. As she adjusted her eyes to find where she left off on the page a shadow darkened the right upper corner of her book. Not wanting to call attention to herself, she traced the darkness of the shadow without moving her head and immediately recognized the source. She recognized the belt buckle, specifically, the 3D image of a horse. She didn't need to elevate her head to know who held the ticket for row 27, seat B.

The gentleman clad in an expensive, tailored business suit, renting the seat on the aisle, stood begrudgingly mumbling something under his breath about hating people who couldn't follow directions and load in the proper sequence. Graciously thanking the man in seat C for making his entrance into the row less cumbersome he, the gentleman she admired in the terminal, quickly stored an item beneath the seat in front of him and wrestled to find both ends of his seatbelt. Once both men were seated, he straightened his cowboy hat so it still rode low on his forehead and he spoke of the elderly woman near the front of the plane who at that moment was still struggling to make her way between the narrow space provided to reach seat F. He spoke of how she stumbled with her bag in hand as she moved toward the ticket counter and was not only weak in walking, but visibly displayed signs of fear. With a small smile, maybe more of a smirk, he described her condition as if he was an insightful shrink. She didn't just need someone to carry her stuff, she needed someone to carry her emotional baggage and tell her it was okay to be afraid. Decisively moving the brim of the hat towards the aisle he added, "Sometimes there are things more important than following directions."

She had to work to keep her mouth from dropping open or from bursting forth in laughter. In that moment she knew her radar was correct again. She had honed in on him and locked in in order to inspect the unique and intriguing gentleman. He was filled with complexities and oddities that were a contradiction, but with him only increased his attractiveness and desirability.

Listening to him speak for the first time, there was softness to his pitch and a level of perfection as he enunciated each word with precision. His manner of speech, the words he employed fit the stereotype of an educated person, but the image of his movement and his selection of clothing challenged such a definition. The intensity of his speech never wavered from when he spoke of the elderly woman to when he ripped the business aristocrat in half. His body did not display signs of tension related to the words he offered, but there were indications of pain and discomfort. She wanted to hear his voice again, but she also didn't want to call attention to herself. She wondered if he recognized her.

Directing his attention away from the center aisle, the brim of his hat did not stop until it was slightly past the center of his seat. He wasn't looking directly at her yet he was clearly acknowledging her presence as he tugged ever so lightly on the brim of his hat. He carefully, as though each inch of his torso's movement was scripted, leaned back until he touched the leather of the seat. The movement ceased, he expelled air, and then his boots became visible as he pushed first one leg and then the other away from his seat. By the time the plane rolled back from the terminal and the enormous wheels rotated towards the assigned runway for take-off, his breath was shallow and consistent. She had the urge to sneak a peek to see if his eyes were shut but she was too afraid to add to the number of times he caught her watching him.

As the plane left the tarmac and the nose tilted from a thirty-degree angle to a forty, and eventually, a sixty, the force inside the plane pushed the bodies back into the seats. Somewhere between forty-five and fifty degrees his hand clinched her right forearm as he grimaced in pain. As quickly as he latched on he removed his hand and with a rigid jawline he apologized, "I am so sorry. Please, accept my apology."

"No." was the only word to trickle out until she got ahold of herself. Then she could continue, but only in a whisper as though she didn't want anyone to interrupt the moment, "Really, that's okay."

Again the adolescent feelings of giddiness, of being overwhelmed, radiated through every organ in her body. She was speechless, her heart was racing, her vision lacked clarity, tiny beads of sweat bubbled forth from her skin. There were other parts of her body that were flushed with warmth as blood rushed to fill the capillaries and engorged her feminine physique, but she wouldn't allow herself to acknowledge the sensual side of her body. Even though his hand had been removed her skin offered a reminder of his touch and she could feel the weight, the warmth, and the strength of his grip. She wouldn't be surprised if he had the power to snap her arm with his clinch. But, her emotions were not being driven by fear. She was not scared of him, she was attracted to him. *ATTRACTED*? The word swirled in the cortex of her brain. She wanted to pull the blanket over her head and sort out these feelings, this notion of attraction, but she also desired to learn the reason behind his touch.

Pulling her right leg up and tucking the toe of her shoe behind the knee of her left leg she shifted her position in order to face him directly. In the voice she used to probe and comfort her children when they tumbled from their bikes or were rejected by their best friend, she asked him, "Are you alright?"

Rather than simply turning his head to reply, he brought his shoulder to the center of his body in a crude manner, like Frankenstein's creation, and he offered a response. She didn't hear, or rather, she didn't comprehend a single word for she was mesmerized, yet again, by the intensity of his gaze. My God, she had never felt anything like this before. Was he human? Was he some sort of hypnotist and had he put her under a spell? In the silence that followed she realized that it was her turn to speak. Not having any idea what he said she needed him to repeat his answer. "I'm sorry, it's so loud back here, could you repeat that?"

"The force of the takeoff jolted me against the seat and irritated a nerve. Again, I am sorry for grabbing your arm. I just instinctively reached out and grabbed for the first stable thing."

Displaying her best flirtatious smile she answered, "You can grab on anytime you need." With a brief nod that moved his hat up and down she decided to continue the conversation so as not to lose his attention. "Do you mind if I ask the source of your discomfort? I'm not trying to be nosy or anything, I'm just curious. My best friend is a massage therapist and so I have heard many stories about pain." As she spoke her brain kept telling her to shut up but her mouth apparently refused to obey. Finally she found herself apologizing to him. "I am so sorry, the last thing you probably need is someone talking your ear off."

"No, actually the conversation is a good distraction."

She couldn't resist the playful opportunity presented to expose the double meaning behind his comment. "So, my conversation is a distraction, ha?"

"No, no, that's not what…"

Before he could complete the sentence she cut him off as she waved her hand. "I know, I'm just play'n with you."

"Oh…yeah" accompanied a half-hearted laugh, which produced a winch of pain the severity of which was confirmed by his eyes pressed shut for a few seconds.

Reaching out, this time she placed her hand on his arm. She wanted to express empathy and acknowledge the degree of his pain. "You really are in tough shape. You sure you are going to be ok?"

"Yeah. Actually, it's getting better." With her professionally polished finger nails blending into the fabric of his plaid western shirt his gaze lingered before returning his eyes to her face.

"If this is better I can't imagine what it must have been like before." When he didn't respond to her comment she gathered that the extended interlude of silence didn't bother him as he methodically examined every feature of her face.

The intensity of having him carefully peruse every inch of her face, including every pore, every scar, every blemish produced a raging inferno inside but she was not about to interrupt the moment. When he reached the tip of her chin he started to speak even though their eyes had not yet met. "I was serious, the conversation is a practical form of distracting my mind from the pain. Please tell me about the book you are reading. If you don't mind."

She paused to carefully select her words. She removed her hand from his arm and, grazing it across the yellow dust jacket, she concluded that the lead character, Bob Slocum, in the pages of the novel, had been replaced by a character his polar opposite. "Are you familiar with Joseph Heller's first work, *Catch-22*?" Chastising herself for such a stupid question she quickly moved forward without allowing him to answer. "Well, this is his second book, *Something Happened.*" That sentence made about as much sense as the first, he could read the bold black print on the cover. Her mind raced to offer up a pithy, intelligent comment. "The book was released less than a year ago and already it is streaking up the best seller's list. Critics have suggested that this is a masterpiece twelve years in the making. Can you imagine spending twelve years on writing a book? I suppose there are those who turn out low level thinking, quick read books every six months and then those who only write one or two books their entire career, but are hailed as sages for the ages." The inanity of that phrase caused her clammy palms to press down on the book until it restricted the flow of blood in her legs and created discomfort. She justified the discomfort as warranted based on the worthless conversation she offered. "Here I go again, doing all the talking. I'll stop now if you promise to say something."

If only her mouth would listen, just once, to her mind. She was, after all, a very intelligent woman who graduated Summa Cum Laude from a very highly respected University in the south. She studied literature and science, gravitated to the nursing program and even published a handful of articles with a college professor, but at that moment she sounded anything but smart. What made matters worse was that she seldom behaved in this matter. In many circles she intimidated men because of how she carried herself and could entertain any topic with confidence. Trapped in the second row from the bathrooms she concluded that every word spoken should be flushed as she merely babbled.

Graciously ignoring the majority of what she said, she heard him comment, "Yes, I read that Heller had released his second book, but I have not had time to pick it up. Is this book also a satirical analysis of some event or component of life?"

"Let me read you the blurb from the back of the book." That had to be easy. How could she mess that up? All she needed to do was read. With her professionally trained voice she read each word with clarity:

Bob Slocum was living the American dream. He had a beautiful wife, three lovely children, a nice house...and all the mistresses he desired. He had it all -- all, that is, but happiness. Slocum was discontent. Inevitably, inexorably, his discontent deteriorated into desolation until...something happened.

As she read the words slowly so as not to rush he closed his eyes and absorbed not only the word but also her voice. He sat motionless, undisturbed when she finished reading. She wondered if he had fallen asleep, but that was hardly possible, she only read a few sentences.

"You are lovely." He delivered the words with his eyes still shut.

"What?" She questioned if she heard him correctly. There was no context for the words he spoke. She was sure she had not heard him correctly.

Opening his eyes as though startled from a nightmare he stammered a reply. "I, I mean, I meant to say, 'You have a lovely voice.'"

"Thank you. When I first entered college my major was theater, drama, acting, you know. I thought I was going to be the next Julie Andrews on Broadway. So in addition to acting classes I loaded my course schedule with speech and voice classes. After the first year I discovered that my passion was less with the performance end of theater and more with the text. So when I returned to campus in the fall of my sophomore year I drifted over to the English department and found a home in literature classes, until my junior year when Chemistry captured my heart." She wasn't sure why she rattled on other than to avoid determining if he was telling the truth but she knew she was not ready to pursue his initial comment, flattering though it was.

"So, the book is a satirical look at the American dream through the eyes of, what was his name, Bob...?"

"Slocum." Obviously he too had decided to drop any further discussion of the gaffe.

"Right, Bob Slocum."

"Based on the first third of the book I have read, yes, I would say that is the focus of the work. But what I appreciate about this work is how literally every sentence is carefully crafted. The opening pages immediately capture the reader and Heller sets the stage by toying with the book's title, *Something Happened*."

Looking directly into her eyes, after stealing a glance at his watch, he made a simple request. "Seeing that we have the better part of the flight left, would you mind reading the opening pages of the book?"

Even before she cracked the binding and read the opening words, *"I get the willies when I see closed doors,"* she sensed there was something sensual about reading to him. Listening to her own voice utter the words Heller skillfully scripted she heard the husky tone an octave lower than normal. It startled her for a moment, creating an awkward pause in the middle of a sentence. She recovered and discovered that, as she read the account of how Bob's older brother had sex on the floor of the coal shed with a girl from the neighborhood during their childhood, her voice grew sultry. The combination of her voice, Heller's words, and the man seated close to her fueled the sexual tension she felt and smelled in the air between the two of them. The words on the page, *"something happened,"* created a fantasy that something happened between the two of them on the floor of the plane. Her internal temperature bubbled up each time she lifted her eyes from the written word to see him smiling. She wondered, had he lied, did he know the opening accounts and that the scenes were filled with sex? Was he the true actor here and had he just played her? Something happened yet she wasn't sure exactly what. But, no matter what it was, she liked it, and she wanted more.

CHAPTER 4

The well-lit vending machine stood there as though it had been sent to mock him. What he needed was a water fountain, but such a device had been placed in the most inconvenient location in order to make the pop in the vending machine more appealing. Although rows twenty through twenty-eight had been summoned for boarding he needed something to wash down the muscle relaxant capsule. While the Coke in the machine right across from gate 12 would have been convenient there was no way he was about to dole out 50 cents for a can that cost 25 cents anywhere else. He knew well the principles of scarcity, the economics of supply and demand that justified the price inside the wall of the airport. He previously refused to accept the logic associated with gas rationing and driving the price of gasoline upward two years earlier, he wasn't about to conform now. The oil embargo of '73 was nothing but a well-manufactured ploy to rob the poor of their hard-earned cash.

Returning from the fountain where he swallowed a horse-sized pill, he saw that the gate area was empty except for an elderly woman and a businessman in an overly expensive suit sprinting past the woman to reach the ticket attendant. It didn't really bother him that the gate area was empty, he couldn't move any faster if he wanted to. As long as the door was open, things were fine. He had a seat reserved.

After stumbling and regaining his balance by running into an all too familiar pillar he noticed that the elderly woman had not been so fortunate in her attempt to regain her balance. When he reached her side to assist her up the attendant also arrived and together they hoisted her to her feet and then to the closest plastic seat. Even before asking if she was ok he inquired about her daughter. "Where is your daughter?"

"Daughter?" She looked confused as though she was unable to comprehend his question.

"Yes, your daughter, the attractive woman seated next to you. Did she leave you? Is she already on the plane?"

"Oh, sonny, that wasn't my daughter. Just some woman who shared space with me."

The attendant inquired about the woman's condition and readiness to continue making her way to the plane. "Do you feel up to walking? Do you think you can make it to the plane?"

"Yes, I can walk, but I don't know how I feel about getting on the plane." With each word delivered she shook her head as though saying, "No! No, I don't want to board any plane."

"Are you traveling to Seattle to visit someone?" He thought if he could remind her why she purchased a plane ticket in the first place it might persuade her to put one foot in front of the other.

"Yes, my grandson and his lovely family. Tommy and Suzy have three children. The third, Emmy Lou, named after my late husband, Louis, and of course, me, will be a month old tomorrow. They are having the baby baptized on Sunday. I don't know why they had to move so far away.

This is the first time I have not held one of my grandchildren within the first day after their birth. How is the child suppose to bond with me if I don't hold it and coddle it?"

"Sounds to me like you have plenty of reason to not be afraid of flying. You haven't held your granddaughter yet."

Leaving the elderly woman to enter her row near the front of the plane he spotted the familiar head of frosted hair. He couldn't see the person's face, the individual was crunched down in the seat and leaning against the wall of the plane. Next to her was an empty seat, or a seat holding a small child not visible from this distance. Each shuffle down the long aisle brought him closer to discovering that unless the child was a baby, the seat was open. It wasn't enough that the seat was empty, the row number and seat letter needed to match those listed on his ticket stub.

Despite his inability to hold the stub stable while he progressed toward the back of the plane, the large bold print assisted him, **Row 27 Seat B**. Confirmation of his seat assignment spread a surge of relief through his core.

When the gentleman, a term employed very loosely, seated in seat C finally, with great reluctance and mumbling into his chest, agreed to stand permitting him access to his seat, he recognized the guy as the person who was responsible for the old woman landing on the floor.

He shared the account of assisting the elderly woman with no one in particular, but with the hope that his aloof flying partner for the next several hours might recognize that his actions had consequences. When that tactic came up short of yielding the desired outcome he decided to be direct, "Sometimes there are things more important than following rules."

Turning his attention away from the aisle he reprimanded himself for allowing this guy to irritate him to the point that he totally ignored the woman who, only moments earlier, he couldn't wait to see. Since she had not witnessed the last time he acknowledged her presence he was determined to not allow a repeat performance. Without stopping to complete the mandatory tasks associated with flying he grabbed the tip of his brim and nodded slightly. He fully intended to accompany this action with words but a spasm gripped the lower region of his back the moment he opened his mouth to speak. He had done all he could do to not hurl the contents of his stomach as waves of nausea raged through his entire body. He even curled his toes inside his boot to keep himself grounded and not concede to the power boiling forth in his abdomen. "Breathe, breathe" became the mantra.

Obtaining an inner peace and relaxing to the point where the spasms ceased, he was about to open his eyes when the increased power and torque lifted the nose of the plane towards the clouds. The force thrust his body against the seat and, for few brief seconds, he viewed himself as an astronaut commanding an Apollo flight destined for the heavens. The increased pain deluded his thoughts of experiencing the pressure of 10 gs. In such a state he grabbed at the first thing his hand struck and he clamped on like a vice grip.

Feeling the soft, amble texture of skin rather than the cold metal armrest that separated passengers from one another, he released his grip and withdrew his hand. He knew he needed to apologize at once to say he didn't mean to touch her but, truthfully, he did enjoy the physical exchange. What concerned him more was that the rough, hard calluses at the base of his fingers would scratch and mar her impressionable, silk like skin.

"I am so sorry..." As he uttered the apology, within his very core of existence he set out to convince himself this was silly. He had touched the skin of countless women, both intentionally and by accident, so why was he so attune to hers? Yes, her hair was that of a model. Yes, her facial features were aligned to perfection, and yes, her eyes were simultaneously inviting and mysterious but that was no excuse for a 35-year-old college professor to behave like many of his college students pumped up on testosterone. He had a gorgeous wife whom he loved dearly and two daughters whom he would literally give his life to protect, he shouldn't have been so preoccupied with this woman nor should he have enjoyed the feel of her flesh. Just when he felt confident that he had pressed past such juvenile emotions his ears burned as her sultry voice whispered, "You can grab on anytime you need." Like a child seated on the lap of Santa Claus overwhelmed by the gracious offering to deliver anything one requested, he could only nod his head. For some unexplainable reason, what he wanted Santa to deliver was her hand. He wanted to reach out and hold her hand as he had done twenty years earlier seated in a movie theater with Betty Sue watching *Rebel Without A Cause*. It didn't get easier for him as she inquired about the intensity of his pain and her eyes wheeled empathy. She not only saw his pain, she felt it.

Was this what some referred to as a midlife crisis, unable to think clearly, unable to use logic? It surely didn't feel like a crisis and he certainly wasn't middle age, at least he hoped not. His only salvation was to occupy his mind with something other than what he labeled as adolescent infatuation. Thankfully she wasn't shy when it came to talking and, although he loved listening to her husky voice, a discussion about the book resting in her lap would force his mind to focus on the book and not on her. "I was serious, the conversation is a practical form of distracting my mind from the pain. Please tell me about the book you are reading. If you don't mind." The distraction was not only for the pain in his back but also to distract him away from the threatening word, ATTRACTION.

For a period of several minutes, it worked. He narrowed his attention to only the words she shared related to the book. The sterilized words drove him back to the academic realm and he commented, "Yes, I read that Heller had released his second book, but I have not had time to pick it up. Is this book also a satirical analysis of some event or component of life?" All was good again; order had been restored…until she offered to read the description from the back of the book.

Her delivery of the written word shifted ever so slightly into a soothing, rhythmic cadence. The pattern seduced him into a trance and before she concluded the first sentence he closed his eyes and permitted the taut lasso around his feelings to loosen until eventually he mumbled the words he had thought from the moment he first saw her, "You are lovely."

Lovely? What had he said, what had he done? No, no, he must say, "You read lovely." Scrambling to not embarrass himself any further he corrected his words, "I, I meant to say, you have a lovely voice." Yes, yes indeed that was what he meant to say. Although she seemed to accept his explanation, he could not persuade himself likewise. He meant precisely what he said. The truth was as clear as the scene outside the plane, she was lovely. She literally made him feel like a kid, like a young innocent lad unaware that love seldom arrives without strings or that love will never be as good as that which the mind conjures. She will never hear these words, because, well, because this was no longer the 60's, a time of free sexual expression. They lived in an age of respectability, of proper respect for the other. It was a time when the country witnessed President Ford stumble down the steps of Air Force One while on a trip to Austria and Time Magazine explained the mishap as the result of a bum knee rather than clumsiness.

His mind babbled on in the realm of infatuation but he needed to keep the conversation moving in the realm of reality. It was time to improvise. After offering what sounded like an intelligent comment, "So, the book is a satirical look at the American dream through the eyes of, what was his name, Bob…?" he invited her to read again. What he didn't realize was the content she was about to read.

Something happened, as the book's title suggested, when she delivered the printed word from the page to his waiting ear. The simple task of wetting her finger in preparation to turn the page mingled with the sexual episodes from the book stroked his libido. The realm of reality melted beneath the heat that fired within. Thoughts danced in his head and pounded through his body of what he desired to do *to* and *with* her. His only recourse was to smile. The smile was one of anticipation that he dreamt would be replaced by a smile of satisfaction.

CHAPTER 5

"Please return your tray to it's stowed position and bring your seat to an upright position. The pilot is making final preparations for landing. We should be on the ground in a few minutes."

The inflight announcement tattooed a sense of urgency on both of them. Yet their immediate attention was not focused on one another but on the passenger in seat C. The businessman to their right sprawled out sound asleep was quite a spectacle. In addition to the annoying gurgling sound that accompanied each expulsion of air there was a string of drool reaching from the corner of his mouth to a small pool of saliva on the lapel of his expensive suit. Papers, apparently legal documents, some bearing an official stamp, covered the plastic makeshift table while his second whiskey and soda left tiny droplets of caramel colored stains on his notepad. Without removing an eye from their fellow traveler they discussed, in hushed tones, the merits of informing him that preparation had begun for landing or allowing the stewardess to perform her duties. The consensus reached in the midst of suppressed snickers was he would awaken the moment the stewardess dumped his five-dollar drink in the garbage.

Offering her a stick of Juicy Fruit to ward off the stress of pressure in her ears a light flashed in the recesses of his thoughts like an aura before a migraine, he didn't know her name. He couldn't believe that he had spent three hours confined to this small space and never once did either of them inquire about the other's name. As he employed his tongue to roll the gum, now a pebble of wax, from one side of his mouth to the other and back again it unnerved him slightly that the topic never arose. Rather than offer an answer it was his custom to turn to questions. Why was this the case? Was it because they would never see one another again and so why bother with a name? Was it because knowing the name of the other would have no impact on the conversation that ensued? Or, was it just the opposite, by knowing the other's name it had the potential to alter the conversation that ensued? He enjoyed contemplating such scenarios under normal circumstances as he easily became bored when life was black and white. But this wasn't normal nor was there time to become lost in some philosophical inquiry.

Just as words were being formed an additional thought numbed his tongue so he couldn't speak the question, "what is your name?" What if the reason both of them engaged in playful flirtation was precisely because neither spoke their name? Knowing the other's name added another layer of intimacy. It was no longer just playfulness; it had the potential to create an air of actuality and certainty. When meeting a stranger one inquires, "What is your name?" for the purpose of moving from stranger to friend. To know another's name is to establish a certain level of connection with that person. For her to know his name or for him to know her name granted each a degree of power over the other. He was already smitten with the woman seated only inches away, hearing her name wouldn't lessen the attraction, it would only increase it, personalize it, and that was dangerous. To hear his name coming from her lips would be like going over Niagara Falls in a barrel, little chance of surviving, and little chance of him holding it together.

Before he could resolve the grayness of the matter surrounding their names, she alerted him to the stewardess' arrival with a brush of her finger to the back of his hand and then pointed to his right. Together they secretly watched the stewardess clean up after their neighbor. Disappointment struck when his drink hit the garbage bag and he never stirred. It wasn't until the stewardess carefully placed a hand on his shoulder, after speaking directly to him to wake up, that his eyes opened and he lunged forward as though being attacked from behind. Fortunately the tray was still down creating a ledge to stop his momentum forward or he may have nosedived to the floor. Unable to ignore the comical display both snickered as they inquired if he was okay. With the wave of the back of his hand he brushed his travel mates off and directed his attention to the stewardess.

By the time the gentleman reined in his anger and need for vengeance Betty, the stewardess, had completed the necessary requirements for landing. The hydraulics rumbled against the floor of the plane as the wheels dropped into position. Esme decided that the combination of these events provided the perfect transition. She leaned in close, savored for a moment his musky aroma and tilted her head slightly upward to align her lips with his ear. "I don't know your name."

"Gunter," he replied even before he completed the turn of his head to face her. And staring into her eyes he asked, "And yours?"

The lids of her eyes slowly dropped concealing the beauty he yearned to hold indefinitely. As the light blue dusted lids rose she gently swayed from side to side and whispered her reply, "Esme."

They smiled at one another for a moment and then both of them positioned their bodies in their respective space and stared at the items collected in the pouch of the seat in front of them. Neither spoke during the remainder of the flight, not even when the wheels bounced on the tarmac, or when the wing flaps dropped and the brakes were applied bringing the mammoth bird to a rolling halt. Gunter never reached out even though the physics of slowing the plane placed stress on his back and Esme didn't attempt to do any people watching from the corner of her eyes. Even though they didn't utter a single word their internal voices never stopped.

Esme wondered, during those final minutes, if she had done the right thing by asking him his name. But, she wanted to know. She needed to know, she couldn't say why, she just did. She also decided that she was not going to analyze why, instead, she would just ask him.

Gunter couldn't believe how easy it had been to initiate the exchange. He actually was annoyed with himself during those final minutes that it never occurred to him to declare a statement as opposed to asking a question. He concluded that this was not merely clever on her part, it was ingenious. She did nothing more than speak the truth, "I don't know your name." And what did he do, he told her his name without a moment's hesitation.

Passengers pulled the seatbelts from their laps and jumped into the aisle even before the plane came to a complete stop despite the stewardess' directive to remain seated with your seatbelt on until the Captain turned off the seatbelt sign. The guy in seat C was the ringleader as he had his leather briefcase swung over his shoulder and was pressing towards row fifteen before his exit was blocked.

"Are you in a rush to deplane?" Gunter was able to again use his normal voice as the engine roar ceased.

"Not at all, I will have to wait for my luggage. I would prefer to just sit here and wait until the crowd thins and then get off."

"So, are you returning home or visiting? If you don't mind me asking." Gunter had lifted the armrest that separated seat B from C and slid towards the aisle so he could turn and face Esme.

"No, I don't mind. I am here visiting and hopefully able to complete some family matters."

"You have family in Seattle?"

"Yes, I suppose you could sort of say that." Esme broke eye contact and stared at the floor.

Sensing a lack of comfort Gunter elected not to press the issue for clarity. Even though logically it did not make sense to say, 'sort of.' Either one did or one did not.

Smiling, Esme once again satisfied the cultural norm of making eye contact with Gunter and in the process shifted the focus off of herself while she playfully continued the conversation. "Let me guess, you are not returning home either, but visiting. Am I correct?

Gunter appreciated her willingness to banter with him and therefore rather than simply provide an answer he urged her to explain the reason for such a guess. "What makes you think that I am not from here?"

Twirling her hair between three fingers that extenuated the size and color of her diamond ring against her brown frosted hair she crafted an answer. "Well, let me see, first, I wouldn't guess Seattle to be home to many cowboys, and second…" After an extended pause she admitted, "I guess I only have one reason."

"You are correct. I am visiting."

"Since you know that I am not returning home, do you want to guess where I am from?"

"The south, your southern drawl gives you away."

"Yes, but, where in the south? You do know that there is a difference in the drawl, don't you?

"Actually, no, I didn't know that, but let me guess nonetheless. Not Texas, since you didn't fly into the Denver airport from Houston. I am guessing you had a layover in Denver otherwise you would not have been sitting at the gate when I arrived, therefore not driving distance from Denver. Based on the thickness of your drawl I will guess Kentucky."

"Well, good guess, but no."

Gunter quickly cut her off before she could identify her home. "Hey, the plane is nearly empty, we better collect our stuff and head out before they throw us off."

Walking through the airport it was evident that Esme altered her natural stride to step more slowly and permit Gunter to keep pace. Approaching a set of public restrooms Gunter stepped laterally toward the wall and Esme drifted with him. Using the wall to support his five foot eleven inch frame and provide an interlude of relief for his back, Gunter reached out with his left arm and lightly stroked Esme's right shoulder as he spoke. He thanked her for making the flight enjoyable and timeless. He also wanted to assure her that she did not need to feel obligated to escort him to baggage claim. Once he used the restroom he would navigate his way through the airport just fine. He informed her that he was slowing her down and hindering her from reaching her final destination. Without granting her an opportunity to rebuttal he pushed himself away from the wall, stole one final lingering look at perfection, and made his way around the corner and into the men's room.

Secretly stepping from the bathroom several minutes later, he hoped that she might have waited for him. He enjoyed her company. She was easy to talk to, she was gorgeous, and… he really didn't know what else there was, but there was something else. Unfortunately, as he surveyed the terminal's walkway, her five foot four inch frame with voluptuous curves in all the right places was nowhere to be seen.

Reaching the baggage claim area suitcases were dropping down the shoot and passengers stood crowded together holding their claim cards. Something he thought was totally ridiculous since no one ever checked if a passenger departed with the correct bag and if the claim card was meant to assist in locating a lost bag, good luck.

The thinning of the crowd enabled Gunter to make visual contact with his suitcase. By the time he reached the turntable platform the conveyor drove his bag for another trip round the table. When the Samsonite bag made its return he slid his left hand under the handle and heaved the suitcase from the conveyer. Before the suitcase fell to a natural state against his side he felt another hand encompassing his. It turned out that another passenger reached for the hard sided suitcase at the precise moment that he did. Even before he turned he knew to whom the hand belonged.

"I believe you have my suitcase." The man from seat C spoke with speed and confidence.

"I am pretty sure that you are mistaken, this is my suitcase." Gunter stood his ground without releasing his grip of the suitcase.

"Check the numbers on the claim card and you will see they match mine."

"I find that rather difficult to believe," Gunter was spitting the words into the face of his fellow traveler, "because you see, when I was packing this very suitcase last evening my daughter placed a blue ribbon on the suitcase so I could easily locate it. Does your suitcase have a blue ribbon like this one?" Gunter lifted the suitcase in spite of the spasm attacking his back so it was only inches from the guy's nose.

As the fellow walked away Gunter heard a familiar voice. "What, was he trying to steal your luggage?"

"No, merely accusing me of stealing his." He was amused by the fact that he filed her voice in his memory bank.

Releasing the handle and using his knee to push the suitcase to the side he turned to face her and discovered she was laughing. She couldn't remember how long it had been since she laughed so many times and in such a short span. He couldn't remember a laugh so inviting and therefore contagious.

Like a puppy mesmerized by its first encounter with a cat he stood still and stared at her beauty, yet again, and attempted to measure the likelihood of success. Acknowledging it was now or never he cleared his throat several times and only then slowly, cautiously proceeded into unchartered territory. "This is really forward of me and you certainly may ignore the question entirely, but are you heading downtown by any chance? I rented a car and I thought, well, if you needed a ride and it wasn't too far out of the way, well, I could drop you off." She drew two steps back and he quickly stopped the invite and became apologetic, "I am sorry, you probably have someone picking you up, or rented your own vehicle."

"No, no one will be picking me up. Remember, I only sort of have family and he doesn't drive." She immediately chastised herself for sharing more than she intended. However, she couldn't ignore the fact that he was so easy to talk to therefore things just spilled forth. Moreover, he listened to her for the purpose of understanding her and not merely to insure that the conversation continued or because it was the gentlemanly thing to do. It was this attribute that held her captive. When he told her not to wait outside the restroom it made her want to wait all the more. She felt safe in his presence, something she didn't experience with her husband until two months into their relationship. As ludicrous as it sounded in her mind she accepted his offer on one condition, that they have dinner together.

She couldn't believe her own voice. Not only had she said "yes" to his offer but she also heard herself ask him to join her for an evening meal. When she counted the hours backwards she realized she had not eaten anything of substance for nearly eight hours which she used to rationalize her invite to him. On another level she attempted to convince herself the invite was rooted in the selfish desire for food, but she was fully aware that the desire was rooted in more animalistic desires than food. Fortunately for both of them, they were still in the airport and not yet seated in the rental car when Esme suggested dining together or Gunter probably would have put them head first through the windshield by pressing the brakes through the floorboards. As it was he stumbled slightly and ended up taking a seat on his suitcase. It was a graceful move and didn't invoke attention from bystanders.

Before he accepted or rejected the idea of extending the evening by sharing a meal she attached to the invite that they go Dutch.

Looking up at her, stilled seated on the suitcase, he said, "I will consider this option, but first, you must explain the origin of why sharing the expense of a meal is referred to as, "going Dutch."

Smiling as she recognized the playfulness connected with his request she lobbed back the question, "Is our dining together contingent upon the accuracy of my explanation?"

He spoke as he carefully tightened the muscles in his legs and hoisted himself up. "Not necessarily, I am merely intrigued by the phrases and sayings we employ without understanding their history. I find that many such phrases actually have a very negative connotation. I am simply curious if this is the case with this phrase."

Extending her hand to offer support as he rose, which he waved off, she spoke in a carefree manner. Since I don't have an idiom dictionary in my possession at the moment I am throwing darts off the wall hoping to strike the target. A negative slant might include the stereotype of the Dutch as being tight fisted cheapskates and therefore not willing to pay for another's meal. I would also imagine it would be equally valid to infer that this phrase is reflective of a cultural norm. Maybe in the Netherlands the custom or practice was such that couples dating were responsible to their own expenses. What do you think?"

"Truthfully, I want to believe that the cultural norm was the origin but I suspect that the misunderstanding of the norm resulted in the opinion that Dutch people are cheap or stingy. And therefore the idiom is a subtle or perhaps, not so subtle, prejudice."

"Surely you know that was not my intention." With her eyes cast downward it was as though she was begging forgiveness.

Without a moments delay he acknowledged her sincerity. "Oh yes." It pained him to think that he might have been the cause of her distress, yet he couldn't keep himself from pontificating on the subject. "But you do see how using a phrase such as this one keeps alive the stereotype without taking responsibility for promotion. Naiveté can never be an excuse. In fact, many people may be supporting a notion or a prejudice they oppose because they don't know the meaning behind the phrase or the word."

Dear God, what was wrong with him? Why did his mouth keep moving? He knew he should shut up and yet… 'change the subject,' were the words pounding in his brain and finally it delivered. "We probably should find the car rental place and pick up the car."

After retrieving the car from the rental counter he yielded to her wisdom concerning the best location to eat in the city and how to navigate from the airport to a downtown location. She confessed that she wasn't very familiar with the city and the few times she was here she used taxicabs but, with the map supplied by the rental agency opened and spread across her lap she directed his driving. She thought it rather unique that he accepted her assistance with something generally reserved only for men. Gunter, on the other hand, found it refreshing that she was willing and able to select the restaurant without saying, "I don't care" and that she served as a copilot.

The 15-mile trek from the airport to downtown took 30 minutes due to Gunter's efforts to orientate himself to the city. Fortunately it was a Thursday and close to 9:00 pm, therefore the streets were not crowded with cars or pedestrians so driving at a snail's pace endangered no one. The façade of the restaurant caused Gunter to rein in a small portion of his skepticism about the quality of the establishment Esme selected. The image that danced about when she shared the restaurant's name was less than positive. He joked about the type of food they would be served, the service they would receive, and the size of tip he would leave. In response she merely asked him to reserve his judgment until he saw the restaurant and tasted the food. Rather than becoming upset or being offended, she liked the idea that he was comfortable enough to joke with her. It wasn't as though she had dated a lot of men, but those she had dated either attempted to use humor to mask their nervousness, which never worked and seldom was funny or insightful, or they avoided humor and joking around all together, which was her husband's approach. But with Gunter it was different, it came naturally and fit the moment and that put her more at ease.

The restaurant Esme selected was a twenty-four hour restaurant named, 13 Coins. In spite of pestering her to identify the significance of the name, she challenged him to guess the meaning of the name once he saw the place.

Tucked in a quiet corner, at Gunter's request, away from a surprisingly large crowd despite the hour, he constructed his hypothesis for the name of the place, as they waited the arrival of their drinks. Since the only thing that awaited both of them was a lonely hotel room on opposite ends of downtown and summer reruns on TV, neither one seemed too anxious to place an order for food even though they were hungry.

Swirling the burgundy liquid around in his glass to assist in the breathing of the wine, Gunter leaned his chair back from the circular table, savored a sip of the house Merlot and confessed, "I suppose I could offer up some academic dribble on the historical importance of 13 coins, but honestly, I would rather have you tell me." Returning the front legs of the captain's chair to the floor he leaned forward, extended his right arm with glass in hand and waited for Esme's glass to clink against his.

The closeness of his face distracted her momentarily as she could almost taste the dryness of the wine on his breath.

Lifting her glass, responding to his nonverbal request, a shiver streaked through her body, caused not by the chilled glass of Chardonnay, but by his ability to pluck the strings of her spirit, perhaps, her heart. Pressing the glass to her lips to taste the crisp, yet slightly sweet white wine she stared at his lips and wondered how two very different combinations would blend. Lifting her gaze from his mouth, she realized that once again he caught her staring, but rather than turn away she responded, "Yes?"

Smiling, he wasted no time in taking advantage of the opportunity. "A penny for your thoughts? Rather, let me make that 13 coins for your thoughts?"

Her nervous laugh was covered by a second gulp of wine. She never anticipated that he might press her to share what she was thinking. What man ever asked her to share her thoughts? Dare she be honest? The questions swirling about didn't stop. Where was this leading? Where did she want this to be leading? My God, what did she know about him? Could he be trusted, should he be trusted? When the waiter returned to their corner he discovered that her glass was empty and in need of a refill.

Holding her glass in front of her chest as though creating a shield of protection she spoke. "13 coins, ha? Well, just so you know, it will take more than 13 coins to hear my thoughts. But, concerning the name of the restaurant that sort of connects with the story, sort of. The tale goes that a poor young man loved and wished to marry a wealthy girl. Her father asked what he had to offer for his daughter's hand in marriage. The young man reached into his pocket. He had only 13 coins, but assured the father he could pledge undying love, care and concern. The father was so touched, he gave his daughter's hand and "13 Coins" has come to symbolize unyielding love, care and concern."

"Since you demand more than 13 coins are you implying that I am not poor? Are you suggesting that to hold your hand I must empty my pockets?"

Esme's redemption from answering arrived in the form of dinner plates heaped with food accompanied by two bottles of wine, one red and one white. In between mouthfuls of delectable food washed down by glass after glass of wine the conversation danced from topic to topic avoiding the one issue that consumed their thoughts and sent blood pulsating through every corpuscle and capillary of their bodies, the issue of attraction.

Although the alcohol was testing her ability to restrain herself she wasn't drunk enough to cover that territory again. ATTRACTION. Carefully watching the last drop of chardonnay strike the bottom of her glass while holding the edges of the table so as to steady her body, she informed Gunter that there was no reason to stay if the restaurant ran out of wine.

Gunter also felt the effects of alcohol and purposefully kept his hands beneath the table top for fear he might reach out and take her hand in his own or, worse yet, he might runs his fingers through her hair. As much as he desired to know her thoughts he was afraid if she shared he would be required to do likewise. And that scared him because he couldn't remember a time when he was so smitten with a woman.

With the bill split equitably they made their way out of the restaurant and into the misty night air. Cupping a street pole Gunter considered for a split second doing a Fred Astaire impersonation of *Singing in the Rain* but contained his actions with the realization that he didn't need to scare Esme any more than he already had. And yet, the desire to break out in song, any song was powerful and the ironic thing was, he didn't really enjoy singing. But there was something about this woman that...

Her voice, now reaching a slightly high octave interrupted his thoughts. "Do you think it is safe for you to drive?"

"Drive? Oh yeah, drive. Where is the car again?" Before closing her door, which he opened as a gentleman, he inquired. "Well, where exactly is your hotel?'

"It's on the north side of the city, and yours, where is your hotel?"

"In the opposite direction."

Acknowledging the stupidity of driving they decided, under the influence and wisdom of alcohol, to share a hotel room for the evening.

Attempting to search the sky of the city through the side window Gunter shared, "When we were driving to the restaurant I remember, I think anyway, that I saw a bright sign a couple blocks over for the Vance Hotel."

The couple of blocks were closer to half a mile, but the fresh air did both of them good. As they strolled through the front doors, into the lobby, and up to the reception desk, something happened.

CHAPTER 6

Twisting the key and shoving the door inward an amber glow radiated from a small lamp on the nightstand next to the bed. The somber mood light melded with the sterile brilliance of the fluorescent light from the hall and, combined with the poignant effects of alcohol, created a Star Trek moment of warping between two worlds. Even in this strange and unique location no longer belonging to the hall or the room, Gunter saw that the comforter was turned down and mints rested peacefully on each pillow. He chuckled for only one of the two beds was prepared for use. Esme, still belonging to the world of the hallway, immediately inquired as to what was so funny.

"Two beds, as we requested when registering, but only one is useable."

"What?" Her voice was louder than she intended, nearly the volume of shouting, making her single word question drag longer than usual. The lingering influence of alcohol undoubtedly muted her hearing and resulted in her speaking with great vigor.

Stepping aside Gunter created a clear line of vision for Esme to peer inside. Once she grasped what "useable" meant, she snickered. "Oh well, I guess we better follow the rules and use the one bed. One can only break so many rules in a single day."

Gunter didn't need another invite. He knew perfectly well what it meant when his favorite horse met him at the gate as opposed to chasing a horse round the pasture.

Inside the door, kicked shut with the heel of his boot, their two bodies became one. The weight of Gunter stumbling forward onto Esme's body sent her reeling backwards until she was sandwiched between Gunter and the wall. His chest became one with her breast where the firmness and size surprised him as the colorful, even flamboyant sweater vest, the two sides of which were held closed over her breasts by a single string, concealed her God given nature. As she pulled him closer she reached for the back of his straw cowboy hat and sailed it across the room. She spread her fingers through his thick brown hair while his mouth explored the softness of the skin on her neck and his nose was pleasured by the sweet fragrance of Chanel Number 5. His *olfactory* receptors detected the scent immediately as it was the first bottle of perfume he ever purchased for a girl. It was the typical love scene of adolescence; only days after purchasing the expensive gift his young lady friend dumped him. Even though he embraces the fragrance he vowed to never purchase another bottle of Chanel Number 5 in case the bad luck was connected with the perfume.

Unable to support his weight and weary from striking the back of her head against the paisley wallpaper, Esme gradually slid to the floor and enabled them to twist their bodies like pretzels. Consumed by the passion and the heat of the moment neither Gunter nor Esme noted the ease with which Gunter moved and molded his body to conform to Esme's. The adrenaline, mixed with muscle relaxant meds and topped off with alcohol masked any pain. And even if Gunter had experienced a spasm it was doubtful it would have stopped him. Hands moved rapidly without purpose or rational objective. It was like a kid in a candy store - completely overwhelmed not knowing where to start or what to select, and sticking his hand into every canister of candy just to feel it.

Esme was still on her back and Gunter straddled her as he elevated his torso from her body and gazed into her eyes. "I am sure you have heard this a million times, but you have the most beautiful amber eyes. Your hair reached out and grabbed my attention but it was your eyes that took control of my breath."

Esme wanted to say thank you but with her body pressed into the carpet and looking up at a man she met less than five hours earlier it seemed trite. Her cheeks were flushed and she knew the upper portions of her chest were covered with red blotches. It happened every time she became excited. The only way she could express what stirred within was to reach up and wrap her arms around him and pull him back to her body.

Drifting back down on her and with his eyes closed he kissed her for the first time. Their lips barely touched and Gunter pulled back slightly, only long enough to breathe, and then repeated the kiss a second and third time. It wasn't a peck like a grandchild to a grandparent, it wasn't a passing brush of lips like two friends greeting one another, it was passionate, it was sensual, and it was intense as though fanning the flames of desire. It was so intense that after the second kiss Esme's eyelids sprang open in panic and she gulped for air. The fourth kiss lingered timelessly to the point where it was no longer discernable when a kiss started or ended.

Near the point of euphoria Gunter wiggled his body down slightly and rested his head between her ample breasts. He listened to the slashing sound of blood beating through her heart, a heart he was falling for. When he finally lifted his head he smiled and Esme immediately asked, "What?" while smiling in return. Slowly he traced the side of her figure with his right hand until he reached the side of her breast. As he brought his mouth back to hers and darted his tongue into her open and waiting mouth he cupped her left breast firmly. As he fondled her through several layers of clothing he noticed her lift upward and push against his hand. Their tongues took turns counting the other's teeth and darting in and out and there the final hint of red and white wine mingled. It was all very romantic and very animalistic.

The numbing effects of a back spasm forced Gunter to wedge himself between Esme's legs in order to rest in a more prone position. Even before he completely lowered his hips Esme pushed her butt off the floor so her hips might meet his and together they could slowly drop to the floor. Still in midair, Gunter felt how Esme rocked her pelvic area from side to side rubbing against his groin, teasing him to reach his full manhood. With her backside on the carpet he pressed himself against her and, in spite of the barrier of clothing; he imagined that they were a perfect fit. Similar to a child riding a rocking horse Esme and Gunter rocked in unison, slowly and calmly, until excitement gave away to aggressiveness and their movement against one another became more animated. As hands frantically searched for any openings to explore exposed skin they playfully bit one another on the neck, the ear lobe, and the lips.

About to reach the point of no return, Gunter pushed himself off of Esme and knelt beside her. Carefully placing one arm under her neck and the other in the crease of her legs he lifted her from the floor. Resting her body against his chest he stood and moved toward the bed. Despite her objections to put her down he just smiled and continued to place one foot in front of the other. At the side of the bed he swung her body from side to side like a discus thrower preparing to launch the object into the air. She bounced atop the comforter and before she stopped moving she clutched the collar of her blouse and pulled outwardly. The first two buttons flew toward Gunter.

Gunter fell on top of her and seized her wrists. He stopped her as she started to rip the clothes from her body not because he wasn't overcome with animalistic desire, he was well beyond that point, but because he wanted to savor the slow titillating discovery of her body. He wanted her to tease him, to slowly reveal each inch of her goddess like body. He wanted her to enjoy the moment. Already his mind constructed an image of her nakedness; he wanted to measure how accurate he was. Removing her hands from her blouse, already missing a third of the buttons, enough to reveal the lacy white brassier, he leaned close to her face and whispered, "I want us to enjoy every minute. Or should I say hour? I want to watch you slowly undress and become excited."

Esme had never been the recipient of such a request. She was left wondering who this man was. Every person she had spent time with couldn't wait to scale her body, to climb on her and reach the climax. Every male had only been interested in meeting his needs and using her and her body to make that happen. She realized, as was always the case, everything she had done to that point was to service him. She acted as she had been trained to do and Gunter stopped her. He requested that she proceed slowly, something she always wanted, something she knew she needed for herself, for her own pleasure, but… she was embarrassed that she never had the nerve to share or state what she needed. As much as she fought to hold back the tears, they formed and dropped from the corners of her eyes. The salt water rolled down her cheeks and pooled in her ears.

Feeling his thumbs drying her face she looked up at him when she heard him speak. "I'm sorry. I didn't mean to ask you to do something that makes you uncomfortable. I only wanted to cherish this moment and you because you are so beautiful."

In between the crying, she put forth, "No, you don't understand. I mean, no one has ever stopped me, no one has ever made this about both of us; it has always just been about the guy. And then you…" The tears were more than Gunter's thumbs could wipe away. The corner of the sheet was pulled that he might wipe her tears and again he said, "I'm sorry." At the sign that the first tear was about to fall he wanted to wrap his arms round her body and hold her close, but he feared such an action might be misunderstood and make matters worse. All that was left was to say I'm sorry.

"Please, don't apologize; it is so beautiful that you desire this to be about more than a single second of pleasure."

"Well, before you get too carried away with thanking me, all I know, is that you are beautiful and I am totally smitten with you, and I want to enjoy every aspect of this and I want you to enjoy it as well. It's really nothing all that special…"

He was unable to finish his thought because her sobs drowned out his voice. When she reached a point of only whimpering she spoke, "See, you don't even recognize how kind and gentle you are, because that is just who you are."

"Well, again, I'm nothing specia…" His voice trailed off and the words hung in the room as neither one knew what else to say. Next to one another they laid for several minutes without moving. Eventually, Gunter rolled towards the nightstand and switched on the radio. The DJ from the local radio station introduced the next song as the latest hit from Jim Cocker's newly released album, *"I Can Stand A Little Rain."* The lyrics, combined with the simple yet moving melody from, *You are so Beautiful*, had Esme's and Gunter's bodies once again locked together.

The next song became nothing more than background noise to drown out the simple yet moving melody as Gunter repositioned himself a foot away from Esme and rested on his elbow to give her the space she needed. Esme sat up, crossed her legs and undid the few remaining buttons of her blouse before she removed the sweater vest. With her hands holding the bottom of blouse she pulled each side of the white garment back to grant Gunter full view of her breast cupped by the brassier. The cleavage was deep and long as her breasts were full and round. Passing a single finger over the sheer texture of the bra and then circling, outlining the complete fullness of each breast in a caressing manner, first the right and then the left, Esme understood completely how her breasts had been a blessing and a curse.

Even though more than twenty years had passed, she pictured herself back in middle school, in sixth grade specifically. She was the first of the girls in her class to develop and the growth felt freakish as she moved from no bra to an adult bra, skipping the training bra, in what her memory told her was overnight. Instantly she became popular with the boys, those in her grade and those much older. Her body became something to be squeezed and poked as she moved through the hallways. Girls on the other hand were jealous and made up cruel stories of how she rubbed breast enhancement cream from the jungles of South America on her boobs each night. When her mental and emotional age finally caught up with her physical maturity she understood that she had not done anything wrong. She understood, even at the age of thirty-five, that men stared at her chest and usually it made her angry, but not with Gunter. She wanted him to look, to see what tingled beneath the lacy fabric. She wanted him to be excited at the sight of the white lace stretched slightly by the size contained within.

Both thumbs had hooked the straps of the brassier at the shoulders and started to pull downward when she stopped. After a momentary pause Esme pushed the straps back up, smiled and said, "Not just yet." Gunter took it as additional teasing, but Esme's intentions had nothing to do with teasing, at least not at that moment. What she really desired was for Gunter to see the matching set of undergarments.

Dropping back onto the bed and spreading her legs Esme worked the button through the eyehole carefully and seductively as though in rhythm to her hips that moved from side to side. With the button freed Esme traced the line with her finger, dripping with salvia, from her opened jeans through her bellybutton, where she stopped and circled several times, and back up to the pink ribbon positioned perfectly in the center of her breasts. The temptation raged within to secure possession of Gunter's finger and retrace her movement but her body was already on fire and she feared she might explode under his touch. With both hands she followed the seam of the jeans between her legs down as far as she could reach without lifting her back from the bed. Through the dense denim material she felt the warmth rising between her legs as she continued to stroke her thighs. Lifting the flap with one hand and using the other on the zipper was no match. With the additional space Esme squirmed her body free of the skintight jeans. Pressing her legs together to hide the dampness she rolled toward Gunter that he might notice how the panties matched the brassier. She never would have imagined twenty hours earlier as she selected her undergarments that a man, other than her husband, would see the matching set.

"They are lovely, you are…" He stopped himself, he was about to say lovely.

"Thank you, I hoped you would notice. It's funny how something that hardly anyone else ever sees can make one feel sexy."

"Oh, there is no question, you are sexy. The placement of that pink bow on those panties adds to the sex appeal, but I am guessing that what's beneath is even sexier."

"So, you want to see more do you?"

"Yes, please."

The playful banter offered an interlude from the foreplay. They both knew perfectly well where this was headed, what they didn't know was what path would carry them to that destination.

Sitting upright in the center of the bed with her legs stretched out straight she reached behind her back, unhooked the brassier and, for a second time, placed her thumbs under the shoulder straps and playfully slid the straps back and forth over the curve of her shoulders. With the bra free from restraint each time her thumbs passed the edge of her shoulders her breasts threatened to push out from beneath the brassier. Just as the bra was about to drop Esme pulled both straps up, freed her thumbs, and placed her right forearm across her chest to conceal what was beneath.

Grinning as though she just thought of the answer to the sixty-four thousand dollar question she informed Gunter that she didn't think it was fair that he remained dressed while she was about to be completely undressed. She shared her solution to correct the situation. She would ask him a series of questions, if he answered correctly, she would remove a piece of clothing However, if he answered incorrectly, he had to remove a piece of clothing of her choice.

Knowing full well that he would accept her proposal he thought he should, at a minimum, ask a clarifying question or two. "What type of questions will I be expected to answer? Are you certain that you know the answer to these questions?"

"As for your second question, yes." Her laughter when responding made him a bit nervous to a point where he felt flush. "Concerning the type of questions, you will have to just wait and see. Are you game?"

"What do I have to lose?"

"Your clothes, I hope!"

The fingers of her left hand combed the long strands of her hair so it draped down her chest and covered portions of her arm and hand holding the brassier in place. Gunter felt as though she was purposefully distracting him so he couldn't concentrate. The first question took him completely by surprise and he laughed out loud. He couldn't believe Esme's boldness. The question was so simple yet ingenious, and, of course, she knew the answer. He realized that he had a fifty-fifty chance of answering correctly, assuming there were only two choices. He wished he had paid better attention in sex ed. class back in 7th grade, although he doubted this topic was covered.

"Well, I am waiting, what color are my areolas?"

"Do I get a hint? I mean, how specific do I need to be?"

"Excuse me, who is sitting here half naked and who is fully clothed? Times up, what is your answer?"

"Okay, Okay, they are…pink?" The answer came out more as a question than an answer.

"Let me see, the boots have to go, but that's footwear and not clothing, so remove your shirt was well."

Swinging to the edge of the bed he pulled off his boots then stood and pulled the snaps of his shirt and tossed it on the chair.

His chest was mostly free of hair, well defined, she assumed from the labor of tending to horses, and his stomach was firm but not rippling with muscle. His arms, as she noticed earlier, were larger than the average man's, again, probably the result of caring for horses. Her smile revealed that she clearly enjoyed the added wrinkle to the foreplay and she asked if he wished to try a second time.

He was totally confused now because he assumed there were only two options, pink and brown, but there must be more, or why else would she offer the same question a second time, unless of course, it was a trick. He stopped himself. He was over thinking the question again. "Brown." he stated with confidence.

Her right arm slowly moved away from her breast and Gunter knew he got it right this time. Rather than using her thumbs Esme shook her shoulders back and forth and the straps under the force of gravity followed the slope downward and the bra fell to her lap. While gravity had done its work on the bra it had spared Esme's breasts. They were firm and full and round and Gunter could think of nothing but gently cupping each one.

After a second extended interlude of silence Gunter finally spoke. "Everything I want to say sounds so childish, other than repeating what I said, you are beautiful."

She had more questions to ask but at that moment, as Gunter had said, it seemed childish, if not silly. She waited for him to reach out and touch her nakedness but he never moved. Without removing her amber eyes from his she took his right hand and place it on her left breast. Gently but firmly he squeezed. It was the same action as earlier but now there were no layers to restrict the warmth of his hand. Her eyes closed when his mouth located her nipple and the first of many orgasmic shivers spread through her body. She pulled his body closer and deeper into hers and together they fell back onto the bed.

Neither remembered the specifics of how it happened but eventually Gunter rested atop Esme in complete nakedness. Both were fully aroused and both were past the point of being polite or cautious as they yearned for the final act of penetration.

As Gunter aligned himself to enter her in one smooth and long thrust, Esme quickly moved her hands from his buttocks, where she had been pulling him closer, and placed them on his chest, stopping any forward movement. She uttered only one word. "Protection."

Completing half a push-up his chest lifted away from hers in order to look directly into her eyes and he spoke. "Esme, I had a vasectomy roughly a year ago and I have not been with anyone other than my wife."

"I am on the pill and I have never had any disease."

Brushing the hair from her face he used the opportunity to ask a question he previously had never asked a woman. "Are you okay with this?"

Esme didn't need to ponder her answer, she was more than ready. "Yes."

He kissed her passionately and as his tongue darted between her lips he thrust himself inside of her. It took a few awkward minutes to discover a rhythm that felt right and pleasured them both. Gunter told himself repeatedly, "Go slow, go slow." The first time he had intercourse, the night of his junior prom, it lasted all of two minutes and he could not remember anything other than the mess afterwards. A repeat performance of that magnitude was not what he desired or what the goddess under him deserved. As he focused his attention on pleasing Esme it surprised him how long he was able to continue.

The orgasms of varying intensities were nearly nonstop. Each movement of Gunter whether deep or barely inside her made her quiver with excitement. Her entire body had reached a point of total exhaustion, even her vocal cords were hoarse from the deep guttural sounds she made. Both bodies were wet with passion and from the labor of shifting her pelvis centimeters to the left and the right without his awareness. The continued shifting pushed Gunter beyond the point of controlling his actions and he collapsed in exhaustion with his head nestled in her hair, he was totally spent.

In the silence and darkness of the room, resting comfortably with her head on his chest and her naked body pressed against his nakedness, she had time to contemplate. The consistency of his breathing was a drastic contrast to the rapid and shallow breaths he took less than fifteen minutes earlier. For a handful of seconds she felt betrayed and found herself questioning his authenticity, if he really wanted this to be about them, why was he so reserved and quiet afterwards? She stopped herself and defended him, acknowledging the obvious; he was tired, and chastised herself for being overly sensitive. She too should have drifted off to sleep as quickly as he, but in spite of closing in on twenty-four hours without sleep she was wide awake. His name, Gunter, was the first thing to fill her thoughts. She couldn't recall ever having met anyone named Gunter. A German name, she thought, but self-doubt arose and she found herself in the attic of the house rummaging through dusty boxes in search of the baby name book. She had purchased the book days after she discovered Mark and she were going to be parents. Mark! It was the first time since she left him asleep in bed that his name rolled through her mind. She was naked, totally vulnerable next to a man she met only hours earlier and yet guilt was not the word to describe what she felt. Sadly, his name only appeared in her thoughts because she was trying to learn more about the man with whom she had had incredible sex. Her thoughts prodded her to consider, was the absence of his name a sign that she didn't love him anymore? A more disturbing question rushed forth, had she ever loved him? She silenced the conversation in her thoughts, for it was too much, too heavy, too overwhelming. Pulling back, retracing her path, she questioned how it was that Mark's name arose and the reason for the review of their marriage. The answer was very simple, the baby book about names and Gunt... The stream of consciousness faded and there was nothing.

A twitch of her right arm yanked her back from the edge of sleep. Embarrassment flowed through her body when she realized that her body left the bed for a second. Like a sniper she laid as still and lifeless as possible to determine if her brief moment of levitation woke Gunter. Confident that he was still very much asleep she decided, first thing in the morning…

CHAPTER 7

The sounds of the city bellowed into the room and jarred Esme awake. After a disconcerting interlude to orientate her body and remember where she was she extended her left arm expecting to touch the man who awoke her sexual energy during the early morning hours, but her efforts merely awarded her with a handful of sheets cool to the touch. Gunter was not beside her in bed. The morning sun jetting through the window diminished any attempt to survey the room. With only one resource left she whispered, "Gunter, you still here?" The soreness of her throat reminded her of the ecstasy her body experienced and she shivered even though she wasn't cold.

"Yeah, I'm right here."

Creating a visor with her right hand she located his silhouette in the upholstered armchair that previously held a number of their garments. The clothes had been pushed to the floor creating a pile next to the base of the chair. Esme couldn't tell if he was in his birth suit or had gotten dressed, but she was confident he was wearing his hat. "How long have you been sitting there?"

"Oh, not long, maybe 15, 20 minutes at the most."

"You mean you have just been sitting there all that time?"

"Have you ever watched someone sleep? It is amazing what you discover."

Totally confused with what Gunter was talking about she stammered forth an answer. "Yeah, when the kids were young, I mean, really young, babies, and they didn't wake up for their normal feeding I would enter the room and stand there and watch them sleep. I can't say I stood there for 15 or 20 minutes, I left after making sure they were breathing."

She couldn't see his face but she knew from the tone and delivery that he was smiling. "You can learn so much more than just if a person is breathing by watching them sleep."

"Well then, mind sharing what you discovered while watching me sleep?"

"Did you know that you do this wonderful thing with your nose?"

"With my nose? What do you mean?"

"You sort of," he paused for a moment searching for the perfect word to paint an accurate picture, "wiggle it."

"Wiggle it!? What are you saying? I think you are making this up." As she spoke she sat up to gain a direct line of vision and challenge the honesty of his comments.

She had learned that he enjoyed teasing her whenever possible.

"No, seriously. Did you ever see Samantha on *Bewitched*?"

Hearing the title of the 60's TV sitcom she pulled the sheet up over her shoulders so that her entire body was covered. "Oh, so now you are calling me a witch?"

"No, the movement of your nose, it is so cute. I wish I had a movie camera to film you."

"Just what every woman wants, to be filmed sleeping. Lovely, just lovely. No makeup, hair looking like a rat's nest and you want to film it?" Lowering the sheet a few inches she tucked it just below her underarms and proceeded to cross her arms over her chest.

"It is, I mean, you are lovely." Standing on the seat of the chair Gunter launched himself toward the bed, landed on op Esme, and drove her down onto the bed.

Esme observed, as he was about to reach her that he was naked and, even though she had yet to touch him, he was already overcome with excitement. She had felt his size when he entered her earlier however, now in the light of day she saw that he was at least an inch longer than average, but what startled her was the girth. Thinking back it made sense why, with every stroke, whether in or out, she exploded with excitement.

Ripping the sheet from her body and exposing her nakedness, he grabbed both her wrists and lifted her arms over her head. He straddled her body and forced himself between her legs. Aggressively he inhaled small portions of her skin, first on her neck, then on her upper chest, and eventually he reached the sides of her breasts. As his mouth covered her left nipple the sucking became biting. He bit hard enough that she moaned in discomfort and attempted to bring her arms back to her chest. She tried to fight, to roll him off, but the more she fought the tighter his grip became and the heavier he made his body on her. The very moment she planted her feet flat on the bed, bent her legs to provide leverage and hoisted her hips upward, he took advantage of the position and inserted his throbbing, thick manhood.

Unlike hours earlier his movement lacked rhythm. It was wild, rough, and forceful. He bounced on her and drove himself forward as far as her body allowed. He threw his hips to the left and repeated the forward movement and then to the right and then again in the center. Esme continued to fight. She freed her left hand and placed it on his butt where her long painted nails pressed into his virgin skin. She used her hips as a weapon against his movement. When he went right she swayed left and then right when he pushed left. The instant his left hand relaxed she placed both hands behind his necked and pulled him into her chest and held him tight as he bucked riotously like a star rodeo bucking bronco.

The entire wrestling matched lasted but five minutes yet both fighters were drenched in sweat and Gunter was lifeless atop Esme as she kissed the crown of his head and gently rubbed his back. Lifting his head from her breast he reminded her that she was beautiful whether awake or asleep and then he inquired, "Shower or bath?"

"Together or alone?"

"Well, I was hoping together," Gunter said, "but I understand if you prefer alone."

"Bath and together, that is assuming you like bubbles?"

"Bubbles? Where are we going to get bubbles?" Gunter answered in complete honesty.

"You leave that to me. Give me three minutes to use the bathroom and warm the water and then come join me."

Holding her hand as she squirmed from the bed he asked, "What am I supposed to do for three minutes without you?"

"Sweet, but I'm not buying it. See what's on TV at 7 in the morning."

"Hey, wait." He called out just as she closed the bathroom door. "Do you want coffee, orange juice, or both?"

"Juice, grape if they have it. I can't do coffee."

"Wait, wait, you what? Seriously, this could be a deal breaker here. You can't do coffee? How do you survive?"

As the door swung shut a second time she shouted, "I gotta pee. I will explain later."

Gunter's body entering the tub raised the water level and the bubbles lapped up against the underside of Esme's 36D's. Gunter wasn't complaining but the distraction had him wondering two things. First, did the bubbles tickle the bottom of her boobs and second, in the pool did those gorgeous breasts act as a floating device? He knew he was being completely silly, but every now and then one had to allow the kid inside to come forth and ask the questions everyone else was thinking but were too proper to ask. But rather than ask either of those questions he stuck to the script. "So, you want to tell me how you created the bubbles?"

What Gunter had no way of knowing was that the kid in Esme was equally active. As she watched him reach over the side of the tub, first with his right leg and then with his left the two things she wondered about were, did he need to purchase special underwear to fit properly and did the expansiveness, that didn't appear to shrink, create a problem when riding a horse?

She was thankful that Gunter inquired about the bubbles because she needed a diversion. "It's called bubble bath."

"I know what it's called."

"If you knew, why did you ask?"

He ignored her jocularity. "Where did you get the bubbles?"

"I packed it. I knew the trip had the potential to be stressful and I thought I might need to relax. I just never dreamt I would be sharing my bubbles."

Scooting forward in the tub Gunter created small waves that washed up over Esme's nipples. Moving within inches of her body he leaned forward and lightly kissed her and then lowered his head and kissed each nipple. Pulling back slightly he apologized. "I hope they're not sore from me biting them."

Horses in Heaven

"Actually, my kids bit harder when nursing." What was she saying? Why had she spoken of her children? The sentence, like an early morning fog in the springtime, floated atop the bubbles and created a moment of darkness and distance between them. Esme considered offering a follow-up comment as she watched him move away. Her first instinct was to say, "I'm sorry," but that didn't sound proper because she was not sorry about being a mother, therefore, she said nothing.

Gunter contemplated following up with an inquiry about her family, but decided he would rather enjoy having her all to himself. He pushed his body back against the end of the tub and stretched out his legs on each side of her body.

For the longest time they both leaned back and allowed the steam and bubbles to wash over their bodies. They watched each other carefully, but neither said anything.

When the water cooled Gunter pulled the drain plug and Esme, understanding Gunter's action, opened the hot water valve. They had not been in the presence of one another for a total of twenty-four hours and yet they were developing their own form of nonverbal communication.

When the water threatened to spill over the edge Esme reluctantly closed the water valve. She informed Gunter that the sound of running water was as relaxing as the actual water. Gunter suggested that he could make her relax more than any sound of water running. Looking at him suspiciously he provided additional details. "I know what you are thinking and that's not it. Turn around and allow me to put these bubbles to constructive use."

Carefully she twisted so as to not increase the waterfall. Gunter waved his hand at her. "What's a little water on the floor, we have plenty of towels and if we need to we can call for more."

As the one always stuck cleaning the mess in the bathroom after bath each night, Esme just wouldn't allow herself to be reckless and splash water everywhere. Gunter, armed with a washcloth, scooped mounds of bubbles from between them and layered Esme's back. The oil from the bubbles created a slippery surface so Gunter discarded the washcloth and proceeded to massage her back. As her shoulders drooped and her head titled forward Gunter asked, "So, what's the deal with coffee?"

Without pausing to consider her reply or lift her head she answered, "It makes me pee."

"Of course it does, it's a liquid." Sarcastically his words were absorbed in the mixture of foamy suds and water on her back while his hands rubbed in circles away from her spine.

"No, I mean, I pee immediately after drinking a single cup. I don't just pee a cup, it makes me empty my entire bladder. Seriously, I can live just fine without it. But, I am guessing you can't."

"Nope. I start the day and end the day with a cup of joe."

With great skepticism she spoke each word slowly. "You end the day with coffee?"

"I will admit it sounds a bit unusual. For most people caffeine gets the blood pumping, but after so many years of drinking the stuff coffee has a calming, soothing effect on me." Oblivious to how his hands massaged Esme he transported her back to the beginning of his coffee drinking youth. "I started drinking coffee at age 8 and never stopped." It was his grandpa who served him his first cup of coffee during morning lunch out in the bean field. Grandpa parked the tractor at the end of the row and waited for his firstborn grandson to deliver lunch. Grandma had prepared two sausage sandwiches wrapped in wax paper to keep them fresh, four dill pickles also wrapped in wax paper, two squares of banana cake topped with creamy peanut butter frosting nearly half the height of the cake, one piece slightly larger than the other, and steaming hot coffee poured into a mason jar. The entire lunch had been carefully packed into a kettle and covered with an embroidered dish towel to keep the contents free of dust and dirt as the kettle swung inches off the ground during it's half mile journey to grandpa. Grandpa noticed halfway through his cake that Gunter didn't have anything to wash down the cake and offset the sweetness of the frosting. Gunter was handed the mason jar and never stopped drinking.

Not having been raised on a farm, Esme was not familiar with the vernacular of morning lunch and asked more questions about the eating habits on the farm than Gunter's drinking habits. She concluded that there were probably worse habits Gunter could have developed even though twelve cups a day did seem excessive.

With the soapy film rinsed from her back he gently pulled her against his chest and together they reclined against the tub. He threaded his hands under her arms and tenderly cupped her breasts. He didn't move his hands, he didn't reach for her nipples, he simply held each breasts in his hands and rested his head against hers.

Although she felt the excitement surging through his penis against the small of her back she eventually understood the act wasn't meant to serve as a prelude to sex. Appreciating the moment of total relaxation she realized it was the perfect opportunity to learn about his name. "Gunter? I don't believe I have ever met another person named Gunter. Any specific reason for your name?

His head and hands remained comfortably positioned as he answered. "My parents are both of Germanic origin and they believed in the importance of a name to carry on the tradition. Therefore, my name technically bears an umlaut over the vowel u. The story goes that at the time of my birth they had not reached an agreement on what to name the baby. If I had been a girl the name given would have been Hertha. If for no other reason, I'm glad I am not a girl. Upon hearing that she gave birth to a boy, my mother wanted to name me Rudolph, after her father, since he always wanted a son but only had daughters. But my father said the name needed to leave a lasting image in people's minds. He suggested the name Gunter, which means warrior. Plus, my father informed my mother that when he saw me in the hospital nursery through the glass I looked like a Gunter and not a Rudolph. I still find the whole thing humorous since I am the furthest thing from being a warrior."

When he laughed she again felt his appendage rubbing on her back. She discovered that when he carried on with the conversation the movement created more excitement within her than him.

"So, Esme? Any specific reason for the name?"

Staring at her toes that she had propped up against the end of the tub to keep from sliding down she spoke. "The story in some sense isn't all that different than yours. I arrived rather late in my parents' life and they were hoping I would be the son they never had, or so I was told, in order to carry on the family name. To make that happen my parents only selected male names thinking they could influence the outcome. Well, when their daughter arrived they had to scramble to find a girl's name. My mother, Esther, and my father, Melvin, thought they were very creative when they came up with Esme. You get it? "Es" for Esther and "me" for Melvin? Don't get the wrong idea, they loved me dearly and provided for me until their untimely death in a car crash."

"I'm sorry."

"Oh, don't be, it was many years ago. I was only 14 at the time. Fortunately, my mother's sister was willing to take me in."

"I am guessing based on your earlier comment, 'or so I was told,' that there is more to the story. At least I sensed a bit of hidden agenda connected with those words."

"Very perceptive. Yes there is more to the story. In fact this is why I am here in Seattle." Delivering the remainder of the story with her back against him didn't feel right, she needed to measure his reaction. Repositioning herself Esme faced Gunter and continued. "My aunt, after I graduated from high school and was preparing to leave for college, informed me that I had a brother. I was stunned. Eighteen years and never once any mention of a sibling. Over the course of the next few days a steady stream of questions poured out. Is he alive? Where does he live? How old is he? What does he do? What about at the time of the funeral, did he come to the funeral? Does he know our parents are dead? Does he know I exist? Unfortunately, the answers did not flow in response quite as smoothly. What I learned over an extended period of time is that he, Melvin, aka Junior, is 20 years my senior and he suffers from schizophrenia. The amazing thing is that he is still alive. He was institutionalized for a considerable part of his life however, after my parents died, that changed and for the last twenty some years he has been living on the streets in various cities. On Tuesday afternoon I received a phone call that Junior was on the streets of Seattle, avoiding the police but creating chaos. For whatever reason, Seattle has become the place where he returns. It has been five years since the last time I had any contact with him.

Reaching out and taking her hands in his he asked, "Your plan?"

"Hopefully find him and get him the help he needs and a place where he will be safe."

"Is he a threat to you or himself?"

"Himself? Yes. Schizophrenics tend to be prone to attempt suicide. Others? Occasionally. Me? It has not been an issue to this point. With his illness one never knows."

Before the words came out he thought about how best to frame them. He had no right to suggest she be careful, but he was concerned for her wellbeing. "Will you promise me that you will not take any unnecessary risks?" That came out sounding more forceful than he desired, but it was reflective of what he felt.

"Yes, but you needn't worry. I don't plan on getting hurt." She smiled as she answered.

"What's so funny?"

"Funny? Nothing, it's not funny at all. In fact, it's really sad. Here you are, we just met, and yet you are worried about me and my safety."

"I don't understand. How is that sad?"

"I have been married nearly twelve years and the only thing Mark, my husband, was concerned about when he heard the news about Junior was the added responsibility he would have during my absence." She couldn't look at him as she spoke because she knew she would start to cry. She cried once before him already and that was enough.

He stretched out and pulled her close to his body in order to hug her. She ignored the water cascading over the edge and melted against his chest when she heard him speak. "For that, I am truly sorry."

Blushing she offered a word of thanks and then, as she pulled away, quickly added "but enough about me. How about you, why are you here? And if you already told me I apologize, I just forgot."

Pulling a towel from the rung on the back of the door he spread it out to soak up some of the water pooling on the tile floor. His eyes fixed on the towel darkening in color; as it lied heavy with water, he spoke. "You didn't forget. I have been avoiding any discussion of why I am in Seattle."

"Okay, now you have my attention. Is there something illegal connected with your visit? Or, are you running away from something or maybe someone and you hope to hide, to relocate here? And the pain in your back wasn't the result of being thrown from a horse, you probably can't even ride a horse, but it occurred during your act of fleeing." She was teasing him because she saw the burden he bore on his face and she had hoped to lighten the mood and make him smile. She loved his smile even though he didn't show it very often. She remembered during dinner at 13 Coins when asked why he didn't smile more, he said something about not wanting to wear it out from overuse.

Without smiling he responded. "Aren't you the funny one? No, my visit to Seattle has nothing to do with any illegal actions nor am I fleeing anyone. I am here for a meeting with a dead man."

"Excuse me?" The water temperature dropped another ten degrees as Esme's body shivered with the thought of the unknown.

"At two o'clock this afternoon I am going to visit a dead man."

Without thinking she looked at her left wrist to determine the current time, but her watch had been removed prior to stepping into the tub. Still confused she asked for clarity. "Care to elaborate and fill in the missing details?"

"Late Monday afternoon, my friend and college roommate for four straight years fell over dead. The doctor said that he was dead before he hit the ground as his heart just sort of exploded."

Nodding her head as the pieces fell into place she stated, "And the funeral is this afternoon."

"Yes. I got the call Tuesday midday that the funeral was today and his parents asked me to serve as one of the pallbearers. One doesn't think about death at our age until it smacks you in the face. I feel guilty that I didn't take the time to stay in touch with him and now it's too late. The list of excuses is endless, but seriously, how long does it take to pick up the phone and call someone?"

Feeling empathy for one another bonded them in a manner that sex had not. As the bubbles dissipated they stepped cautiously from the tub and onto the wet tile floor partially covered with towels. When Esme reached for a dry towel on the sink she felt Gunter wrapping a towel over her shoulders and patting her dry. As she turned to face him, Gunter pulled her close to his body. He pushed her hair, still filled with droplets of water, back away from her face so that he might behold her entire face. Gazing down into her amber colored eyes he kissed her cheek softly and then spoke. "I would like you to stay the night again. In fact, I will be in the city until late Sunday afternoon and I would like you to stay with me that entire time." He left the invite simple, he did not want to overburden her and he certainly did not want to force her.

Rocking forward onto the balls of her feet she kissed him. Falling back only slightly she answered, "I would like that very much." And then she rocked forward again to kiss him deeper and more passionately.

Reclining on the bed Gunter went about cancelling the

reservation he booked at another hotel and postponed Esme's arrival at her hotel until Sunday afternoon, as she planned to stay in Seattle until the following Wednesday. The room, their room in the Vance Hotel was reserved for another two nights with a simple call to the front desk. Gunter returned the room phone to its cradle on the nightstand and rolled back to face Esme who wore nothing but her smile. Gunter couldn't resist, he smiled and Esme declared, "That's what I want to see."

"I think we probably have 30 minutes before we need to get dressed and find something to eat and I head out in search of the church and you in search of your brother.

Any ideas on how to spend the time?"

"Actually, I do, and I think it will bring another smile to your face."

CHAPTER 8

The doors of the elevator scaled apart and Gunter stepped from the metal floor to the carpeted hall and sensed the absence of normalcy. He felt the weight of air as his shoulders slumped and drove him forward so that he stooped like an old man. He heard the darkness as the sound of emptiness pounded on the drum in his ears. He tasted the stale crunch of defeat even though his mouth was empty. He witnessed the anguish of despair when his eyes watered in the absence of another human walking the hall. The trek down the long hall was surreal; he paused before he reached the room to consider if the ecosphere that swirled about was an outcrop of his afternoon with a dead man or mirrored Esme's afternoon in search of her brother.

The mood was such that as the room key slipped into the keypad and aligned with the tumblers and freed the lock Gunter knew that Esme's day had been as exhausting as his. The hollow thud of the deadbolt liberated from the doorframe clutched his throat and he labored to maintain focus as the door swung inward and gloom flooded past him and escaped into the chaos in the hall. The lives of two dejected and disheartened individuals were about to crash and bump up against the other. The looming question was, would the empathy from the morning sustain them and bond them as a united front again in the evening?

Esme laid on the chair curled in the fetal position burrowed beneath a comforter she pulled from the bed. Mascara like tracks in the river bottom where pick-up trucks had gone mudding lined the length of her cheeks. Her hair suffered from the endless drizzle that blanketed the city.

Without interrupting Esme's self-designed sanctuary Gunter perched himself on the arm of the chair and tenderly brought her head to his lap. He ran one hand along the outline of the comforter where he believed her arm was while the other hand fluffed the strands of her matted, frosted hair. Her head in his lap while he busied his hand with the long strands of her hair, reminded him of the scene when he spent the night cradling his daughter after she received news that her best friend had been kidnapped, raped and left to die in the woods. There were no words to explain to a nine year old why her best friend no longer existed, or why her life ended in such a cruel and horrible manner. There would be plenty of time in the future for speaking, what she needed at that moment was the closeness of another human being who loved her. Gunter had nothing to offer in the form of words, because Esme had not yet spoken, what he had to offer was his presence and a willingness to be patient. What transpired with his daughter, he was confident, would happen with Esme; that before night's end she would share the events of the day.

When his legs grew numb from the combination of not moving and the weight of Esme's head he carefully lifted her head to reposition his body on the arm of the chair. He respected the solitude as much for her as for himself as it provided him time to reflect on the events of his own afternoon. When the opportunity presented itself he too would speak of the afternoon not for the purpose of securing answers but to unburden his spirit.

As the sun set behind the skyline the room was lit by the glow of the city lights. When Esme's stomach rumbled a cry for food Gunter slid off the arm of the chair and knelt before her so that he might meet her eye to eye. His cheeks rose slightly as he half smiled at her, kissed her forehead and, rather than ask if she was hungry, knowing she would decline any offer of food, said, "I saw a Chinese restaurant with takeout a few blocks down the street. I am going to pick up an order. Do you have any specific requests?"

She answered, as he knew she would. "I'm not hungry."

Holding her chin in his right hand he spoke, "I don't believe I asked if you were hungry, but if there is something in particular you want."

After several minutes of silence and avoiding his eyes she sat up, looked directly at him and said, "Well, if I have to eat, I like sweet and sour pork."

"Sweet and sour pork it is. White or brown rice?" As the comforter fell from her body he noticed that she was dressed in what appeared to be a two-piece pajama set. He couldn't help but noticed how she made even a simple blue and white cotton twill weave pair of pajamas sexy.

"Rice?" A slight wrinkle appeared between her amber colored eyes.

"Yes, you know, the small stuff about a fourth of an inch in length that's either white or brown in color."

With a partial smile she sassed back, "Yes, I know rice."

"Good. I was beginning to wonder who this woman was that I had allowed myself to become attracted to." He knew perfectly well what he said. The moment demanded honesty even though it was framed in the context of playful banter about food.

Leaning forward she kissed him. The meeting of their lips was not long, forceful, or riddled with passion, yet both realized that something was very different from every other exchange that had occurred up to that point. Although neither said it, they both understood that this "relationship" had the potential to become extremely dangerous and neither could predict the outcome. Therefore, when their eyes slowly opened they saw the other person differently.

After a moment of clumsy stillness Esme spoke first. "Thank you for being here. I am not sure how I would have survived without someone as understanding as you."

"Don't sell yourself short. You are a gifted woman and you would have done fine. But, it's nice to share things, including a meal. I'm going to get the food and something to drink. I should be back shortly." As he stood he bent over the chair and quickly kissed her, grabbed his hat, and was out the door.

The brown paper bag was three-quarters filled with small white boxes each tightly packed with a Chinese specialty. A second brown bag held four bottles of wine, two white and two red. From his shirt pocket Gunter produced two sets of disposable chopsticks wrapped in paper.

"Please don't tell me you didn't pick up a fork, a knife, or a spoon."

"Alright, but here you go anyway." Gunter presented her with her own chopsticks.

Shaking her head, Esme joined Gunter on the floor next to a petite coffee table. "I can't do it Gunter."

"Have you ever tried?" Gunter asked as he attempted to model her seated position of crossing her legs.

"Not really, but I know I can't."

"Can't or don't want to?"

"Both!" Her answer was quite emphatic.

"Your other option is your fingers and that only works once the food cools."

"Well, professor, how did you master the use of chopsticks? I don't know many cowboys who use chopsticks."

"And just how many cowboys do you know?"

"That's beside the point."

After fumbling with the chopsticks, still joined at the top, she tossed them on the tabletop as she spoke. "I'm serious; I don't think I can learn how to eat with those things."

"Half the experience of eating Chinese is using chopsticks." The thought occurred to him and he needed to ask. "You have eaten Chinese haven't you?"

"No..." Hesitation followed as she cast her eyes downward and then she finished, "Not really!"

He reached over, rested his hand on her thigh suggesting it wasn't a big deal and again handed her the chopsticks. "Here, take the set and break them apart at the end. First, hold the upper chopstick like a pencil, about a third of the way from the top." Gunter waited as Esme carefully followed his directions. When she had placed the stick in her hand he continued. "You know, it's the little things that one notices in the beginning stages of a relationship that as the years pass are taken for granted. And yet, it is the little things that keep a relationship exciting, fresh, and healthy. For example, I noticed in the airport how you held your book in your left hand as you read and how you cradled the fork gracefully in your left hand as you eat."

"Being left handed in a right handed world has been challenging. But I wonder, is it all the little things that are noticed or only those that are out of the ordinary? Would you have consciously noted if I held my book or fork in my right hand?"

"Precisely, that is the question. Will there come a time when the act of you twirling a few strands of your hair with your right hand will go unnoticed? How you prefer to sit with your legs crossed and your toes hidden? Which, by the way, is killing my knees. Or how your chest becomes red with blotches, or…"

She interrupted him that she might make a point. "I would have to say yes, because that is the difference between infatuation and stability. One doesn't need to notice all the little things every single time because the relationship is stable."

"And stable is good? It's enough?"

"I don't know. I will tell you when I get there."

"We better keep the lesson moving or you will be using your fingers. Next, place the second chopstick against your ring finger, holding it with the base of the thumb. It should be pointing the same way as the first chopstick. Are you good? Can we move to the last step?"

"Yes, and please hurry before these sticks fall to the carpet."

"Move the upper chopstick with your thumb, index, and middle fingers. Grab a piece of food between the lower and upper chopsticks." Passing the open box of sweet and sour pork he offered her the opportunity to practice. "Here, try and grab a chuck of pork."

On the first try she successfully transported a piece of pork from the box to her open mouth. Together they laughed and Gunter applauded the initial success. Esme patted her mouth with a cotton washcloth and wiped away remnants of red dye from the sweet sauce.

Since he basically ignored her earlier question she asked him again, "So, how is it that a cowboy has mastered the art of using chopsticks?"

"During my senior year in high school we had a foreign exchange student from Japan who became a good friend.

I taught him the fine art of snipe hunting and he taught me how to use chopsticks." Watching her struggle with a second smaller piece of breaded pork he said, "And when the skill fails you, and it will, you use my method that I call, shoveling it in."

"Shoveling it in?" With both hands pressing down on her thighs and Esme straightening up it was obvious she wasn't buying the new terminology.

Gunter quickly responded and, to add validity to his words, he demonstrated the act. "Hold the plate, bowl or, in our case, the box, close to your chin and quickly bring the stick to your mouth before the items can fall off."

Reaching for a new box of food to test the method Esme worked the sticks and spoke at the same time. "Which is about half a step above the finger method."

Over the sweet and sour pork, among a variety of other Chinese items, Esme shared the details of a sour afternoon of traveling the city streets, hitting the places where Junior had previously been. She attempted to speak with people who were intoxicated, people who were delirious due to the lack of a consistent diet, the use of drug substances, or the absence of prescribed medication, and people who reeked from the filth and the dirt that they lived and slept in night and day. Each conversation proved as worthless as simply searching the underpasses, the bridges, and the back alleys. She went to various homeless shelters and discovered that Junior had spent part of Monday night at one shelter but because he was loud and vocal and scared the other people staying there, security called the police. By the time the police arrived Junior had vanished into the night. That incident activated the call on Tuesday.

The search would need to expand beyond the city proper and into the outer ring of the suburbs. Esme's body language attested that she was not thrilled with that thought, there was no guarantee Junior had not left the city entirely because he was fearful of being arrested or killed. Tossing the empty box of sweet and sour pork and her chopsticks on the coffee table, Esme announced that she was finished eating Chinese. Which came as no surprise since all the boxes were at least half empty.

Gunter, totally riveted by the details of her afternoon and the angst placed on her both physically and emotionally, blurted out without much forethought, "Where else has he traveled?"

A glass of Chardonnay in hand she scooted back against the bed for back support. "San Francisco, Portland, LA once, I believe. Since I was first introduced to Junior some fifteen years ago he has stayed on the west coast. I think, and I don't have any evidence for this, I just think he likes the milder weather and generally people are more willing to tolerate homeless folks. But, honestly, I don't always know where he is or where he has been.

"Canada?"

"Never, that I am aware of.

Transporting two bottles of wine and his own glass, Gunter joined Esme on the floor at the foot of the bed. "So, where do we start tomorrow?"

"We? What do you mean, we? You don't need to go with me to search for him."

"What else am I going to do, and seriously, I want to help you."

"Is that comment based on your afternoon?"

"What, that I want to help you?"

"No, that you have nothing else to do. You have all of Seattle you could visit. There are countless attractions right outside the front door of this hotel. Yet, you want to go searching for my brother? Maybe it's your turn to tell me about your afternoon and your visit with a dead man."

"I don't know where to begin, it was all too crazy and disappointing and humbling."

"Humbling?" The inward dip of Esme's eyebrows confirmed her confusion. "That's not a word I would expect to be linked to crazy and disappointing."

"Humbling because for the first time I honestly thought about my own death. I mean, we think about death, but not in a serious manner. We know we're not invincible and yet the vast majority of the population live as though they are. There are a limited number of days I, you, anyone will spend walking the face of the earth. Each morning I awake I am one step closer to it being my last day. It is humbling to think that I can control so many aspects of my life but I can't control the end. Sure," with the wave of his hand he continued, "we attempt to use heroic measures to avoid or postpone its arrival, but in the end the truth is that no matter the number of days life is extended, it still IS going to end."

"I don't mean to be judgmental with this question, but is this humbling or depressing?"

"See, that's part of the struggle surrounding death, to honestly address our mortality is labeled as depressing or suicidal. I am not depressed, at least I don't think I am, and I know I'm not suicidal. I am merely coming to the realization that if I were to live to the age of 70, I am already at the halfway point of my life. Today, sitting in the church, having stared at the waxy complexion of a man who was my roommate for four years, a man with whom I did many stupid things, a man with whom I discussed philosophical topics deep into the night, a man who no longer breaths, will no longer play and laugh and build things, I realized that could be me. There are no guarantees. As the five other guys and I carried Bradley's casket to the cemetery I found myself asking, did his life make a difference? Was there a purpose to his existence? As the pastor threw a handful of sand that came from a plastic tube and mumbled some words about being earth and dust, I heard my inner voice asking, does my life make a difference?"

"Does it have to make a difference?" Seated at his left side she spoke without looking directly at him.

Pausing a moment to consider the question he replied in a mellow tone. "I never actually considered that option."

"Consider my brother for a second; is he any less of a human being because of the manner in which he lives? If nothing changes between now and the time of his death would his existence have been meaningless? Simply because Bradley was not able to fulfill all his dreams doesn't mean he didn't make a difference."

"I guess that's what's so humbling, I don't have the answers and therefore I must live by faith."

Her head leaning against his shoulder, she listened as he spoke of the craziness that unfolded as the family assembled. The whole event became uncomfortable. Rather than gather to celebrate Bradley's life, they fought, they bickered, they made excuses to justify why he was dead. It was the worst nightmare Gunter had experienced until the actual funeral service started. The pastor could have seized the moment to offer a word of hope and comfort, or at the very least, to speak well of the dead, instead it became an opportunity to scare the people.

"The entire afternoon was so disappointing because I was looking forward to hearing stories about Bradley's childhood, his return to Seattle, and I was hoping to add to the collection. I had hoped that by attending the funeral I could offer a gracious word to the family and I could reminisce about a chapter of my life and turn the page, unfortunately none of that occurred."

"This might not be the right time and I might be totally off base, but…" she inhaled deeply, "…at least for me, it feels like a page has been turned and a new chapter is being written."

"It's so weird you should say that because I was thinking something very similar when I brought back the Chinese food. Earlier this afternoon when I returned to the hotel everything seemed slightly out of balance and then tonight, even though I knew nothing from our day had been resolved and probably wouldn't be resolved, the moment I stepped from the elevator into the hall it was different."

"So…" with hesitancy she continued, "you don't think I'm crazy?"

"Good heavens no!"

"You feel it too?"

"Esme, I felt it the moment I saw you and it has been growing ever since."

Smiling as she spoke, "That's so funny Gunter because that is exactly how I felt and feel at this moment."

She wanted to say more but instead carefully, without moving her head or shifting her body, she placed her hand inside of his and weaved her fingers between his. Even though, as he tightened his grip she felt the ring on his left hand, she wasn't about to let go. They sat together on the floor against the bed in silence, sustaining one another when no one else could provide them the support they needed.

Thinking she had drifted off he whispered, "Are you awake?"

"Oh yes! I am just inhaling the moment."

"The last part of a Chinese meal, American style that is, is the fortune cookie. You select which cookie you want. My daughters informed me one day, although I think they were making this up on the fly, that you can't read the fortune until after you eat the entire cookie. That is of course if you want the fortune to come true."

"Well then, we best follow that practice. I will take the one in your right hand." After quickly consuming the sweet vanilla flavored cookie Esme read the note. "'Our greatest glory consists not in never falling, but in rising every time we fall.' I think these words pertain more to you than me considering your current physical state."

At Gunter's turn he first read the fortune to himself and before reading it aloud he said. "I think this one not only fits well for you or me, but for us. 'Life is not a mystery to be solved, but a reality to be experienced.'"

"Us, I like the sound of that. I have no idea what us means, it just sounds nice."

"Since we received a third cookie should 'us' open it together?"

Similar to a turkey wishbone at Thanksgiving each took a corner and pulled upward. The cookie crumbled and the white slip gently floated to the floor. They ate the crumbs and together they read, "Practice makes perfect."

Without a moments pause Gunter's words sounded as though they belonged with the fortune, "I'm ready."

"Really? First let me ask, how is your back?"

"Honestly, it is quite painful, but I am still game."

Taking both of his hands in hers she asked, "Would you mind if we switched places and you allow me to create the motion?"

"I'm dreaming of the view already."

As they raced to the topside of the bed Gunter's elbow knocked the radio and it struck the base of the lamp and music woofed through the speakers. Apparently the radio had never been turned off; the volume had only been turned low so they hadn't noticed. As Esme straddled Gunter the room filled with the words, *You Are So Beautiful.*

Gunter whispered as he stared into Esme's eyes that were only inches from his, "In so many ways, in so many ways."

CHAPTER 9

Esme stirred, forced open her eyes and established the source of her discomfort. What actually woke her was the need to empty her bladder. Knees pressed together, as though bonded by superglue, she hoped to buy a few additional minutes in bed. With her left ear buried in the pillow the first thing that came into view was the clock radio that read 10:07. She rubbed her right eye and squinted to narrow her focus and read the numbers a second time convinced she had misread what appeared to be the first two digits. She was unable to remember the last time she slept past 9am, even 8am pushed the extreme. She had two kids and a husband after all. The second reading yielded a similar result, 10:08. Unable to control the need to pee her legs swung free of the bed and the moment her feet struck the carpet she made tracks towards the bathroom. In her haste she failed to notice that Gunter laid flat on the floor stretching out his lower back.

Similar to a cartoon character, Esme stopped midair with her left leg positioned to descend directly onto Gunter's midsection. In slow motion she attempted to redirect her foot beyond Gunter's body. The effort, while laudable, failed to yield the desired result. Esme's left heel struck the side of Gunter's ribs and when her foot reached the carpet it skidded even further away from her body. Her right foot stayed planted which caused Esme to slowly drop lower and lower until she was performing the splits with her pelvis resting on Gunter. Time was of the essence, to linger with an explanation or an apology would have been disastrous. Using his torso as a pommel horse she pressed down with her hands as she pulled her legs inward. The moment she regained her balance she leaped over Gunter and sprinted to the bathroom not wasting time to swing the door closed.

Gunter couldn't resist the opportunity to tease her. "I told you I would be able to give you ten reasons why sleeping in the nude was good for you. What's this one, number 8? You don't need to waste precious seconds to pull down pajama bottoms when you gotta pee really bad!"

"You know, just because the door is open doesn't mean I can hear you very clearly. Did you say I don't need to waste time with pajama bottoms because you are going to join me in the shower?"

Even though he couldn't see her Gunter heard the smile as she spoke. He too cracked a sly smile as he noted an opportunity to propose reason number 9. "No, that's not what I said, but I like the idea and your suggestion gave me reason number 9, one doesn't have to undress to take a shower."

He stood in the doorway, when she turned back from starting the shower and before she greeted him with a kiss she informed him that as the numbers became greater his reasoning became lamer. She warned him that number 10 needed to be a homerun to sell her on the idea permanently.

The clock radio displayed 10:54 and once again the volume had been turned down to a level only a dog could hear, although neither of them could remember actually touching the device. Gunter placed a glass of grape juice on the bathroom counter. Esme thanked him and inquired about getting some food. Gunter said he saw an advertisement for a café, Three Girls Bakery, at some place called Sanitary Market. Supposedly the bakery existed since the early nineteen hundreds and, based on Gunter's logic, that meant the food must be tolerable. Both agreed to use breakfast as a time to discuss how and where to search for Junior.

Over a bagel smothered with cream cheese Esme began to speculate locations surrounding Seattle that might attract Junior, especially if he was in a state of panic and overcome with fear. Gunter was stunned to learn that Junior had an attraction to water. He momentarily stopped chewing his Bismarck and nearly choked when he attempted to speak. "I'm quite shocked that someone who lives in a world of paranoia would perceive water, especially large bodies of water, as anything but threatening."

Reaching across the tiny circular table with napkin in hand Esme brushed crumbles from Gunter's chin and shared how she too questioned how her brother could find solitude and sanctuary in the presence of water. "I initially didn't believe Junior when he requested that I take him to Mercer Island in order that he might walk the beaches and wade in the water. Even as I watched the waters of Lake Washington lap over his bare feet and as he marched knee deep into the lake, I feared that he would not stop walking and this was merely a suicidal swim. Yet as he emerged it was as though he did so transformed, bathed clean, made whole and I no longer questioned his relationship with bodies of water."

"Any idea why water? Is it some religious connection, perhaps, a washing of uncleanliness? A baptismal moment?"

"I couldn't comprehend the oddity of it either until we visited Luther Burbank School on Mercer Island. I don't know for certain, because he refuses to confirm or deny it, but I think he attended the school. What I know for certain was that being on the island and roaming about the grounds of the old school relaxed him in a way I had not previously witnessed. Not just physically but emotionally, even spiritually, if I can say that."

"What do you know about the school? Is it still open?"

"No, the school closed several years ago. After some research I discovered the mission of the Luther Burbank School was straightforward; assist neglected, indigent, and unfortunate children." After a cynical laugh she continued. "Sounds like something that would fit the needs of Junior doesn't it, especially if he had been caught by social services wandering the streets of Seattle during his early adolescent years?"

"So you think we should head to Mercer Island and the old school grounds to find Junior?"

"As strange as this is going to sound, I have to say, no." To make sure there was no confusion Esme shook her head as she spoke.

"No?" Gunter couldn't believe his ears. He thought the choice was obvious. He had even felt confident that Junior would be located before day's end. "But, you just said…"

"Yes, I know, but you need to understand, Junior is extremely intelligent. His IQ is in the realm of highly gifted. The day he shared with me his sanctuary he lost his place of solitude. I didn't understand it at first but the request to visit Mercer Island was a selfless act, perhaps the greatest I have ever experienced. He invited me into his sacred space knowing that my presence would defile its pureness. The private became public. The moment I stepped foot on the Island with him he knew it would be the last time he would."

"So where does that leave us?" Gunter's face bore the marks that he grasped the depth and weight of frustration

Esme must have felt yesterday, if not every day, when searching for her brother.

"On the other side."

"The other side? I don't follow."

"If Junior is still in the Seattle area my guess is that he has found another island to provide him the sanctuary and solitude needed. We need to go west. Bainbridge Island."

"Doesn't that require a ferry trip?"

"Yes, that's the quickest route. I know what you're thinking, but remember, Junior is extremely resourceful."

Draining the final swig of liquid, blended with a few grounds, from the coffee cup Gunter said, "Well then, Bainbridge it is."

Before he could stand Esme clamped down on his hand and kept him from moving. "I want you to know how much I appreciate this. Thank you. I also want you to know that I want to spend the time on Bainbridge not just looking for Junior but spending time with you in public. I want us to have this afternoon together."

"Esme, as long as we can be together, I don't care what we do. If it's possible to be tourist and detectives in search of Junior, I'm all for it."

To keep from crying Esme's amber eyes dropped to the tile floor and she lifted her hand from Gunter's arm. It had been so long since anyone spoke to her with such passion. What was it about Seattle that put her on the receiving end of selfless actions? She knew she didn't deserve this kindness.

Leaving Three Girls' Bakery Gunter scooped Esme's hand into his, kissed the back of it, and together the two walked effortlessly to the rental car.

At the Bainbridge Ferry Esme suggested, in hopes of adding to the romance of the moment, that they not take the car onto the island. They could walk or rent bicycles to traverse the island, plus either form of transportation would allow access to places a car never would.

Less than a block after departing from the Bainbridge Ferry the couple had to decide between the selections of a bicycle built for two or two individual bikes. Gunter rationalized that two bikes would be better if they needed to separate to give chase or corner Junior. Never having met Junior Gunter recognized that he was limited to the picture Esme painted of her brother with words and that created a vacuum as he attempted to envision what might unfold when and if Junior was located. He also wasn't sure how Junior's presence might influence the last twenty-four hours of his stay in dahlia city. He thought it was strange that a city would identify a flower to represent itself, but before he publicly commented he thought it best to determine if other cities acted in a similar manner. What he knew for certain, based on observation, was that the city proudly displayed their flower of choice everywhere possible. The idea of dahlias fit much better with Esme than Junior in Gunter's mind.

Pedaling northwest from the bicycle shack the couple discovered that the transition from tourist to detective was extremely difficult. The solar rays intensified the pigment of Esme's and Gunter's skin as a gentle breeze heavy with moisture drifted inland from Puget Sound and enabled them to ignore the unusually warm day. The fourteenth of June seldom delivered such perfect conditions. The difficulty of remaining focused was compounded as the initial blocks were littered with cute storefronts and enticing window displays that attracted Esme and Gunter. The first hour on the island Esme and Gunter spent as much time off the seat of their bikes as on.

Dizzy from wandering hand in hand through bouquet stores, specialty shops, and bookstores, and full from an ice cream parlor adventure complete with every possible flavor imaginable the handlebars of their ten-speed Schwinn's pointed south. Blakely Harbor Park became the point of destination. As they left the commercial sector and spun through the residential areas dotted with large two story houses Gunter questioned Esme, "Why Blakely Harbor?" She described in detail that in addition to the bay, the solitude created by the abandoned Port Blakely Mill, the former site of one of the world's largest sawmills, provided the ideal location for Junior to seek refuge.

The journey to Blakely Harbor was not long but the ride, at least for weekend cyclists, was challenging as the terrain was anything but flat.

Gunter recognized the signs immediately, failure. Esme's shoulders slumped, her stride shortened, her arms were idle and tight against her body as she walked. Forsaking the bikes several hundred yards from the water to more thoroughly investigate the ground and surrounding area for any signs of Junior revealed that he probably had been there but was not currently.

Frustration mingled with sadness skewed the delivery of her words. "Missed him again."

"How do you know he was here?" Gunter didn't doubt that Junior had been in this location but he wondered how she knew with such confidence, especially since he couldn't see anything beyond footprints.

"See here?" She pointed to marks in the sand next to what had been a fire pit. "Junior has a slight limp, or really, a bum right leg that he drags. The accident occurred when he was in his early twenties. He was running to latch onto an empty railroad car and just as he reached for the ladder and placed his right foot on the first rung the train lunged forward and just as quickly rocked to a stop. The force of the unexpected movement forward drove Junior's body against the ladder and his foot through the rung. The sudden and violent stop hurdled his body backwards but his right leg was stuck on the backside of the ladder so he hung upside down banging his head on the rocks lining the tracks. The fierce action resulted in Junior dislocating his hip and severely damaging his femur. Being homeless his long term health care was minimal and he was harnessed with the physical limitation."

Gunter internally chastised himself for worrying about trying to catch Junior if they saw him. He felt compelled to say he was sorry, but he really had nothing to apologize for, so he said, "Do we wait here hoping he will return?"

"No. This is going to sound cold and callus, but I learned the hard way early in my search for Junior not to set up camp hoping he would show up at a particular location. It doesn't work that way, at least not for Junior. There are too many variables driving his life. There are variables I can't begin to imagine. No, either someone gives me a lead on where he is or I see him like I had hoped we would here."

The pain hovering just below the surfaced connected to the reality to which Esme spoke cut Gunter to the core. His first impulse was to reach out to solve her dilemma, to offer a word that would make everything alright, but there was nothing he could say or do that would provide a solution. The best he could offer was his presence in the form of a hug that lingered beyond the counting of one Mississippi, two Mississippi, three...

The fragrance along with the soft texture of her hair against his neck functioned as an aphrodisiac. It was not the first time he experienced a heightened sexual attraction to a woman in need and it bothered him. As they stood, arms draped round each other he questioned why he would be aroused. Was it his masculine demeanor raging forth to rescue the damsel in distress? Did it feed some carnal instinct of male dominance and female fragility and servitude? Both options angered him for he labored not to fall victim to the macho image driven by the media. Yet, there was no denying his level of arousal, both physically and mentally. To save Esme and himself embarrassment he twisted slightly to avoid contact with her lower body until he eventually pulled back, took her chin in his hand and asked, "Are you ready to search other sectors of the island?"

The ride to the western side of the island lacked the energy and excitement previously displayed by both riders. Esme's expectations for a miracle had been tapered. Reality seized control of that portion of her brain that was filled with optimism and she informed Gunter that Junior would only be found if and when he wanted to be found. Boarding the ferry for the thirty-five minute return trip to Seattle they acknowledged that their stay on the island was considerably shorter than either expected.

The positive side, at least in Gunter's mind, was that the early departure eased the level of stress experienced as they prepared for a night out on the town.

Entering the room a few minutes before six o'clock Gunter informed Esme that he made a dinner reservation for eight forty-five and that they would need to leave the hotel by eight-fifteen. He apologized for the lateness of dining but it was the earliest a table was available and even then they were next to the kitchen door. Esme, having used the ride across the water to settle her disappointment looked forward to spending the evening with Gunter and didn't care where or when they went out. In her mind the time worked well.

"That's actually better because I can take a relaxing bubble bath, alone this time if you don't mind, and I can call home."

Gunter pretended to pout that he was not invited to share the bubble bath, but Esme assured him that there would be plenty of opportunities later in the evening for sharing, including a whole lot more than just bubbles. She pledged that this was about her. She needed the time for herself because she wanted to surprise him with a dress she couldn't explain why she even packed. Having addressed his sexual desires she continued, "Do you mind if I call home? I haven't spoken with my kids since we arrived in Seattle. I am feeling both guilty and lonely for them."

Gunter ignored the question and directed the conversation in another direction. "Have you spoken with your husband?"

Feeling like a skier attempting to out race an unexpected avalanche Esme stuttered initially. "N...o..." Taking a moment to gather her thoughts she asked, "Why do you ask?"

"You said, 'I haven't spoken with the kids'...and... well...I thought maybe...it doesn't matter." Her question made him realize that he was attempting to use her request to call home for his own motives.

Having nothing to conceal Esme proceeded in an effort to offer clarity. "In Denver I called home since when I left early Thursday morning everyone was asleep. I wanted to say good-bye to the kids. When I called mid-morning Mark was already off to work."

"Mark?"

"Yes, my husband's name is Mark." An edge not previously displayed materialized in Esme's voice. "Have you called home?" She decided if he could press her she could return the favor.

"Yes I did, yesterday after the funeral before returning to the hotel I stopped at a phone booth."

"Well then, you understand why I want to call my kids."

Both hands held up as though surrendering, the pace and the volume of his voice increased. "I never said you shouldn't or couldn't."

"I'm sorry, you're right you never did. I suppose I just needed to hear that it was okay with you."

"It's okay with me." Gunter paused for a moment and then added. "But I'm still interested to hear about your husband."

Esme who was en route to the bathroom stopped, rocked back on her heels and spun like a horse sorting a cow from the herd. "Why?"

"I'm not sure other than I'm curious what he does and who he is." The longer he talked the clearer his reason became. "I think I am curious because by learning something about him I might gain a better understanding of you."

"Of me?" The confusion drove Esme to take a seat on the edge of the bed. She needed to hear an explanation.

Seated in the chair with his boots firmly planted on the floor he calmly offered a reply. "Yes, of you. You married him, and from what I have deduced, together you have two kids. By hearing about him I will also discover what you like, what you value, what you..."

Leaning forward nearly sliding off the bed she interrupted him. "Let me stop you right there. The logic of your argument is extremely flawed."

"How so?" Gunter had an inquisitive look accompanied by quick short shake of his head.

"First," she used her fingers to count out each point,

"you assume that because we are married that represents what I like or even love. Two, you assume that my values are the same as my husbands. Third..."

"Okay, point well taken."

"But I'm not finished. Third, you assume..."

"Is it necessary to continue? I understand, you don't want to talk about your husband. I simply wanted to know what the man does for a living, sorry I asked." Crossing his arms he pressed back against the chair.

After a sigh and a relaxing of her back muscles that lowered her shoulders slightly, Esme crossed her legs and spoke calmly. "I still don't understand why that should matter to you."

Gunter wasted no time in responding. "And I don't understand why this is such a big deal. Is there something I am missing here?"

She uncrossed her legs, her shoulders rose and she pushed back further onto the bed and sat silently. When she eventually spoke each word uttered appeared heavy and immediately dropped to the floor. "Mark is a lawyer, a damn good one." She processed in her mind before the word was delivered that this was the first time she swore in his presence.

"Esme, it was never my intention to force you to tell me anything."

"No, I want to, or I should say, I need to. I'm just not sure how much I can tell."

She inhaled deeply and pushed the air out slowly. "We met when I was a junior in college and he was in his first year of law school. It was a blind date. I remember how nervous I was and how I couldn't wait for the evening to end."

"Obviously, there was a second date."

"The first date didn't end until after breakfast the next morning. I had too much to drink and ended up spending the night at his apartment. Honestly, the next morning I had no idea if anything happened. He was pretty drunk as well." Lifting her head up from the bedspread she looked across the room and directly into Gunter's eyes. "Don't look at me like that, I'm not proud of it, but that was nearly fifteen years ago."

"I'm not judging, believe me, I have done stupid things of which I am not proud." He remained in the chair determined to give her the space she needed.

"I didn't hear from him for several weeks and then one Saturday night several of us were out at the bar and he was there with his buddies. We sort of hooked up that evening with the understanding that we would not end up repeating our first date. I think he was equally embarrassed that he got so wasted."

"The two of you started dating at that point?"

"Yes and no. We dated but there was no consistent pattern. If there was a social event we accompanied the other. If we needed a distraction from our academic studies, we called."

"Working on a college campus I can tell you things haven't changed much." He couldn't explain why but questions continued to pour forth. "Was that your choice or his?"

"I initially thought it was my choice, the chemistry was lacking and there were no sparks, my leg never raised when he kissed me. A few years after we were married I began to understand our dating ritual was actually his choice."

"Did you date other people during that period?"

"I didn't, but I discovered, again years later, that he did. But that's getting ahead of myself."

"Sorry I'm distracting you with all my questions. I'll keep quiet, I promise."

"So you know, you may ask any questions you want, I can always refuse to answer." She smiled but since she didn't elevate her head Gunter never witnessed the nonverbal cue connected with her words.

"Following graduation I got a job at a small rural hospital some hundred miles from where Mark was about to start his final year of law school. I was excited because nurses were expected to work every station within the hospital and it would give me a wonderful opportunity to sharpen my skills and narrow my selection if I decided to specialize at some point."

"And have you selected an area?"

"I think so, I really enjoyed neonatal care. I haven't worked for a while, I took time off to be at home with the kids, but as they are getting older it is time to return. I hope to start a master's program within the next year."

"Good for you."

"Thank you. I only wish Mark felt the same way now and back then. When I moved he immediately started pressing the issue of marriage, which was something we hadn't previously discussed. By Thanksgiving we were engaged and a June wedding was in the works. Mark could never understand why I didn't immediately quit my job. At first I thought he was threatened by my possible success as a career woman, but eventually I understood it wasn't the career that he questioned, but my leaving the house."

Gunter moved to the bed and positioned himself next to Esme without touching her. Softly he stated, "I don't understand."

"Like I said, I didn't either. His jealousy wasn't about a career, my god, Mark was streaking up the lawyer ladder well on his way to becoming the youngest partner in the law firm. Mind you, this was no small firm. No, his jealously was rooted in questioning my fidelity."

"Did he have reason to be suspicious or jealous?"

She laughed so hard she snorted several times sounding like a pig. "I was the one who should have been suspicious but I was too trusting or blind to see the signs."

"You mean…"

"Yes, Mark was having an affair with his secretary so naturally he assumed I too was having an affair. It was at that time that I unearthed the reason during our early days together that we didn't see each other more, he was dating, or to be blunt, having sex with multiple partners."

"Not to be judgmental, but it sounds like a pattern, why did you stay with him?"

"When I finally learned what was happening, I was six months pregnant. It is difficult enough today to be a single parent, imagine what life would have been like for a child and me in 1965. I hoped that once it was exposed we could address his issues and it would be resolved."

"I'm sensing it wasn't?"

"Like a typical man he swore it would never happen again. He was sorry, on and on. But, it happened again. And from what I can tell, I think it might be happening again now." As she lay with her head resting on her left arm tears from her right eye rolled to her nose and dropped to the bedspread like droplets of rain falling from a roof.

"Esme, I am sorry." He narrowed the space between their bodies leaned his head forward and kissed her forehead before pulling back.

"I don't want to discuss this any further." She pulled her left arm toward her body so that she was now resting on her elbow and elevating her torso. "Would you mind showering first? I'll call my kids and then I'll hop in the tub for a quick soak."

"No, I don't mind."

An hour and half later Esme gracefully glided from the bathroom causing Gunter to nearly spill his glass of Merlot. She wasn't only beautiful she was breathtaking. The red dress clung to her body as though Michael Angelo painted it on. The silk like material captured the light and offered a glossy sheen. The dress, if it could be called such, complimented her shapely figure. The plunging neckline accentuated her cleavage, the perfectly centered belt rested against her flat stomach while calling attention to her curvy hips. The slit in the skirt, three quarters of the way up from the hemline, teased would be viewers with the hope she might extend her stride and lift the slit higher across her thighs.

Seductively her tongue grazed across her upper lip that had been highlighted with lipstick to match the dress. The act was followed with the question, "What do you think?"

"I can't think right now my heart is racing too fast." Reaching out he pulled her against his body and whispered, "You look stunning. If we plan to dine out we better leave immediately or…" He left the sentence unfinished leaving her imagination to run wild.

Their reservation for the evening was at the Space Needle and while the food was superb, and the atmosphere couldn't have been more romantic. Each time their eyes met they soaked in the presence of the other; the weight of their mood carried the shadow of the afternoon conversation. Even though neither spoke the name Mark, and even though he was 3,000 miles away probably fast asleep, it felt as if he was seated at the table with them. Therefore, the dinner conversation was limited.

With an after dinner drink to settle the food they held hands and quietly watched the city below them as the needle circled. They eaves dropped on the conversation of those seated close and smiled when intimate words were spoken. Esme blushed when a man at the neighboring table described in specific detailed what he planned to do to his dinner date when he got her home, to which Gunter merely winked and continued to smile. Gunter nodded his head toward the waiter, who stopped frequently at the table to inquire if additional services were required, in order that Esme might notice how the young man enjoyed admiring her body. At one point, with their drinks nearly gone, Gunter leaned forward to speak but Esme squeezed his hand and whispered, "words aren't necessary." And so he smiled, nodded in agreement, leaned back slightly, and absorbed the beauty before him, the beauty he was certain had been captured in the eye of every male in the room.

CHAPTER 10

The return to the Vance Hotel and entrance to the room unfolded completely opposite from their first arrival only two nights earlier. Rather than thrashing about wildly, Gunter took Esme in his arms and danced about the room. The radio station played the latest hits, not all easy to dance to, but that didn't seem to bother the couple as they swayed back and forth occasionally in rhythm to the music and other times not. As they moved past the corner of the bed carefully, so as not to bruise their shins, Glen Campbell's newest hit filled the room. Esme pulled back from Gunter's chest, stared up into his eyes and announced, "I love this song and until this very moment I had no reason to. You are my 'Rhinestone Cowboy'." As she sang along Gunter listened to her and ignored the radio even though he enjoyed Glen Campbell.

With her arms wrapped round his neck and with her high heels on, she could tip him forward so she no longer needed to raise up on her toes to kiss him. The coming together of their lips started soft and playfully but grew with intensity and purpose. When she released him from her grip her body remained pressed against his and she whisper a second time, "You are my Rhinestone Cowboy."

"That's cute and all," Gunter was embarrassed by the unsolicited attention, "but I'm not so sure the rhinestone image fits me too well."

"Don't sell yourself short there cowboy it…"

"There, in all honesty, just cowboy fits me a whole lot better."

"Cowboy it is then, but you will always be my rhinestone cowboy."

Gunter bent forward a few inches more and nuzzled her neck and when her eyes closed and her head drifted back he scooped her up, in spite of the stinging pain piercing his back, and he carefully placed her on the bed. He climbed on the bed, straddled her legs and lowered his body until it met hers, then he resumed kissing her neck. Slowly working his way down her voluptuous figure with his tongue he peeled the red dress from her. Inch by inch the dress crawled down her frame revealing skin waiting to be kissed and licked. Gunter did not leave a single patch of skin untouched.

In response to the sensual stripping of her body, Esme moaned with enjoyment whenever Gunter's tongue struck a nerve of excitement. The gentleness of his touch and tardiness of his movement caused Esme to arch her body away from the bed and into Gunter's mouth inviting him to move more aggressively and with greater pressure. Yet, aware of the impending movement of her body upward, from the years of anticipating a horse's movement, he lifted himself up thereby expanding her frustration and ecstasy simultaneously. The lighter his touch and the slower he moved the more her body tingled and ached.

With the dress resting just past her hips Gunter sat up, reached out with his right hand and touched her body to the right and inches above her pubic hairline. "Is this a tattoo or a birthmark? I can't believe I did not notice this until now."

"Birthmark. Silly, isn't it?"

"Silly? It is wonderful."

It became clear that she was uncomfortable with the potential for where the conversation might go so she controlled its direction. "The official description of the mark is 'Café au lait," coffee with milk."

"Whatever it's called, I like it."

Resting on her elbows in order to make eye contact with him, as he had positioned himself between her legs, she asked, "You like it because of its location or because it was unexpected?"

"I can't lie, the location" shaking his head ever so slightly "is magnificent. But what I really like, and I am sure you have heard this before, it looks like a heart."

Without smiling, so he couldn't read that she was joking with him, she asked, "What, do you think I have slept with every Tom, Dick, and Harry?"

"No, no, I, I," he stuttered as he attempted to clarify what he meant.

Before he could defend himself adequately she informed him she knew what he meant, and yes, a heart had been stated before. She also described the source of her defensiveness concerning the birthmark.

"I made the mistake one day in elementary school, in spite of the warning my mom had delivered, of showing the mark to my best friend in the bathroom. During recess the blotch and I became the topic of conversation. The initial attention was great; I was the most popular kid on the playground. I stood in the middle of a large circle of kids and one by one they stepped forward to see the mark. Eventually we attracted the attention of a teacher who quickly dispersed the kids and escorted me to the principal's office. Miss Anderson, the principal's secretary, had me take a seat and wait until Mr. Jackson returned from lunch. I remember that every fifth or sixth word Miss Anderson typed she would stop and tell me that I had nothing to worry about I was not in trouble. She went so far as to give me a stick of gum and placed my chair next to hers. I must have looked terribly scared. If I close my eyes I can still smell her perfume. Unfortunately, Mr. Jackson wasn't quite so considerate. He asked me to follow him into his smoke filled office. To this day I can't tolerate the smell of cigars. With the office door closed he told me that my actions on the playground were not appropriate behavior for a third grader. He told me several times that I wasn't in trouble I just couldn't go around showing that part of my body to other kids. He then informed me that he needed to see the mark in order to confirm the story. He stopped me as I raised my dress to show him and said I needed to take off all my clothes so he could determine the seriousness of the situation. I knew it wasn't right but how does a third grader say no to the principal? Needless to say, Mr. Jackson was not the principal the following week."

All Gunter could say was, "That must have been horrible. I am sorry that I..."

Pressing a finger against his lips she stopped him and said, "You had no way of knowing. That was a long time ago and I have dealt with it. Now where were we?"

Her smile told him he had permission to continue.

The moment he directed his tongue south of the café au lait she dropped to the bed and the blood again pulsated in her groin. She moved her hips to the right and then left so that his tongue might strike the perfect spot and push her past the ultimate ecstasy. The more she moved the less his tongue touched her. It wasn't until she stopped forcing the moment that he surprised her by licking the most sensitive spot on her entire body. She shivered with excitement and wanted more but he pulled back and continued to strip her body from the red dress.

It was not until he reached the soles of her feet that he moved back between her legs and yielded to her demand to make her eyes roll back into her head. But even then just as she was about to experience the floodgates opening he stopped, making her beg for more. It wasn't until she pleaded, "Don't stop, don't stop," that his tongue pressed on and made her scream.

After another fifteen minutes and the intensity of screams magnified three more times, her hoarse vocal cords were begging for him to stop. With the palms of both hands flat on the crown of his head she pushed downward and repeatedly croaked like a frog, "Stop, please stop, I can't, I can't go on it's too," squirming uncontrollably each time his tongue grazed her body she paused to capture her breath and then continued, "too sensitive."

At that point he pulled back and took his place at her left side. Like an overcooked noodle her limp body conformed to his. Portions of her body that previously had been firm and tight were loose and elastic. She was exhausted. Even when he placed his left hand on her right breast she never moved.

The purpose of his touch was not to tease or excite her further but to hold her, to cuddle, so he slid her tighter against his body. For several minutes they rested beside one another and neither attempted to speak but merely listened to the other breathe and felt the others' body. They resembled the Chinese symbols of Ying and Yang.

Some seventy hours earlier, for all practical purposes, these two people were complete opposites if not contradictory forces moving towards Seattle and yet they became interconnected and interdependent. Ying and Yang. In Gunter's mind the escapade was more than just falling into bed with a beautiful woman, there was something of depth and meaning to the brief encounter. There developed, in a matter of hours, a new level of connectedness that resulted in Gunter's question. "Why are you here?"

In a state of total relaxation Esme wasn't sure she heard or understood Gunter's words and therefore she endeavored to clarify what she thought she heard. "Why am I here?"

Gunter assumed that Esme had requested some rationale for the question. "I suppose what I am asking is, are you here because this is a way to even the score with Mark?"

She immediately rolled her upper body far enough away from him in order to look him directly in the eye. As his hand dropped from her breast she asked him, "Where is this coming from?"

He proceeded to explain that since their conversation earlier in the evening he found himself wondering if the reason she stayed with him was to get back at her husband."

Her first reaction was anger. "What type of person do you think I am?" Before he could answer she continued with less tension in her voice, but still gritty from screaming. "If that was the reason, I could have left Friday morning."

"I'm sorry. I didn't mean to suggest that…" Gunter stopped himself. After a few seconds he confessed, "I'm not sure what I meant, I just think we need to think this through, or at least I do."

"Honestly, I have been asking myself the same thing, and not just for myself but also about you. I certainly could ask the same question, 'Why are you here?'" Esme couldn't believe that she was having this conversation completely naked under the glow of a lamp.

"Yes you may, but that doesn't alter the fact that I asked first. I believe you owe me an answer."

"Consciously, I can say that my presence here with you has nothing to do with Mark. Unconsciously, perhaps, that's another story.

"Care to elaborate?"

"From the moment I saw you I wanted to know more about you. I wanted to spend time with you. It wasn't just about the sex. I wanted to learn who that cowboy was laboring about in the airport. And now, I enjoy listening to you and I appreciate how you listen to me. I don't know, maybe all this is somehow rooted in my relationship with Mark. That's what we pay shrinks seventy-five dollars an hour to tell us, right?"

Gunter refrained from responding in case she wanted to expound further. He also wanted to avoid sounding like a shrink by asking a question. After a few minutes of silence Esme directed the question back to Gunter. "Care to offer up your answer?"

Employing a couple of deep breaths and having pulled the sheet over both their bodies he attempted a reply. "I wish my answer was simple and straightforward, but like life, it is complicated. Or, maybe it's just me who makes it complicated. First, I am here because I am physically attracted to you. Second, I think the context of this trip has something to do with it. Thirty-five year olds are not supposed to fall over dead. If it could happen to Bradley it could happen to me. Third, the spring semester was challenging. Classes didn't unfold as I had hoped, completion of the next great American novel was delayed, and the paperwork for my third year review was greater than I imagined. Combine all these events and I was feeling sorry for myself, I didn't want to be alone, and I could justify why I deserved a little me time."

Tucking the sheet neatly under the edges of her backside she lowered her body to rest against him and added, "I understand exactly where you are coming from."

"Yeah, it sounds like all valid excuses. But these are all reasons created in hindsight as an attempt to placate any guilt. The honest answer is, I never thought about it, I just went with it."

"Based on that can you also accept my answer that I too just went with it and that this isn't about Mark?"

He nodded his answer rather than using his lips for he was preparing his lips to kiss her. Following an extended interlude of kissing he pulled back in a similar manner as Esme had earlier in order to look directly into her eyes as he explained that he had planned to share this in the morning just prior to leaving for the airport but that the time seemed right. Before she could say anything he shoved the words forth knowing he was taking a huge risk. "I would like to do this again. I mean, I would like you to meet me here, in Seattle, next year."

"Oh," was all Esme initially said.

"You don't like the idea?"

"It's not that. I'm trying to wrap my head around what you just proposed."

"Do you have questions? You certainly don't need to answer this moment. Please, don't feel pressured into answering."

"I don't feel pressured; it's just that I had not allowed myself to think past tomorrow morning. I guess I was wondering if we would exchange phone numbers, or addresses? Would we wave good-bye, shake hands? Would I become a smile in your old age that no one knew about?" She rubbed her eyes as though attempting to clear the present and see into the future. "And when you say, 'next year' are you suggesting the same time, the same days in June? Are you implying that we don't have any contact with one another until some 360 days from tomorrow?"

"As ridiculous as it may sound, that is precisely what I am suggesting."

"I guess you have given this considerable thought. I must say, I am glad you didn't wait until the morning to discuss this. May I ask why no contact throughout the year?"

"I'm scared what might happen if I see you sooner. I am concerned about your marriage and mine. I need space to understand this, us. I want both of us to have an out if needed.

"So, give me the details of what you are thinking."

"For June twelfth we book a seat on the first flight available from Denver to Seattle after 1pm. If seating options are available, you select seat A in row 27 and I'll select, B. This will enable us to meet in the airport together and fly to Seattle just like this year. I will rent the same room for next year here at the Vance Hotel."

"What happens if you decide not to show up?"

"I will make the reservation tomorrow morning before I leave. The room will be listed under Gunter."

"No last names?"

"Right, and no hometowns identified."

"Why?" Esme was mystified by the restrictions being proposed.

"Because I am weak, curious, and creative and with just a small amount of information I could and would find you. I don't mean to scare you but I am very resourceful. I also know myself well enough to say that if I possessed your address or phone number I would contact you."

Esme nodded in agreement and placed her hand inside of his. "I too would reach out to you."

"Again, the dates are June twelfth through the fifteenth, if you want to stay longer, that's your choice, but this room will only be until the fifteenth."

"This is so well planned, I have to ask, have you done this before?" She wasn't attempting to be funny, the question was meant to be sincere.

"Good heavens, no!" For a moment his hand abandoned Esme's, but slowly it fell back into place and he completed his thought. "But my imagination never stops and while pedaling across Bainbridge this took shape."

"Cowboy, you just confirmed what I knew the moment I watched you ramble across my line of vision. I'm hooked!"

Sunday brought the rain and mist for which Seattle was famous. Gunter had mentally prepared himself to experience dampness every day of his visit but the skies never cooperated until that moment. The damp gloominess punctuated the somber mood radiating from both Gunter and Esme. The level of tolerance for considering the other person's thoughts was nearly nonexistent. Esme refused to accept any part of Gunter's logic concerning why she should not accompany him to the airport and Gunter flushed Esme's passionate description of why it would serve them well if she went to the airport. It was only when each tackled the question, "why are we doing this?" that they both realized that in an effort to protect the other, they were in fact creating a more painful situation. Although they eventually were able to respect each other's position and acknowledge that sadness was weighing heavily, it didn't remove the solemnity within their hearts or upon their faces.

Seated in the concourse of the Seattle Airport both Gunter and Esme concentrated their people watching skills on each other rather than on those surrounding them. Both commented on the irony of having come full circle from the Denver Airport and seeing the other from a distance to the current moment of sitting close to the other and seeing the distance that threatened to separate them in a matter of minutes.

A voice bellowed through the intercom announcing boarding instructions, which disrupted the intimacy of the two in spite of being surrounded by more than one hundred and fifty strangers. Esme's reaction was to tighten her grip on Gunter's arm, while Gunter's was to reach for his briefcase, pulling him away from Esme. Having retrieved the case he returned to her side that he might whisper and not be heard by those surrounding them.

"I have a small gift. One that I hope reminds you of me, and just what you mean to me. You may also note how fitting the title is." He carefully extracted from the leather case Joe Cocker's latest album entitled, *"I Can Stand A Little Rain."*

The moment she saw the cover with Joe Cocker front and center tears streamed down her face.

"It is the album with the song, *"You Are So Beautiful."*

Struggling to speak she whispered "Thank you" and "I didn't get you anything" simultaneously.

Wiping the wetness from her cheeks with his thumb he iterated that she had given him the greatest gift possible, herself.

As his row was called for boarding they stood and clung to one another one last time. Before she released him she thanked him for the gift and promised to play the record every day. Then she said, "This has to last for an entire year," and she kissed him as passionately and aggressively as possible.

As Gunter rambled toward the gate entrance she saw the top half of a book cover peeking out from his briefcase. She recognized the jacket immediately as belonging to Joseph Heller's, *Something Happened.* She prayed silently that he would not think of himself as the character, Bob Slocum. He was anything but. The only person to fit the story of Bob was Mark. Mark? Reality slowly overwhelmed Esme as she watched Gunter's plane leave Seattle.

Cruising comfortably at 30,000 feet Gunter pulled the book from his briefcase, creased the initial pages, and began to read. He read the opening account of Bob's childhood experiences and he contemplated how a singular event, how something happened that could alter an entire life. Closing the book and pulling his hat low to shield out the other passengers he wondered if the chance meeting and subsequent past four days with Esme could or would change his life and hers. In spite of a spasm rippling through his back Gunter smiled, something already had happened. The question was just how great the change would be.

CHAPTER 11
JUNE 12, 1976

Two hundred years earlier on the 12th of June a handful of men assembled in Williamsburg, Virginia and completed two monumental actions. The first was to determine who would represent Virginia in Philadelphia at the Constitutional Convention. The second was the adoption of the Declaration of Rights which less than a month later would serve as the foundation for the U.S. Constitution. The delegation in Williamsburg accepted words that would guarantee life, liberty and the pursuit of happiness. As the book, *Alistair Cooke's America,* dropped to his lap, Gunter chuckled and shook his head as he sat in a crowded plane destined for Denver. It was doubtful that any of the men gathered in 1776 could have imagined the transformations that occurred to the U.S. He wondered if they would condone the citation of the preamble in support of a wide variety of issues. He wondered if their intentions would support his current pursuit of happiness. He was not naïve, he could acknowledge that there were limits and boundaries to the pursuit of happiness. As a critical reader of history Gunter also recognized that the four hundred pages of *Alistair Cooke's America* narrowed the definition of what counted as significant American history.

Pressed against the interior wall of the plane due to the size of the woman covering seat E and portions of D and

F, Gunter directed his attention out the port style window and surveyed the jagged terrain some 30,000 feet below. He contemplated the seldom-recorded history of the formation of another country also during the year of 1776. Unlike the assembly in Philadelphia this gathering occurred outdoors before an audience composed of family members who endured hardship and loss as they moved from the wind-blown flat grasslands to an area where the rugged granite stretched to the sky. These people too desired to live with the guarantee of life, liberty and the pursuit of happiness. Closing the Cooke book and holding it tight against his chest he questioned if the second delegation, those living on the scarred ground of the Black Hills, could have imagined the transformation, if not denigration, of the land they called home? He wondered how those innovative people of the earth would understand life, liberty and the pursuit of happiness when they were referred to as Sioux, "little snakes." Their name, in fact, was Lakota. He wondered what those pioneers would say of his personal pursuit of happiness? He wondered...

The bag of peanuts tossed by the stewardess landed on the pull down tray and served as a bridge between 1776 and 1976 transporting him back to the present. A quick flash of his LED watch informed him that it would be an hour and thirty minutes before the plane would be on the ground. The events of 200 years earlier couldn't compete with the excitement that swirled in his chest. The smile was accompanied by a nervousness he had not felt since defending his dissertation. He thought about purchasing a drink to dull his senses but the price gauging kept his wallet hidden in his back pocket. Since he had no idea what awaited him once he stepped off the plane, he attempted to play out every possible scenario but realized that was impossible so he narrowed the focus down to three highly conceivable situations: Esme was waiting for him; she was not present but would arrive soon, thereby pressing him into the role of greeter; she was not present nor would she be coming. But of course he had no way to know. The foul body odor from the perspiring woman next to him distracted him as he toiled to construct a response for each until he discovered he spent more time manufacturing the aroma of Esme splashed with Chanel. Eventually he gave up. He concluded that it was futile to script how he would respond in the airport since it had been three days short of a year since he last held her, or for that matter, spoke with her. Frustrated he covered his face with his hat in an effort to filter the disgusting air and create a darkened environment that he might snooze and quicken his arrival to Denver.

Each step up the walkway from the plane to the terminal became more challenging than the previous. He imagined he was carrying a saddle and striding up alongside a two-year old horse that had never been tacked. Thoughts and emotions ran the gamut from extreme caution to exuberance, from patience to uncontrollable eagerness. His foot crossed the threshold of the doorway and his senses and heightened awareness kicked in as though he was placing his foot in the stirrup for the first time ride. No matter the amount of preparation and ground work performed it was impossible to predict how a horse will respond the first time they experience the weight pressing down on the saddle and a leg swinging over their back. One had to be ready for anything and that required the cowboy to see, hear, feel, and smell the moment or the only thing he will taste is a mouthful of dirt.

When Gunter's second leg swung through the door he was firmly seated in the saddle of the moment and all five senses were at work. The emotions were raging and he silently told himself to breathe and focus. His jaw had worked the stick of Juicy Fruit aggressively during the plane's descent so the rubbery texture offered nothing but stale, non-sugar flavor. The multitude of voices, complete with varying tones and pitches vibrating off the walls and ceiling, made it difficult to distinguish Esme's voice, if indeed she was present to call out his name. The crowd, pressing forward like groupies at an Eagle's concert, hampered his sight. Forced to amble behind his seatmate he was convinced his olfactory system had been momentarily damaged making it impossible for him to detect chemicals floating the air. As sensitive as his mucous membranes were to Chanel Number 5 he doubted he could smell it or anything other than the nauseating aroma of body odor. His senses were not serving him well.

The moment an opening appeared he removed himself from the stream of passengers surging forward and held up next to a family silly with nervous energy as they prepared for their first flight. Determined to rest from sensory overload the logical section of Gunter's brain engaged and within seconds it produced an "Ah-ha" moment as though a light bulb switched on over his head.

He grumbled to himself as he rubbed his forehead and realized that he had acted totally irrational. Agonizingly, he admitted that he had allowed his emotions to cloud his thinking. It was the sort of thing only weeks earlier he challenged his students not to do as they prepared for their professional careers. The simple truth was, it was not reasonable to expect Esme to greet him at this gate. She had no idea his point of origin or what airline he flew. For one of his senses to locate Esme's presence meant she just happened to be strolling by on her way to their exit gate.

He had a greater chance of being struck by lightning on a sunny morning than to see Esme at the gate. He had to be careful with the nonverbal cues he displayed, he didn't need to appear too strange to the children of the family surrounding him. They didn't need any additional reasons to fear flying.

Prior to falling into step behind the flight crew, who had a several hour layover before making the return trip north, Gunter handed each child a five pack of Juicy Fruit and explained how he never flew without gum. Beneath the warm smile from the children's parents he wished the family well on their inaugural flight and set off in search of the gate for the connecting flight.

"A Firebell in the Night," the sixth chapter from Cooke's book retained Gunter's attention as he was determined to distract himself from the anxiety of the hour. The phrase, "firebell in the night," originated with Jefferson in 1820 when he wrote a friend and lamented the decision to allow Missouri, the *Show Me State,* to gain statehood as a slave state. The Missouri Compromise, as it became known, was an attempt to maintain the balance of free and slave states. One hundred and fifty plus years since The Compromise and more than one hundred years since the battle to end slavery and he wondered what comprises were being crafted behind closed doors, or worse yet, on the floor of congress to ensure that equality came with conditions.

Engrossed in the issues from the pages of the text combined with his acute awareness of the inequality of the day made Gunter oblivious to the small hamlet of people that had drifted into the gate area. The thought that people continued to face prejudice and acts of discrimination in the last half of the twentieth century dulled his senses so that the sweet fragrance of Chanel Number 5 went undetected.

He thought the gentle weight of slender fingers stroking his shoulders originated from the brim of his hat. It wasn't until the sexy, husky voice inches from his ear puffed, "Hi Cowboy" that it registered. Without confirming to whom the voice belonged, he twisted sideways firmly, grabbed the tiny waist and dropped her body into his lap that he might behold her beauty and taste her presence. She assisted with the kiss by draping her arms round his neck and pulling him close. Lips locked and the pages of *Cooke's America* crinkled on the terminal floor. Gunter was embarrassed to admit how easily he could ignore the social injustice of the day for the pleasure of a woman, yet not just any woman, but this one, Esme.

For the extended period of time the two of them resembled mannequins suggestively intertwined by an overly sexually excited stock boy. There in the midst of a crowd of strangers impatiently waiting to board a plane, they held one another, stared into the eyes of the other, probed the tonsils of the other, and respectfully avoided being the first to speak. In part because they were not sure what to say, what would function as the appropriate initial conversation after a year of separation. The only words that stirred in Gunter's mouth threatening to push past his lips were, "Thank you for coming," but that didn't sound suitable. As he searched for something pithy to share, he realized how scared he was that she wasn't coming. He had not allowed himself to seriously consider that he would spend the four days alone in Seattle. He finally accepted that he had to come to terms with t just how bad he wanted, needed her to come. So rather than say something silly or stupid, he squeezed her more tightly.

Esme, doing her best to pull back the salty water that threatened to roll from the corner of her eyes, also desired to express gratitude for Gunter's presence, but when she spoke the words in her head they sounded trite and childish. "Thank you for being here." So she too said nothing, until...

Quite unexpectedly it was Gunter who provided the content for a lighthearted yet authentic conversation.

Gunter felt it immediately as her body shifted ever so slightly away from him and in response he leaned back, as much as the chair allowed, in order to read Esme's intentions. What he discovered had nothing to do with Esme but everything with him. Gunter realized that he was smiling, in fact, his face hurt from smiling so hard.

It wasn't that he didn't like to smile, as he on occasion had been accused, or that the facial muscles lacked development from under use, rather the explanation for why the facial muscles worked on a limited basis was quite straightforward. Gunter's grandpa had always told him to be leery of a man who smiled too much. Grandpa would say, "A man will smile while he reaches into your pocket and steals your wallet. A man will smile when uncomfortable to convince others, and at times even himself, that he is secure. A man will smile to your face as the knife is plunged into your back." Gunter, throughout his life, reserved his smile because the last thing he wanted was to deceive someone. But at that moment if he stopped smiling he would burst.

Before Esme leaned back in and tucked her head under his chin she offered up, "You will never know how much I missed seeing that gorgeous smile."

Gunter's ears turned red as he blushed momentarily at Esme's honesty and then proceeded to broaden her understanding of his smiling. "You may not believe this, but I found myself smiling at the most unusual times. I would be strolling across campus in search of a cup of coffee, I'd pass a set of classroom windows and see my reflection and there would be this person smiling at me. I would be shaving and sure enough the half lathered face in the mirror staring back at me was smiling. Armed with a pitchfork, sweating, and feeling the strain of my muscles as I tossed another scoop of horse manure into the manure spreader, I was smiling. Honestly, the first eight months I smiled because of last year. I would see you naked and tripping over me as you rushed to pee. I saw you sipping wine and working to enjoy it. I saw the perspiration coating the tank top between and under your magnificent breasts as we pedaled bikes. I saw the moonlight dance off your hair as you slept and I smiled. The last four months I smiled in anticipation of today and the thought of seeing, no," his head was shaking, "no, kissing your birthmark. Esme, you showed me it's okay to smile."

There was no barricade strong or high enough to hold back the salt water. Beneath the menace of chapped cheeks Esme shared her similar experience. "I know exactly what you mean. I would be standing at the kitchen sink washing dishes and a tingling wave would flood my inner core and shortly thereafter I would feel your embrace or your weight pressing down on me. As the months pressed on my skin struggled to feel you, but your smile never faded, it never grew dim. Perhaps," she stopped herself.

Gunter prodded her to continue. "What is it? Tell me."

Shaking her head she justified her stopping in mid-sentence. "No, you will think it is silly. I think it is silly as I listen to myself say it."

Pulling her closer, as though that was humanly possible, he challenged her. "Let me decide for myself. I promise if I think it is silly I will tell you."

"I know, that's the problem, you will tell me."

"What?" Placing his cheek against the crown of her head he admitted he would never understand women. "Okay then, I promise not to say anything."

Laughing she finished her thought. "As I was saying, I never forgot your smile. Perhaps the reason is, that in spite of the miles of separation I saw your face each time you smiled."

"You're right, it was silly, but also very romantic. I like it."

With that they fell silent.

Neither one seemed to care that they were making a public spectacle. Gunter had not paid attention to where or what his hands were doing. From the moment Esme landed in his lap his hands never stopped traveling her body. At times his calloused hands, still bearing the dirt deep in the crevasses, were visible but were charting territory generally not covered in the presence of others. At other times his hands played a game of hide and seek beneath Esme's clothes. His hand scaled the side of her bountiful breast and continued northward over the nipple that threatened to poke through the fabric only to stop suddenly when the texture of the brassiere abruptly changed. The lace lining at the top of the bra was tactually pleasing to his fingers and it invited his mind to surmise the color. Black trimmed in red were the colors he hoped his eyes would see in a few hours, but purple was a better guess, since that was Esme's favorite color. He knew it really didn't matter what the color scheme was as he concluded that she purchased a new bra for just such an occasion, well, actually, just for him.

Esme's hands were not nearly as active, instead, whenever she was not speaking, her mouth was exploring Gunter's neck, his ear, or his chest which, mysteriously was becoming more exposed.

The gate attendant summoned all passengers to board the plane, but they elected to ignore the request. When the waiting area was finally empty, accept for a toddler who squealed with excitement as an older sibling was in close pursuit, Esme placed both feet on the floor, stood and waited for Gunter to rise before stepping toward the ticket taker. Holding hands as they narrowed the distance to the gate the realization struck them that they might soon be separated. Carefully each of them located their boarding pass and proceeded to read their seat number aloud, in unison.

"Row 27."

Gunter's smile returned as he voiced, seat A, and Esme said, seat B. Their laughter of relief echoed through the empty gate area.

The moment the plane reached the cruising altitude of 30,000 feet the seatbelt light dimmed and in spite of the instruction to keep the seatbelts fastened while seated Gunter and Esme freed their bodies. With the restraints removed their bodies become one.

Absentmindedly brushing an unruly strand of hair that persistently fell into Esme's eye, Gunter commented. "I love your hair."

"I hoped you would, I let it grow just for you."

"I mean this in all sincerity, you could be Farrah Fawcett's twin."

"And you're the Six Million Dollar Man."

Sensing that she was dismissing his comment too quickly he slowed his delivery and stressed each word. "No, really, I mean it."

Wearing her own smile of satisfaction she responded. "Well, thank you, but just so you know, this hair style requires a few more minutes in the bathroom so don't go planning anything without giving me fair warning."

"Wait, you mean, it's possible to spend more time in the bathroom than last year? I thought…"

She cut him off and her body, rigid like a deer caught in headlights, transported him back to last year and a difficult conversation the two of them had. Nervously he listened, "I'm sorry Gunter but I can't always tell when you are being serious and when you are joking."

"Esme, it was never my intention to confuse you, I…"

Again, she cut him off in mid-sentence. "I know, Gunter. I, I need," she stumbled over her words as she worked to dispense the perfect explanation, "to provide you with a context for my shortness with you."

"Take your time, I'm not going away wher…" he stopped, took her chin in his hand, turned her to face him and kissed her softly. "There I go again, I'm sorry."

"No, that was different and please don't stop your witty comments. It all goes back to Mark." She shook her head as she spoke.

"Mark?" It was obvious her husband's name totally surprised him. He cleared his throat before he continued. "I don't understand. What does Mark have to do with this?"

She spoke without looking directly at him. "Mark has always been critical of the amount of time I spend getting ready. He continually reminds me that I spend too much time in the shower, too much time doing my hair, too much time putting on my makeup, too much time selecting what to wear. And of course, he is not joking."

Gunter stopped himself from offering the expected, "I'm sorry." It was not his place to be sorry. In the silence he noted the irony of their flight moving westward not unlike the trek of the Lakota. While he was not arrogant or naïve to suggest that their movement was similar in rigor or depth he understood that the simple flight westward couldn't free one from the baggage carried. He knew what he needed to share.

"I guess the tapes we play again and again and the interactions with others will influence our relationship. It's not as though we can just switch them off, but we can be open and honest with one another. Esme, if I ever cross the line concerning you getting ready, tell me. For that matter, if I ever cross any line, tell me. Now, to set the record straight, I also need to tell you, you don't need any makeup, and truthfully, while I like your selection of clothing, I love seeing you in the buff."

Turning to look directly into his eyes she promised to be honest with him and then added, "I never thought I would say this, but I like it too. I love being naked for you, it feels so natural."

The plane couldn't fly fast enough into the western sky for either of them in their pursuit of happiness and pleasure.

CHAPTER 12

Gunter handed Esme the key and said she should go up to the room and he would park the car and bring up the remaining luggage. Her objection to leaving him with the burden of carrying the suitcases was met with a tug to the brim of his hat as he turned and stepped heavy as he walked away. She discerned his motive for sending her on ahead the moment she pushed through the doorway.

Although it was midafternoon the room looked more like dusk as the curtains were pulled shut and the most unique shadow was displayed on the wall next to the bed. She stood motionless for several minutes attempting to give meaning to the shadow as she had done as a kid lying on her back staring at the clouds and naming animals and identifying objects as they floated past. But she couldn't see any animals or objects in what appeared to be a jungle of chaos. What frustrated her more was her inability to define what created the abstract art form without sneaking a peek. It was not until she stood in the center of the room that she discovered the source and the items being projected.

Gunter took his time parking the rental car and unloading the luggage, he wanted Esme to have sufficient time to experience what awaited her arrival in the room. After two flights of stairs, he wondered why it was that a woman needed three bags to every one bag a guy needed?

The third flight revealed the stupidity of his decision to get some exercise and not to take the elevator. At the fourth level, as the bags landed on the step in order that he might catch his second wind, he looked at his wrinkled shirt and had his answer. The moment he stepped into the room he forgot about the luggage, the eight flights of stairs, and feeling fatigued. None of that mattered any longer.

The color coordination could not have been planned any better. The possibility always exists when a color with two slightly different pigments are placed side by side that they clash, but such was not the case in this situation. Esme even asked how he knew, to which he shrugged his shoulders because the truth was he didn't know at the time the order was placed. He knew her favorite color and the rest, well; sometimes it was just good to be lucky. And lucky Gunter was.

Esme had stripped down to her newly purchased brassier and matching panties and strategically tucked a dahlia, from the bouquet on the end table, between her breasts as she stretched seductively across the bed. The purple dahlia, the tip of which resembled a paintbrush barely dipped in white paint, matched the undergarments perfectly. The purple bra accentuated by white lace across the top and the panties with a narrow strip of white lace in the crotch had Gunter scaling the bed with his pants stuck at his boot tops. Resting partially on her right side with her left leg bent and foot placed behind her right knee the narrow strip of lace seemed to separate, however Gunter wasn't one hundred percent sure and he wasn't one to stare. The priority at the moment was the removal of his boots and pants, there would be plenty of time to explore and determine the quality of the stitching.

His right boot dusted the corner of the room as his ankle, like a slingshot, hurdled the boot free of his foot. The second

Tony Lama was nearly off when Esme's left hand took hold of his shirt collar and hauled him close, being careful not to damage the flower resting between her ample breasts. Following a passionate kiss of appreciation she verbally thanked him for the flowers and the surprise artwork and demanded to know how he managed such an arrangement. The last thing he wanted was to discuss the conversation he had with the hotel manager two weeks earlier. They had all night to discuss such things, at that moment he wanted her, his body wanted to feel her nakedness, but propping his head in the palm of his left hand he rested next to her and explained every detail, including reciting her comments from the previous year of how she loved seeing dahlias all through the city. He confessed that this was how he loved viewing the flower.

In response to his final comment she moved her arm forward, pumping her breasts fuller and tighter and narrowing the cleavage and pushing the dahlia upward. Without thinking Gunter rolled on top of Esme, pinned her arms to the bed and with his teeth he carefully slid the dahlia until it was free of the purple strap. Still on top of her holding her arms in place he stared down at her until the absence of movement and sound pushed Esme to ask, "What?"

Without moving he asked a question in return. "Do you trust me?"

The wrinkles in her forehead revealed she was totally confused yet she answered his question. "Yes, of course."

Continuing to straddle her as though seated in a saddle he sat upward. "If at any point you want this to end simply say, 'stop' and I promise I will stop."

"Okay, but you need to tell me mo..."

Before she could finish the word the room went dark as she was blindfolded. She never saw it coming, she had no idea what actually served as a blindfold. Her body rolled slightly to the right as he got off her. Without sight her ability to hear intensified. She tracked him as he moved to the head of the bed and fumbled with the pillows or the sheet or something, she wasn't sure. Forcefully with intentionality if not anger her right wrist was taken captive and her entire body was dragged further onto the bed. The clutching grip surprised her and instinctively she pulled her arm to her body but he was too strong and her elbow never reached her torso. The fingers holding her wrist firm were replaced by a cloth, perhaps a pillowcase, tied tight that was then secured to the frame of the bed. Anticipating that her left arm would be tied next she screamed when her left ankle was bound and pulled to the corner of the bed. Playfully she fought as he worked to secure her right leg but it was only a matter of seconds before her leg was immobilized and in spite of preparing to counter attack his next move she laid spread eagle.

Standing at the foot of the bed Gunter grinned devilishly as he noted the white lacy crotch was **not** intact. Careful to not touch the bed or make any noise he removed his second boot and clothes. From his suitcase he pulled a bottle of Merlot which he uncorked and savored as he savored the beauty still clad in purple resting peacefully on the bed. At that moment he decided that purple wasn't such a bad color after all. With his second glass nearly empty it occurred to him that the only thing better would be to combine the two pleasures and enjoy both in the same instant.

The traffic noise from the street below disrupted her ability to focus on his actions and increased her level of irritation. Even so, she was positive he was seated to her left in the overstuff chair and drinking a glass of wine or two. She assumed the absence of a gag meant she had permission to speak and yet it didn't seem appropriate, and so as she waited she tilted her head to the right to expose her left ear to improve her auditory perception.

As the liquid struck the bottom of the glass and splashed against the sides she counted, that made three glasses of wine. What transpired next caught her totally unprepared. She heard him rise from the chair and step towards the side of the bed, she felt the moment his leg brushed against the mattress, she assumed he left the glass of wine on the nightstand next to the bouquet of dahlias, that assumption was responsible for the complete and utter surprise.

The room temperature liquid landed precisely where Gunter aimed. Controlling the amount of burgundy colored liquid that dripped from the glass Esme's bellybutton was filled after four moderately large drops fell. As she squealed in response to her body becoming a chalice he placed his mouth over her bellybutton and inhaled. Before removing his lips, that had created a seal against her firm stomach, his tongue made sure nothing was left behind. The precise moment he touched the core of her belly she sucked in her stomach and rolled from side to side in excitement. The second pouring lacked the precision of the first as several dropped missed the intended target and he continued to pour even though the tiny cup was flooded. As the wine spread he watched with delight as two streams emerged. One stream traveled southward where the top of her panties absorbed the river flowing red while the second, a smaller narrow stream rolled to her birthmark. It was the second stream that became his source of drinking. Like a dog he used his tongue to lap up the wine as it pooled at the café au lait. Initially she pulled back and squirmed as his tongue outlined her birthmark but quickly her body rose to meet his tongue in anticipation of feeling him against her body.

He desperately wanted to share with her the thoughts that rumbled in his mind but he refused to break the silence. He would have to wait and tell her later how much he enjoyed a little wine with his coffee over her heart.

The simple snap of his thumb and middle finger unhooked her front fastening brassier and her breasts jiggled slightly and stood firm with her nipples fully erect as the bra fell to the comforter. Again, anticipating that her boobs would become a waterfall for the wine resulted in the jolt to her body.

There was no liquid, no mouth pressed against her skin, and no tongue teasing the tip of her nipple. The touch that did occur was not on the top of her breast but on the bottom side. Contact with such virgin skin made her quiver while her mind raced to identify the object that gently caressed. It tickled like a feather but the consistency was too firm for a feather yet too pliable to be a finger. With her imagination pounding on all cylinders for a split second she was confident she identified correctly the object, it was his...but the moment she realized that his body was not hovering over her she knew she was wrong. She told herself it was probably wishful thinking that resulted in erroneous conclusions.

Gracefully Gunter started at the underside of one breast and followed the fullness up the cleavage and then back down to the underside of the other breast. The relentless musing from one breast to the other intensified the firmness, as if that was possible. She wanted to inquire the source of titillation but instead she squirmed in an effort to move her body lower on the bed so that the object between his fingers might grace the top of her breasts and possibly even bond with her throbbing nipple. Her efforts were futile until Gunter placed his body next to hers and elevated the movement of the object that circled her nipple while intentionally avoiding contact and purposely increasing the tease.

With his lips next to her left ear he lightly kissed her lobe and then whispered, "You want your nipple touched don't you?"

The moment he spoke she got a whiff alcohol. The oaky aroma of Merlot was unmistakable and even though she had no desire to drink any she wanted to taste the lingering remains on his tongue. Her response was more of a moan than an actual word, "Yes." She assumed it was an adequate response for the circle closed to within centimeters of striking her nipple…and then he stopped.

"No" Filled the space between her mouth and his ear much louder than she expected.

"Then tell me how much you desire your nipples to become the focus of my play. Tell me specifically how you want me to fondle your nipples."

Her silence caused the circle to widen and move away from her nipple. As she groaned as though she might speak he pulled the object closer to the target. She had never spoken during sex, at least not like this or gave instructions and therefore the wall holding back the words she yearned to speak was taller than the Great Wall of China, or so it felt.

To motivate her he continued to whisper in her ear. "I know you want it; I can feel the heat within your body. I can see your nipples pleading."

Tingling with fear and excitement, anticipation and hesitation, she was so turned on a flood of emotion streamed through her body. Even though she knew she was safe, his words and the words he demanded from her drove her to a place she had never experienced. Could she? Would she? Both questions raced through not only her mind but also her very core. It wasn't just about the sex, although that was significant by itself; it was also about the notion that she had the right to state what she desired. She told herself it was one thing to be embarrassed sexually, recovery from such a state was possible; it was quite another thing to challenge the tapes that told her she was to meet the needs and desires of others and never herself. The possibility of recovering from this could be nonexistent thereby affirming that she didn't have a voice. Yet something deep inside told her this was different and he was different. She was creating a new tape, a tape that freed her from a life of bondage and humiliation. Pulling slightly against the cloth that held her restrained she snickered inside for at that very moment she was physically bound yet it would free her emotionally and sexually.

"Touch me, Cowboy." The words were faint and filled with more puffs of air than actual vowels and consonants.

Careful not to disrupt their closeness Gunter nuzzled his nose deep into her neck before speaking. "Esme, I am touching you."

With greater urgency and forcefulness she pleaded. "Please, Cowboy, touch me."

Rather than answer he used his breath to blow softly into her ear and make broad looping circles round her nipples.

"My nipple, play with my nipples!"

The moment the petal of the dahlia graced the center of her left nipple she squealed, "Yes," quickly followed by specific instructions, "don't stop, don't stop."

Following the directive he used the end of the flower to stroke first one nipple and then the other. Occasionally pulling back and creating a figure eight pattern between both breasts. As the petal lost its definition he plucked another from the bouquet.

Before the caress reached the point of irritation and discomforted she commanded him to suck. He complied and placed his lips over the nipple but the sucking was so limp that a vacuum cleaner with a completely clogged hose offered greater suction. She knew immediately that this was part of the game to entice her to say more, but instead she pushed her chest upward and smashed her boob into his mouth. Unfortunately, her efforts yielded no reward. It was not until she said, "harder," that he sucked her nipples as she desired.

Unable to see his face as he shared risqué thoughts and desires made it easier for her to fall into the same pattern and free her tongue to speak what she previously only thought. She found herself, with considerable ease, spitting out words she only heard teenagers mutter.

"Now my panties, remove my panties, but don't use your hands."

The spread eagle position provided him a great view as breathtaking as standing on the rim of the Grand Canyon and beholding the grander. The position however made it nearly impossible to remove the panties. His teeth latched on the top edge of the panties and he pulled downward. The panties slid easily as she raised her hips to aid his labor, but he quickly discovered that he would have to untie one leg in order to fully bare her privates.

With her neatly trimmed hair exposed and her legs again secured she conducted a how to class on satisfying her. It took the college professor only a few seconds to become the star pupil as his tongue and carefully placed fingers had Es, as he continued to call her, unable to deliver coherent and audible words. Her groans and moans increased in volume to a level that would compete with any future Seahawk fan.

Fearful that he would pull back or cease the movement of his fingers at the very moment she needed him to increase the speed and firmness she became a cheerleader in the midst of her ecstasy. With simple words interjected between the moans she hoped to release more of his adrenaline so he couldn't stop, "harder, faster, right there, that's the spot, yes, yes..." Her body became tight and she pressed upward into his face. Even though she was spread eagle her thighs came together squeezing his head. For several seconds she held her breath and her entire body quivered until she screamed and dropped her hips to the bed only to bounce back and forth. In the most demanding voice yet she pleaded with him, "Now, now, f... me now! I need you to f... me now."

It was not the first time Esme delivered the "F" word, in fact during heated arguments with Mark she placed the word together with you. It was however the first time she used the word in the context of sex.

After positioning himself atop of her their bodies rocked back and forth like a small fishing boat catching the wake of a much larger boat. Once they established a rhythm that met both their needs Gunter reached behind her head and untied the blindfold in order that he might look into her eyes. As much as he enjoyed her voluptuous figure it was her eyes that seduced him.

With his ear next to her lips it became her turn to gnaw at the ear lobe and whisper into his ear. She used the same words as before, "harder, faster, right there, yes," but now they were not for her but for him. She marveled at the endurance and ability he demonstrated to prolong the final gratification. In spite of the strangeness of not having her arms wrapped about his body and her legs pulling him tight into her body he was able to climax and the final seconds just before he did so he held his breath and his body became rigid, his toes curled as though digging into the sand to keep from being swept away by the tide about to crash into and through his body. As the tidal wave struck Esme was sure the people two floors below heard him acknowledging the existence of God, "Oh God, Oh God!"

His lifeless body above her, she was intrigued how the body, both male and female, responded in a similar manner to an orgasm. Yet something told her that the feeling associated with the orgasm was different for each sex. Of course, she couldn't prove any of this, as she couldn't define the exact experience for a male. As a nurse, and one well on the way to completing an advance degree, she could describe biologically what happened, but even for herself, she couldn't describe the specifics of the experience other than to use words like, great, amazing, and out of this world. Which made her realize why Gunter's toes curled.

Lifting his head from her pillow breasts, there was no blindfold or any clothes holding Gunter to the bed, yet a single question blinded him and pressed upon him making it difficult for him to move.

CHAPTER 13

Once Esme's arms and legs were freed the two of them rolled to the center of the bed where they enjoyed the nakedness of each other in a sensual, non-sexual manner.

Esme had her head on his chest and Gunter's hand cradled her breast. Prior to Esme's disruption of the sacredness of the moment she tilted her head just enough to look into his eyes. She appreciated the unconventional complexity of the question before it passed her lips and therefore wanted to see his face. "What is your wife like?"

"My wife?" He was clearly dumbfounded. "We just spent ninety minutes in the most intimate manner possible and you want to hear about my wife?" Was this some woman thing? That question never entered the room, instead he continued, "Essy, are you sure this is what you want at this moment?"

Using her fingers as a comb she brushed the hair from her cheek and wrapped it behind her ear as she addressed his question. "Do you trust me?"

"Yes."

"Well then, trust me when I tell you, I want to know about the woman you love and I am curious what you said to get away."

"Boy, where to start?" The question was for him not her. As his eyes drifted the full length of her body, the body he enjoyed touching, he viewed her nakedness in a different light. "I guess I'll start with how I got here. It actually was a suggestion from Emily."

"Emily is your wife?"

"Yeah."

"So you are here because your wife suggested it?"

"Yes and no. Yes, she suggested in mid-April that I should set aside some time just for myself at the end of the school year, maybe take a trip like last year. No, I am not here because of her I am here because of you. Her suggestion merely made it a lot easier to carve out these four days without any justification."

"It sounds like your Emily is a real understanding wife."

"My Emily?" Gunter spoke the words in a cautious manner as he pushed Esme away from his chest that he might study her face.

Softly she answered, "My daughter's name is Emily."

As though he said something embarrassing he offered, "Oh, I'm sorry."

"Sorry? Sorry that your wife's name is Emily or that my daughter's name is Emily?"

"Sounds silly when you put it that way."

With her head again resting on his chest and her index finger aimlessly traveling about his torso she spoke. "Not really. I think you are simply trying to be considerate, which by the way is one of the things I find so irresistible about you. Now, tell me about your Emily."

"We were high school sweethearts. Actually, we started dating, if you can call it that, in junior high. For six years, other than a few brief periods, we were a couple. Following graduation we decided, with considerable coaching from our parents, that our collegiate years should be spent at different schools to test the strength of our relationship. By the end of the first semester we recognized the stupidity of that decision and the following fall Emily transferred. The summer after graduation we were married."

Staring at the ceiling he continued. "Emily is an architect who dreams of starting her own firm someday. That dream was put on hold as she supported me through grad school and with the arrival of two daughters. No doubt, I am bias, but Emily is an exceptional architect. She is creative and has an eye for moving beyond the norm. Emily is a very detailed person, some might say, anal retentive, but an architect has to be."

Without moving Esme interrupted him. "That's nice, but none of that tells me anything. The description sounds like a business partner or in your case a departmental colleague. Someone with whom you work and respect which is fine, but a spouse is more than a colleague."

Her observation penetrated the surface of his skin like an interrogation light. Prickly beads of moisture surfaced on his forehead and his arms felt heavy as though he carried a newborn foal half a mile to the barn. It wasn't her intention to make him uncomfortable but that didn't matter, the sheet beneath him was wet with his sweat.

She was right and at some point he would need to acknowledge such, but he was overwhelmed with attempting to determine what this suggested about his understanding of Emily. Was she merely the mother of his daughters and an architect who was anal-retentive? Was his description reflective of fourteen years of marriage and reaching a level of comfort, in other words, taking the relationship for granted and, sadly, taking Emily for granted? Was this a guy thing, focusing on the economics of marriage? Describing the relationship based on what one does and how one adds value to the household rather than the emotional side? Such an excuse was equally disconcerting as he couldn't use that excuse if he wished to continue to view himself as someone other than a traditional male pumped up on masculinity.

Her final comment continued to echo as though he was riding through a limestone canyon, "but a spouse is more than a colleague." He wasn't so sure.

The conversation took a trail he never imagined when he acknowledged that he had no idea who Emily was. He defended that revelation by adding, "What do you say about someone you don't know, or maybe never knew?" The truth was there was a time in their relationship when he did know her, when he could have told Esme about Emily for hours, but they drifted apart. They had become roommates who share a common space and kids, as evidenced by the lack of intimacy. It wasn't just the lack of sex, although that was part of it, they simply were no longer intimate with one another. They never held hands, they seldom kissed, they never shared thoughts or feelings, and any physical touch was deemed as a request for sex. When sex did occur, once every couple of months, there was no foreplay, no creativity, and certainly no snuggling afterwards. She'd lie there, he'd lie on top of her, and the whole thing lasted no more than 5 minutes.

He thought about sharing a host of reasons why the chasm occurred but he determined it really didn't matter, the truth was he and Emily were strangers.

The pinhole in the ceiling that allowed droplets of truth about his relationship with Emily to fall forth expanded in size and it became difficult for Gunter to stop himself. He described how mealtime resembled a monastery where monks took a vow of silence. If it were not for the girls and stress at work he doubted they would ever speak.

Esme sat up and turned to face him in order to ask the next question. "Do you think she has or is having an affair?"

As much as he enjoyed ogling her breasts whenever she sat up he didn't even notice that her left breast hung slightly lower as her body was tilted toward him. Gunter merely answered, "Honestly, the thought never occurred to me. I can't imagine she would…" he stopped himself for a moment. "I want to say no, b…" He couldn't complete the word.

Esme pulled the bedspread over her shoulders so it hung like a shawl and said "But?"

Gunter reached up with both hands and pulled the bedspread shawl closed and asked, "Are you cold?"

"No, there was just a shiver that streaked through my body. But?"

Without letting go of the bedspread he spoke. "But, as I think about it, I don't know. The kids are at grandpa and grandma's, and she did suggest I take this trip, over the years there have been times when…" again he stopped. With the bedspread he pulled her toward his body and opened the shawl that her body might touch his. "To say anything else would be like the pot calling the kettle black." Beneath the bedspread they snuggled until both drifted off to sleep. The chasm created by time and distance had been closed in a matter of just a few short hours.

"Essy." She heard him but in the haze of total relaxation after early morning sex it took her several minutes to position herself in Seattle and in the Vance Hotel with Gunter.

"Essy, you awake?" Without waiting for a reply he continued to speak. "Essy, describe your brother to me."

Hearing the mention of her brother shook her enough to respond, "My brother? What are you talking about?"

"Describe him, his physical characteristics."

Placing both elbows beneath her torso she elevated her head and located Gunter seated in the easy chair with the Sunday paper covering his lap. "I don't understand."

Lifting his head from the paper he promised to explain once she shared her brother's profile. At the same time he apologized for not remembering the description she provided the previous year, other than his bum right leg.

"Early 50's, streaks of gray, at least the last time I saw him. Sometimes he has a short beard and other times he is cleaned shaved." The specifics did not flow smoothly as she was still consumed with the intent of his inquiry. "He is five ten and weighs between 150-160. What else do you want to know?"

"Any scars you know about or loss of teeth?"

"Cowboy, you are scaring me, what is this about?"

"Night before last they found a guy, homeless, the police are suggesting based on his clothing. Anyway, this guy was found in the railroad yard dead and they are seeking the public's assistance to determine if he was from the Seattle area."

Measuring each word carefully she asked, "There's a description of him in the paper?"

"Yes."

"What are you waiting for? Read it!"

"Read the entire article or just the description?"

"Stop stalling and share!" Seated on the bed with the sheet tucked under her arms her words were pregnant with tension.

"They are not quite sure on the gentlemen's height, they are guessing between five feet eight inches and six feet, and probably weighed…"

"What do you mean they are guessing, they don't know his height?"

Without emotion he answered. "No, apparently the gentleman was attempting to jump the train and slipped which resulted in his lower body being amputated."

In spite of sparse traffic, the ride to the city mortuary felt as though it lasted forever. The description of scars and the absence of teeth along with the long beard didn't fit Junior but it had been more than two years since she last saw him, things happen. *What were the odds* kept circulating through her thoughts, still, she needed to be sure and so Gunter insisted they check it out.

With her hands folded in her lap the range of emotions she experienced surprised her. She wondered, does the label "family" guarantee love? She had only spent a handful of days with Junior over a ten plus year period. Was it possible to say she loved him? Passing through an intersection she instinctively looked both ways to check for oncoming traffic. The moment her head swiveled to the left she captured Gunter's profile. Quickly she lowered her head as a similar question emerged, was it possible to love someone after only spending a few days together? She chastised herself, she was about to view a dead body to determine if it was her brother and she was pondering the idea of being in love with a Cowboy. What was wrong with her?

The sheet peeled back under the direction of a young intern and revealed that the body on the stainless steel plank was not Junior's. Relief washed through her body only to be filled on the backside by worry that next time it might be Junior. Tears streamed down her cheeks that she wiped, without thinking, on Gunter's shirtsleeve as she struggled to gain her balance in the midst of a whirlwind of emotional release. Leaning against him as they departed the cold, smelly room, part of her secretly wished to put some closure to the Junior chapter of her life. She didn't wish for her brother's death, but not knowing where he was or what he might be experiencing was a slow, anguishing death.

When they reached the car Gunter opened the passenger door for her and prior to getting in she thanked him and reached up and kissed him on the cheek. Before her heels reached the pavement of the parking lot she vowed to herself that before their time together elapsed she could tell him that she was falling in love with him.

CHAPTER 14

Gunter pointed the car toward Elliot Bay and Pike Place Market that sat above water's edge. His specific point of destination was a coffeehouse his students refused to forgive him for not visiting the previous year. When he spoke of visiting Seattle during the summer their first question was, did he visit Starbucks? He promised the students that the next time he was in Seattle he would make a point of visiting the trendy coffeehouse. More importantly, in spite of Esme's lack of appreciation for a great brew of coffee he decided that the coffee shop abuzz with Sunday morning caffeine worshippers was the perfect place for her to unwind.

The storefront business located at 1912 Pike Ave was exactly as Gunter had imagined. If one entered with eyes closed the sound was similar to a beehive with the workers tirelessly fluttering about in an attempt to complete their labors and impress the queen. The only thing missing was the queen, but in Gunter's mind she was attached to his arm. Recognizing the limitation of any analogy he kept the image to himself, plus, he didn't want to confuse the moment with any discussion of sex.

Spotting an empty table in the corner Gunter suggested they become squatters and take possession of the space before placing an order. The action defied protocol but rather than squabble customers in line nodded their approval that someone thought outside the norm.

Esme, feeling the eyes of others, whispered across the tabletop, "I think we are the topic of conversation."

"Yeah, well that's what happens when the most beautiful woman in the city enters and then dismisses the necessity of following the unwritten rules."

Blotches popped across her neckline and dipped down her cleavage as she blushed. She should have grown accustomed to his endless compliments but it just didn't happen that easy, not after endless criticism and dismissal from Mark.

Seated directly across from the Public Market Center they nursed their drinks and watched as vendors unpacked the wares they hoped to sell for the day. The aroma of fresh cut flowers mingled with coffee grounds, one sweet and one bitter, inserted another scent to the market already teeming with fish and smoked pork and somehow it increased the attraction of the space. The unique, if not strange, vapors slowly acted as a sponge absorbing Esme's stress from earlier in the morning.

The venue outside the coffee shop provided the perfect backdrop for people watching. The number of homeless people, mostly men sprinkled with an occasional woman, was disheartening even though they had firsthand knowledge of homelessness. They stared as a woman, probably in her fifties but bearing the marks of a seventy year old, hobbled along following a shopping cart that acted as her motivation to move forward. Some members of the disheveled crowd confiscated the remains of cigarettes and with the strike of a match attempted to inhale a hit or two of nicotine while others, similar to seagulls, pecked the cobblestone street in search of crumbs left behind. The setting inside offered similar entertainment.

The crowd of locals and the workers preparing for the day was gradually transformed into tourists as the sun rose in the eastern sky over the mountains. Without breaking visual contact with the throng of people conversation started to flow between the two of them. Esme created stories to fit facial expressions or the hitch in a walker's giddy-up, and Gunter built on the foundation she started.

After purchasing a second cup of coffee Gunter reached across the tiny circular table that separated them, took Esme's hand and inquired, "If you could change one thing, what would it be?"

She worked her fingers between his and delivered her answer. "I want to say Mark, but I can't because without Mark there would be no Scotty or Emily."

Burning the tip of his tongue, distracted by her response, he set the cup down and waited a few seconds for the tingling to stop before speaking. Shaking his head he began, "Essy, I gotta tell you, I never expected that. Tell me about them."

"My kids?"

"Sure, why not? They are important to you so they are important to me."

"Scotty, I mean, Scott, who is now eleven no longer wants to be called Scotty. He informed me the other day that Scotty is a baby's name. He is very much like his father or I suppose I should say, working to be like his father. I tell myself it's just a phase. Like all young males he is struggling to separate himself from me, but honestly, we have never connected."

"That must be painful."

"It was for a long time. I interrogated myself, 'what did I do wrong?' I would sneak into his room when he was asleep and try to imagine what life would be like if our relationship was different. Finally, I came to realize that I didn't do anything, we are just different."

"Different? How so?"

"Scotty," her head dropped as though she was disappointed with herself, "there I go again, it's so difficult not to use an endearing name. Scott is concerned first and foremost about Scott. And yes, I know the stages of development, but his behavior and attitude is more than a stage. He loves money and wants to make more money. He wants to become a lawyer, like Mark, so he can become rich and famous."

"And rich and famous is a bad thing?"

"Of course not, but Scott is not interested in law or justice, but like his father he sees being a lawyer as equal to wealth."

"It's not my place to question you, but he is only eleven."

"Yes, I know, and if this was not consistent with everything in his life I would not be concerned. Scott may be eleven but academically he performs at a tenth or eleventh grade level. His plan is to enter college when he is fifteen and matriculate onto grad school before he turns twenty. Knowing his competitive nature and refusal to fail it wouldn't surprise me that he accomplishes this feat. This may sound harsh and not very motherly, but I pray that Scott experiences failure so he doesn't end up failing at life."

"Surprising, or maybe not so surprising, I have met and worked with many students who exhibit the same qualities. They are not fifteen or sixteen years old but the drive to exceed and avoid failure at any cost figuratively and literally destroys their lives."

Moving her chair closer to his and placing her hand on his leg as though she desired to shut out the world, both faces and voices that surrounded them, she asked, "And what do you do, if anything?"

"Essy, anything I may do with my students isn't a prescription for you to do with Scott."

Twirling a disobedient strand of hair with one hand and squeezing his thigh with the other she said, "I know. I am interested to hear how you address such students. Because, based on what I know about you up to now, I just can't imagine you don't do something or say something to these students."

Tilting his body back and rocking the wooden chair onto two legs he smiled within at how perceptive Esme was concerning him and how she remembered the little things he shared or implied when others, including Emily, either ignored or missed them entirely. He concluded that her request was genuine and not an attempt to secure a quick fix for her son, and therefore she deserved a reply.

"Yes, I do attempt to do something, but it totally depends on the student."

"That doesn't surprise me as I have listened to you speak about your students."

This time he smiled outwardly knowing that she wasn't afraid to let him know he was worth listening to. When the front legs of the chair returned to the floor his knee struck the table and coffee splattered everywhere. As he mopped up the steaming brown liquid with a towel, he described the various approaches employed, and not necessarily because they were successful, but because he understood his job was to make students uncomfortable in order that they might create new options for life.

Leaving behind the dense aroma of coffee beans and crossing the street to the Public Market, Esme described her daughter, Emily, who for all practical purposes was the complete opposite of Scott. Under the shelter of the roof protected from the morning mist Esme stated, "It's hard to believe, same parents, same household, same rules, and yet two completely different children. Sort of challenges both ends of the debate, nature verses nurture."

Carrying a single long stemmed dahlia that Gunter purchased in one hand and the other securely connected to Gunter's hand, Esme designated Emily as the sensitive one, in fact, she suggested that at times her daughter was overly sensitive. Even for a nine year old she was attune to the emotions of others. Without thought she placed the needs of others ahead of hers which Scott takes full advantage of whenever possible. Gunter occasionally probed with a question or offered a comment but for the most part Esme did the talking.

Leisurely they strolled through the entire marketplace drifting towards various vendors when offered free samples or when an item captured their attention. Standing behind Esme, Gunter draped his arms around her body pulling her close as they watched the bantering between a potential customer and salesperson at Pike Place Fish Company. Fish sailed back and forth and the crowd held their breath until the fish was caught. Nudging Esme forward the couple made their way to the front of the crowd where one of the workers hoisted a large salmon and placed it directly in front of Esme's face. The crowd chanted, "Kiss it. Kiss it." With another nudge from Gunter Esme puckered her lips and kissed the fish. Leaning back into Gunter she informed him that now he needed to kiss her and together they laughed.

At the end of a short hallway a terrace, a rooftop flower garden opened up looking over Puget Sound. A few strides past the doorway a large black ceramic pig greeted visitors. In front of the pig rested a plastic bucket partially filled with chunks of colored chalk. The pig wore pithy and not so pithy sayings. Armed with pink chalk Esme scrolled on the left ham, E (heart drawn) G.

As she rose, nervous how Gunter would receive her work, she was engulfed in a bear hug. Pulling back slightly to see his face she whispered, "Cowboy, I think I am falling in love with you." Without a moment's hesitation, as though he failed to grasp the full depth of her words, Gunter responded. "Well then, we need to take a trip to San Juan Islands and test out your feelings."

Reading her expression he knew he derailed her. "You look like a bull rider sitting with their ass buried in the dirt wondering what just happened while at the same time trying to locate the hind legs of the bull."

Reaching the railing of the terrace Esme confirmed Gunter's suspicions. "You could say that." Staring at the tide making its way toward shore she continued, "A little explanation would be helpful."

Without looking at her or touching her he attempted to explain. "When you drifted off on the flight from Denver I paged through the airline magazine and there was an article featuring the San Juan Islands. The writer described the Islands as a location great for romance, specifically, a place for lovers."

Taking in the full western horizon she spoke. "Cowboy, your connections never cease to amaze me and the way you put me at ease…well, that's part of the attraction."

Ease, however, was not the word that would come to mind for Esme or Gunter later that evening. Conversation was guarded and somewhat stilted almost to the point of being unnatural. Television became the means of entertainment or noise to fill the space until bed. Even though they slid beneath the covers naked sex was not on the agenda for either of them that evening, the thought of love had the potential to change everything.

CHAPTER 15

Gunter's hand squeezed her shoulder much to her dismay. It was not the manner she preferred to be drawn out of the deepest stage of sleep. To make matters worse, darkness engulfed not only the room but also the entire city. Drifting in limbo between conscious and unconsciousness she wondered, why is he doing this to me and then, purely by coincidence, he reminded her of the reason for his rude behavior. "Time to get up if we hope to catch the 9:10." Four hours later his hand squeezed another portion of her body, her hand, as he dragged her first to the ticket window and then to the entry point for the ferry heading to San Juan Islands, specifically, Friday's Harbor.

A blond-haired, college-aged girl drowning in a heavy canvas coat to ward off the freezing breeze blowing from the Straits of Juan de Fuca calmed their fears the moment they were within hearing distance. The stress of the moment was that if they were unable to board this ferry the next one did not sail until 11:55. Accustom to witnessing people racing to climb aboard the ferry the young woman assured Gunter and Esme that even though it was past 9:10 the ferry would not sail until fully loaded.

Because the walk up passengers and passengers with bicycles had already boarded Gunter and Esme were required to wait at a holding point a hundred feet from the back of the ferry until all vehicles were loaded. Watching vehicles stacked up more than a quarter mile from the hull of the ship crawl forward and pass within inches of their toes, Gunter observed a similar fear reside in the eyes of drivers who were equally nervous that the ferry would reach capacity before their vehicle was permitted to secure one of the final stalls in the belly of the boat.

Similar to a litter of newborn pups Gunter and Esme huddled next to one another lacking the clothing necessary to keep the wind and mist from penetrating to the core of their bodies. To distract himself Gunter chatted with the drivers as their vehicles crept forward. The conversation with each person was the same. Apparently they all desired to commiserate regarding the traffic from Seattle. Gunter gained an appreciation for commuters who didn't demonstrate road rage on a daily basis and he recognized that he could never drive in daily traffic.

During the hour plus excursion Esme busied herself with reviewing trifold brochures detailing the San Juan Islands and the sights and sounds of Friday's Harbor and Gunter, with a book in hand, questioned the wisdom of traveling to Friday's Harbor under such a pretense. After all, what did he really know about the place other than what some journalist wrote, who for all he knew, was on the city payroll. He was well aware that anything could be made to sound wonderful, even spectacular. He witnessed this first hand reading college students' philosophical exposes in which they described exceptional theories that lacked practical truth. He hoped for Esme's sake such was not the truth concerning Friday's Harbor.

As for Esme's confession from the previous day, what did that entail? As an advisor he heard at least one advisee each semester describe being in love one month and the next month onto the next person. He challenged these individuals to consider the difference between infatuation and love and to recognize that love has a host of meanings and expressions. As he watched the shoreline of an uninhabited island pass close to the ferry he contemplated why he had not pressed Esme for clarity. Was he afraid that her response would be too much or worse yet, not enough for him?

Focusing on a lone bird, perhaps a red-tailed hawk or possibly a broad-wing hawk, soar on an updraft he had to admit that all these questions seeped from his pours and lead directly to him and his avoidance of admitting how he felt, not just what he thought, but what he actually felt.

Passing a small strip of land that jetted away from the island the ferry made a sharp turn portside and aligned the stern of the boat with the dock. The captain announced the ship would be docked in a matter of minutes and all passengers needed to leave the ferry. Esme and Gunter collected a handful of items and proceeded to a lower level in order to exit. Both were startled by the jolt against the stationary dock that halted any additional forward movement of the ferry. Esme commented, purely in jest, that the force of the jolt must have sent a powerful vibration straight upward because the moment they stepped off the ferry and climbed the hill toward Friday's Harbor pockets of sunlight brightened the island. Gunter prayed that it was an omen for a positive and bright outcome to the day's voyage.

As a result of the cold wind swirling about the hills of the island and the forecast that stated it would remain windy and damp throughout the day the couple decided to explore the city on foot and if they elected to venture beyond the boundaries of the city they would travel by taxi.

Esme had stayed in bed until the very last minute with the idea that she would grab breakfast during the 80 mile trip northward but when it became clear time was a factor she was forced to wait. Therefore, the noises her stomach broadcast announced that the first item on the agenda was to fill the void in her stomach. Walking hand in hand down the street overlooking the bay it was decided that they would eat something small to tide them over until they ate a late lunch before boarding the ferry for the return trip.

At the first corner they turned left and followed the street to the heart of the city. Leaving the cement and stepping on a finely sanded and polished wooden floor the couple ordered a ham and cheese croissant to share. Watching the worker carefully slice the airy dough Esme joked that the Vienna style pasty added to the atmosphere of love. With the croissant and a can of coke in hand Gunter and Esme returned to the sidewalk in search of a sun baked bench. Spotting a wooden bench tucked next to a building that offered cover from the wind they planted themselves on each end of the bench with the croissant and coke between them.

In spite of the less than ideal conditions for roaming the city streets and marina Gunter and Esme had a diverse group of characters to select from to entertain them as they savored their mid-morning lunch. Ironically, without informing the other, each gravitated toward the same five individuals interacting in a very passionate manner. At times they shoved and teased one another. They whispered to each other and shouted across the street to each other. They laughed one moment and the next worked to comfort one who isolated himself from the group. Unmistakably these five people formed a family. There was a dad, a mom, a son and two daughters, presumably the children ranged in ages from approximately thirteen to seven.

Watching the family made Gunter and Esme contemplate their own family, specifically their children. Simultaneously, without uttering a word both became aware that their four day relationship once a year had the potential to be life threatening. Lurking, but yet to be named was the truth that the danger escalated in explosive power by introducing the construct of love. Before the croissant became nonexistent both internalized that before they declared love for the other they needed to weigh the consequences for themselves, personally, and for their families.

The island of love became a sphere not necessarily *of* love but *to* define and discuss love. For Gunter this occurred as he pondered what it meant to employ the word love and what such a word once spoken meant for them as a couple.

The idea that love was difficult to define and to explain captured his intellectual curiosity and social cynicism. Gunter was fascinated that individuals would alter their careers, they would risk stability, they would toss aside family and friends, and they would recalibrate their moral compass all because someone mumbled the word, LOVE.

In reality, at least for Gunter, there were no assurances that how one person defined love was the same for the other. Gunter was and always had been skeptical of love being some warm fuzzy feeling. It was just such a position that earned him the title Mr. Unromantic.

It was also this position that led him to question Esme when they left the bench and walked back toward the center of the business district. "Essy, what did you mean when you said you think you are falling in love with me? Let me narrow that question, what does love mean to you in relationship to me?"

She turned her head to get a better look at him and caught a glimpse of her reflection in the bookstore window. She increased her pace slightly to push pass Gunter and view herself more fully in the window. She was surprised to see the age of the woman who stared back at him. She felt as if she was seventeen but the person bundled up, forging against the cold wind swirling down the hill towards the waterfront, looked middle-aged. The image was that of a woman who already had experienced too many moments of disappointment and rejection. The wrinkles at the corner of her eyes were not the result of too much laughter, but from worry, stress, and occasionally crying herself to sleep. Many of the marks she saw on her face along with the emptiness she felt in her heart were the result of the absence of love and therefore to describe love would be easy, simply name the opposite of the life she lived. But rather than answer she tugged on Gunter's arm which brought him close to her core and blocked the woman in the window. When she spoke she chose her words carefully. "You have an uncanny ability to ask incredible questions with perfect timing."

"Does that mean you don't have an answer?"

"No, it means I find myself wondering how you are able to read my thoughts."

As they walked another block and a half the mist, driven by the wind like a dog shaking lake water from its fur, drove the two of them into an antique shop.

Esme immediately found herself in her element. She loved to rummage through places searching for the perfect item to add another piece of history to the house that could gain acceptance on the historical registry. But unlike the artifacts she was accustom to pillaging these wares were maritime connected. Still, the smell, the clutter, the adventure offered Esme sanctuary.

Gunter was not opposed to browsing, in fact he enjoyed a good antique store. However, unlike most scavengers, including Esme, he completed review of the inventory in ten minutes, fifteen if the store had a collection of toys from the forties and fifties. He learned over the years to avoid such establishments with Emily because he would grow impatient and frustrated with her need to view every item. Eventually, what was supposed to be enjoyable and a shared outing lead to an argument. Yet, for some reason it was different with Esme, after thirty minutes of standing at her side and watching her pick through piles of "junk" he was totally at ease. Was that the definition of love?

Did love mean setting aside one's agenda and feelings for the sake of the other? Did love mean placing the joy and happiness of the other before one's own? Was love more of an action than a feeling, or the absence of particular feelings? Or was that the definition of infatuation?

With the white and single red dot wooden "Lazy Ike" fishing lure careful wrapped in an old newspaper for safe transporting, Esme informed Gunter that she was ready for the next store. His response had her believing that he couldn't wait for the next shopping adventure. The mist had given way to a steady rain and Gunter appreciated Esme's insistence that they bring rain gear and an umbrella. Scrunched together under the black tiny walking canopy it took another block and half before an antique store lured Esme off the damp sidewalk.

Gunter could tolerate any type of store with the exception of one that only displayed glassware. With the umbrella folded Gunter saw that the entire store held nothing but old glass; tea cups and saucers, bowls in all shapes, sizes, and colors, dishes, plates, candlestick holders, on and on. The majority of the glass was on display and waiting to be fondled but a few exceptional pieces were behind locked china cabinets. The square footage of the store was twice the size of the previous shop.

Reaching the first table cluttered, in Gunter's opinion, with glass items, Esme leaned into him and whispered, "This is a dream come true. When does the ferry leave?"

Gunter stammered for a second and regained his composure. "Three forty five."

Without skipping a beat Esme sang on. "Well, if I rush we just might make it."

Cautiously Gunter uttered "Okay," with a quivering voice.

Esme broke out in laughter.

"What? Did I miss something?"

"I couldn't resist." Displaying a broad toothy grin she added, "Sorry."

Perplexed by the conversation that transpired he could only shrug his shoulders and ask, "What do you mean?"

"I was only kidding. I don't get into glassware."

Breathing a huge sigh of relief he suggested they leave the establishment in search of stores more to their liking.

Throughout the remainder of the afternoon they visited every store in Friday's Harbor. Some visits lasted just long enough to determine the contents held no interest while other stores offered appealing items of interest. It didn't matter the type of store or the elements they endured on the street, they held hands, they laughed, they kissed, and occasionally they touched one another in a suggestive, teasing manner. Absent, until lunch at the Fish Shack, was any formal conversation about love.

Nursing her second Chardonnay waiting for the arrival of their double order of fish and chips, fish advertised as freshly caught that morning, Esme entertained Gunter's question from the last time they shared food. With the assistance of alcohol warming her core Esme felt confident enough to tackle the question of love. "Cowboy, this has been the perfect day. I have to agree with the author of the article, this is an ideal place for lovers." Without pausing to allow Gunter to respond or distract her from her obvious rehearsed monologue she plowed on like a team of runaway horses. "I wish I could answer your question from this morning with clarity, but truthfully, I can tell you what love isn't easier than what it means to me. That being said, Cowboy, I am falling in love with you." She stopped herself, cleared her throat with a gulp of white wine, looked him square in the eye and finished her piece. "That's not totally true. I am not falling, I am in love."

The Merlot continued to swirl about the glass as Gunter mindlessly created a small barrier between himself and Esme with the smooth but dry drink. As the base of the glass reached the table the waiter arrived with their baskets of Alaskan cod and French fries followed by an assistant waiter, learning the ropes for the upcoming busy tourist season, who delivered a tray of condiments. The invasion of workers in their personal space afforded Esme and Gunter the opportunity to absorb her confession without fear of creating an awkward silence.

A third glass of wine didn't nullify her ambitions it merely made her tired. The conversation that weaved through the deep fried fish and uniformly cut potatoes was causal, a replay of the day including descriptions of interesting people they saw.

Stomachs filled to the point of discomfort and a mild alcohol stupor raging behind their eyes, the ferry ride back to Anacortes, WA was uneventful as both completed the trip with their eyes shut.

The plan was to spend their final evening in Seattle dining at 13 Coins. Once back in room 816 at the Vance Hotel Esme announced that she needed a shower to make herself presentable for any public outing. Gunter challenged the notion of presentable, "Essy you could not shower for a week and wear a sweat suit and be more lovely than any other woman in public."

"Cowboy, I think your judgment is far from being balanced and you certainly are not blind."

Seated on the edge of the bed, Esme tried removing her pants that had been soaked by the rain on three separate occasions. The blue jeans clung to her skin and invoked Gunter's assistance.

The moment Gunter took hold of the bottoms of her pants legs he knew there were basic needs that required attention greater than satisfying hunger. Firmly he tugged on the pants but when movement was nonexistent in spite of Esme's efforts to squirm free Gunter hooked his thumbs in the belt loops and carefully slid his fingers inside the waistline of the jeans. From that position he pulled first with the right hand, then the left until the jeans cleared her hips. He was careful not to move too quickly and to keep her lacy panties in place. With the jeans crumbled on the floor he informed Esme, "Good thing 13 Coins is open twenty-four hours, it will be a while before we leave the room."

"That's fine by me, I am more hungry for something other than food right now anyway."

Half under the covers they stared into each other's eyes and, without looking, continued to undress each other. It didn't seem appropriate in the moment to mention it but both sensed something was different. They knew each other's body, they knew what excited the other person, they knew how to move to increase the pleasure or prolong the union, they knew when the other was about to explode into ecstasy, but as Gunter rolled on top of Esme without breaking eye contact, there was something they didn't know. Neither could predict how Esme's words, "I'm in love with you" would affect their sexual relations.

As they gracefully swayed in perfect rhythm with one another as though they were not resting on the bed but floating in midair Gunter understood, for the first time, the depth of what his religion professor attempted to clarify. In the Old Testament the sexual encounter between two lovers was described as, "to know" while the sexual act between others was described as "to lay with." Gunter had fathered two daughters and had made love to his wife, or so they defined it as love, countless times, but nothing compared to this. Resting his body on Esme totally exhausted he could say that he "knew" Esme as he had never known another woman. Yet, the words did not cross his lips.

Equally as spent as Gunter Esme was not burdened supporting his weight. She actually found it comforting that he trusted her enough to allow himself to be so vulnerable. She could feel his heart throbbing against her breast, the very heart that had captured hers. She desperately wanted to whisper in his ear, "I love you" but she already had revealed her feelings and she didn't want to come off as some scary unstable lunatic who went around saying I love you. Instead she whispered, "Tell me something I don't know about you and would never guess."

His breathing never altered, he didn't move, she wondered if he was asleep. Another minute passed before he turned his head that he might speak to her ear and not the pillow. "I like M & M's after sex."

"Will any chocolate do?"

"No, it needs to be M & M's, specifically peanut."

"Well then, we need to find a candy machine on our way to 13 Coins. And, just to be safe, we should probably buy a couple extra packages. One never knows what the remainder of the night might bring."

Their flights home both departed late in the afternoon on Tuesday and, somewhat ironically, the two planes left within thirty minutes of each other. Forty-five minutes after the last kiss and the promise to return next year both sat silently on their respective planes. Even though they were hundreds of miles apart and the distance was growing by the second, the same internal conversation occurred for both of them. Could they survive a twelve-month separation?

Sitting squished between two large men, Gunter remembered the flight to Denver and thought about the preamble, "Life, Liberty, and the pursuit of Happiness." There was no doubt in his mind after spending the four days with Esme what happiness was. He whispered as though she was seated next to him, "Essy, I love you."

Esme, having the entire row to herself, stretched out and replayed the conversation at the Fish Shack. She was haunted that Gunter never said he did or did not love her. She wiped the tears with her sleeve as she whispered, assuming that Gunter magically would hear, "Oh Gunter, I miss you already."

And then as though on cue from an off stage director both said, "We'll make it, I know we will."

CHAPTER 16
JUNE 12, 1977

It felt awkward to fly on Sunday. Gunter strove to comprehend why the ticket prices were higher for a Sunday flight, especially considering that the flight to Denver was less than half full. Emily had also questioned why he needed to leave on Sunday. He did not have an answer other than to say, "I just am." He thought about saying that it was cheaper to fly on Sunday but decided against it because he didn't want to lie to her. The thought had not vacated the recesses of his short-term memory when he realized that his moral higher ground was extremely shallow considering the words that would be shared.

Gunter had contemplated asking the stewardess if the jet was flying through molasses but with the rash of hijacking during the past several years he wasn't about to increase the crews' level of anxiety. He already felt embarrassed with Erich Segel's latest book in his lap so he wasn't about to call more attention to himself. *Oliver's Story* in part was his story. He had not lost the love of his life, as Segel described in gripping fashion in *Love Story*. However, he was questioning if he loved Emily. Similar to Oliver he too one day met a beautiful mysterious woman who captured his heart and led him to read books authored by Segel. As the jet engines droned on he found himself pondering, was Esme his Marcie, his true soul mate, who would teach him the true meaning of love?

With the book closed and the back facing up so no one could ascertain the title, Gunter understood that none of that would occur until he arrived in Denver where he would put an end to a year of being riddled with guilt. Gunter had emotionally chastised himself for not telling Esme he loved her before they departed. He could only wonder what undo stress he placed upon her and how she must have mulled searching for any evidence to determine if he felt the way she did.

Speed walking the concourse Gunter's cowboy boots echoed through the sterile environment. In spite of the unique sound and image of a man aggressively powerwalking through the crowd Gunter saw Esme approaching the gate from the opposite direction before she locked on to him. Like two medieval knights on horseback charging one another with tremendous determination, minus the lance, Gunter and Esme strategically weaved their way through the crowd. The final few strides were accomplished as Esme threw herself into Gunter's chest and was retrieved by his waiting arms. The force of the embrace sent them twirling as though they were performing a dance on ice. Her maroon pleated Sally skirt puffed away from her body offering glimpses of her matching panties while the off the shoulder black knit sweater held in place by her breast threatened to drop obscenely low. Individuals from the crowd who stopped to stare had no choice but to grant them space or suffer the effects of being struck by the heel of Esme's shoes.

Gunter refused to return Esme to the floor, as he desired that she was close when he spoke the words he should have delivered twelve months earlier. "Essy, I love you. I'm so sorry I did not tell you last year before boarding the plane. I have felt terrible the entire year wondering what..."

With her finger pressed against his lips she stopped him in order that she might speak. Gunter slowly lowered her until she stood firmly. "I knew you loved me, I just didn't know if you would ever be able to tell me. Cowboy, my love for you today is just as strong as it was when we departed. It's silly, I know, we have been apart for an entire year and yet right now none of that matters. I won't lie, it has been a long" she exaggerated the word with her southern drawl, "year. I could have used those words as a source of strength and comfort."

"Do you want to talk about it?"

With a strong and steady voice she answered, "Not right now, but yes, I do want to share the events of the past twelve months and I want to hear about your year as well, but not right now. At this moment I need to hold you and for you to hold me so you can tell me again that you love me, me, Essy."

Before he declared his love a second time he kissed her passionately to the delight of several bystanders who offered approval with applause. Embarrassed that they did not realize that they had attracted an audience they offered a sheepish grin and made their way towards two seats on the fringe of the gate area.

A sheet draped across their hips, a bouquet of purple dahlias on the end table, a bottle of Chardonnay and a bottle of Merlot both half depleted, and two lovers flat on their back gasping for air in an attempt to recover from a marathon session of love-making. Sweat streamed between Esme's perfectly round breasts while her Farrah Fawcett hairdo wilted. Sweat pooled in Gunter's ears as it poured from his brow and his midsection felt as though he forgot to towel off after a shower.

Reaching across his body as excitement still surged through him in spite of nearly hyperventilating, he carefully rolled the tip of her nipple between his fingers. Without delay she pressed his hand flat upon her breast and asked him to just hold her. With her hand restraining him against her breast he inquired if there was something wrong.

Too exhausted to look at him she stared at the textured ceiling as she spoke. "I'm not sure if this is the right analogy, but isn't there some saying about riding your horse hard and putting him away wet and that being a bad thing?"

"Yeah, a wet horse, an exhausted horse, can develop muscle or respiratory issues. It generally refers to someone who does not take care of the horse. So, you're saying you need time to recover."

"You're quick cowboy."

With his hand still held captive atop her breast he rolled toward her and kissed her and told her yet again, "Essy, I love you."

When she opened her eyes she saw that Gunter was only two inches from her face and staring directly into her eyes. Startled she didn't know how to respond other than ask a question, "Yes?"

Drifting back gradually, expanding the distance to nearly a foot he asked her, "Do you always close your eyes when you kiss?"

"I guess so, don't you?"

With complete sincerity he broadened his inquiry. "Why? I mean, why do people close their eyes when they kiss?"

With a chuckle she responded to her bedmate. "Cowboy, seriously, doesn't your brain ever stop?"

"Come on, it's a fair question. Why close your eyes?" After a momentary pause he continued. "Have you ever kissed someone and not closed your eyes?"

"Honestly, I have not thought about it." She alternated her gaze between the ceiling and his face; it was as though the close proximity of his face created a sensory overload.

"Well, think about the various individuals you have kissed, was there ever a time you didn't close your eyes?"

"I don't know, I suppose maybe my kids." With an eyebrow raised she asked her own question. "So tell me, what's behind this question?"

"What do you mean?"

"You know perfectly well what I mean."

"No, really, I don't."

"Oh, come on. You don't just ask a question such as this out of the blue. I am guessing there is some hidden agenda."

"I promise you Essy, no hidden agenda. I am merely curious why people close their eyes. I am wondering if this is a learned behavior or something natural."

"Okay then, become your own subject, what about you, is there a time you don't close your eyes?"

Gunter took his time before replying. "Like you, I would probably say my kids, parents, and my grandparents."

"Which leads you to conclude what?"

"Actually, there is science on this very issue that suggests when a person is aroused the pupil dilates and too much light is let in which may result in the closing of the eyes. The problem with that being the sole answer is, then why do people close their eyes when they kiss in the dark?"

"I don't know, but I am right back where I was when this conversation started, does it really matter why people close their eyes?"

"It might, it just might." Gunter bore a grin from ear to ear. "Consider how you felt when you opened your eyes and saw me only inches from your face. Now add to that feeling kissing someone for the first time. Kissing places a person in a vulnerable position to say nothing of being extremely self-conscious. Perhaps, the simple act of closing one's eyes enables one to become more comfortable with self and the other person."

"Does a blind person close their eyes? Oh god, now you have me asking those mind-numbing questions."

"What a great question. I never thought of that. The answer could credit or discredit my hypothesis. Perhaps…"

"Shut-up Cowboy and get over here and close your eyes and kiss me, your horse is all dried off."

Following a long, lingering shower the couple propped pillows against the headboard and watched a rerun episode of Rhoda. The TV Guide magazine offered the title, "Guess Who I Saw Today" and a brief description, "Rhoda sees Joe with another woman." Gunter was familiar with the name of the show and the lead character as it was a spin-off from the Mary Tyler Moore Show, but he had never watched a single episode. Esme described, during the opening credits, how, like so many Americans, she became hooked the previous season when Rhoda and Joe got married in a cliffhanger of a show and how the current season unfolded as though it was based on her life. When Gunter asked for clarification she merely whispered, "Not yet, let's just watch the show."

Intertwined they watched the comedy, fueled by a few witty one-liners, play out as a drama. During the commercials Gunter would glance over at Esme and notice how she labored to fight back the tears. When the show ended Gunter took the lead and suggested they see if Todd, "their waiter," was working the night shift at 13 Coins.

Strolling beneath the canopy and through the thick, solid wooden door they were greeted cordially by the maître d' who welcomed them and inquired if they wished to be seated at the bar or a booth. Gunter asked if Todd was working and, if so, could they be seated in his section. If necessary they were willing to wait.

When Todd arrived at the edge of their table he introduced himself as their waiter for the evening and proceeded to share the well-rehearsed list of specials. Continuing to speak without disrupting the eye contact he established he shuffled his feet a half a step back to collect his thoughts and determine if he knew the patrons at his table. To afford a greater window of time to reach a conclusion he asked if he could take their drink orders. Before either spoke he knew the order would be one bottle of Chardonnay and one bottle of Merlot. Obviously he knew them from the restaurant, yet he was still at a loss. Returning with the drinks he confessed, "I'm sorry, I know I should know you, but I just can't…"

Esme stopped him, "Unless you have a photographic memory I doubt you would remember us."

While pouring a small amount of clear liquid for Esme to sample, savor, and signal as acceptable, Todd spoke, "I have been blessed with the ability to remember faces which is helpful and can be profitable in this line of work."

Gunter, watching him uncork the Merlot, quickly added, "Understandable, if people are remembered it increases their sense of self-worth and value and that translates into worth and value for you."

"But that's not why I do it. Being able to remember faces is about remembering the stories that people share with me. The dining experience is about more than just the food, it truly is an experience. There are many patrons who dine here weekly and in a very small way I know their story. And there are others who come here specifically to get away, to be secretive, and that too is their story."

Running her finger around the top of her wine glass, Esme asked, "So what is our story?"

Having poured the drinks Todd returned to his statue position. "That's what is pestering me, I don't know."

Looking at each other, Gunter nodded his approval and Esme proceeded to share a small portion of their story. "We come to Seattle once a year, the same four days, June twelfth through the fifteenth. This is our third trip and the restaurant is always part of the trip."

"And I served you last year, yes?"

Esme answered, "Yes." Followed by Gunter who added, "And two years ago as well."

"Well, welcome to the city, again, and to 13 Coins, again. It is my pleasure to serve as your waiter. I will place your order for appetizers and unless you have questions about the menu I will leave you to enjoy the wine and survey the menu to make your selection for the main course."

Sharing a cup of onion soup that had become a hallmark staple of the restaurant the conversation remained light and safe. Esme inquired if Gunter watched the Belmont Stakes the day before.

"I wouldn't have missed it. Probably one of the greatest horses ever to race won the Triple Crown and did so undefeated, quite an accomplishment. Did you watch?"

"I actually did. I have always watched the Kentucky Derby because it was the Kentucky Derby, but I never paid much attention to the Preakness or Belmont. But with a horse named Seattle Slew how could I not watch?"

"The owners, as I understand it, are from Yakima. If I remember correctly, honesty I didn't pay much attention to the prerace hype, the horse was purchased for seventeen thousand five hundred dollars."

"I have no idea, is that a lot for a horse?"

"For most horses, yes, but for a thoroughbred like Seattle Slew, no. That was a steal. He could have sold for one hundred and seventeen thousand."

Giggling she asked, "So you're telling me you never paid seventeen thousand dollars for a horse?"

Gunter choked on his Alaskan cod. Smiling to keep from laughing he stated, "I didn't pay that much for all my horses combined."

Curious she asked Gunter if he ever rode a horse as fast as Seattle Slew.

"Not that fast and certainly not at the distance of a mile and half. I do have a black mare and she is lighting quick, but with her size she could never compete. It would be like a sixteen-year old boy with long legs racing a five year old. The stride and the power of a race horse are incredible."

Savoring her small rack of ribs Esme was silent for several minutes. With the plate pushed to the side, more than half covered with ribs, Esme stretched out her arm and took hold of Gunter. Softly she asked, "Will you take me horseback riding?"

CHAPTER 17

Beaming with eagerness Gunter informed Esme that they would need to locate a stable that offered trail rides or an outfitting company that did trail rides. He warned her that most of these companies have horses that could complete the trail ride without a rider. "It can be less of a riding experience and more of a sitting excursion. It's not the horse's fault, it is merely the result of endless repetition."

Midmorning on Tuesday the clouds separated and by noon the sun was shining and working its magic to dry things off. The trip eastward became more enjoyable as the thought of riding in the rain evaporated. An hour and a half outside of Seattle the rental car was parked next to a freshly painted white picket fence.

"To match you with the right horse we have a couple of questions to assess your riding level." The ranch hand moved to each individual registered for the trail ride asking the same series of questions. "Never rode a horse, rode a few times, ride frequently?" The final two questions were how comfortable are you with riding? And how would you describe your skill level?

Esme didn't wait for the ranch hand to ask the litany of questions. As he approached she blurted out, "I have been on a horse a couple of times. And I will be comfortable if I am next to Gunter."

Directing his attention to Gunter the cowpoke with clipboard in hand continued, "You must be Gunter."

"Yes."

"Where would you place yourself on the riding spectrum?"

"I have ridden a few times."

"And your skill level?"

Shrugging his shoulders he answered, "I'm pretty comfortable."

Esme interjected, "Stop being so modest. He trains horses."

Smiling the ranch hand asked if Gunter would be comfortable riding a horse in training. "She's green, never been out on a trail ride, but she's ready."

Returning the smile Gunter said, "I would love to ride such a horse."

Gunter's horse, unlike the other horses already saddled for the trail outing, had to be saddled. Gunter watched closely as the large, stocky, amply fed, chocolate palomino mare was saddled. He looked for any cues of how the horse responded and how she communicated with those close to her. Handing the reins to Gunter the trail guide offered a simple warning, "She can be a handful, but she has never bucked. She locks up or she bolts. You probably want to ride at the end of the line. It makes her nervous when another horse comes up behind her."

Without making eye contact with the small group of trail riders nervously listening to the conversation Gunter focused on the mare and made a declarative statement in the form of a question. "Bottom of the herd horse ha, pushed around a lot?"

"Precisely." The trail guide nodded affirming that Gunter knew something about horses.

Esme interrupted, "I don't understand what you guys are talking about."

"Horses that are on the bottom end of the herd tend to be nervous because other horses have pushed them around and frequently charged at them from behind. It's not unlike the school playground where the bullies target certain kids and make their life difficult, if not miserable. Consequently, those kids are always looking over their shoulder to avoid being surprised. When necessary they bolt."

Esme was satisfied with Gunter's answer, "Got it."

Directing his attention back to the guide he said, "If you don't mind, it would probably be more constructive for the horse if we placed her in the middle of the group and help her work through her anxiety."

'I agree totally if you're up for it."

"The horse you selected for Essy, he or she is okay with a nervous horse?"

"Yeah, he's an older gelding who was a pickup horse in the rodeo and a horse we use to pony our young stock. There's not much that unsettles Old Joe."

"Good." He looked at Esme to assure her that she would be safe.

The guide spoke the truth. The moment Gunter stepped up onto the mare he felt the muscles across her shoulders tighten. Attempting to place the stocky horse in the middle of the single file line, as though he was parallel parking, the horse started side passing to avoid the position. After several attempts and subsequent circles after each failed attempt, and the trail guides assuring the other riders Gunter knew what he was doing and they were perfectly safe, Gunter positioned the chocolate palomino behind Esme's horse. He instructed Esme that if his horse leaped into the hindquarters of Old Joe or pressed alongside her and rubbed against her leg to grab the saddle horn. He was emphatic that she not pull back on the reins, in fact, she was instructed to allow Old Joe to make the necessary corrections on his own. Gunter trusted her horse more than he trusted Esme to know what to do if and when his horse got pushy.

"We haven't moved yet and my hand is already turning blue from gripping the horn." Esme's level of confidence had deflated. Her left foot slid into the stirrup and Gunter gave her a boost up and she stared at the ground where she once stood.

"Just relax Essy and let go of the horn. Turn around and look at me." Gunter knew that for her to complete that task she would need to let go of the saddle horn. "Good, see, you are just fine. Now, turn back and place your free hand on your thigh or use both hands to hold the reins. You don't need to worry, Old Joe will take care of you. Seriously, the worst thing to do when riding is not relax. Take a deep breath and exhale and enjoy the view."

Esme cautiously, and with a jerky motion, turned back. Her body movement resembled a ventriloquist's dummy's movement.

"Oh, and one more thing and this is the most important thing."

Without turning to face Gunter a second time, without moving a muscle, as though speaking to the rider in front of her she said, "Yeah, what is it?"

"I love you."

As though she was a contortionist she rolled her head past her shoulder, that never moved, smiled, blew him a kiss and said, "Cowboy, I love you too."

Gunter wasn't sure who was more nervous his horse or Esme.

The large chocolate palomino did surprisingly well for the first half mile at a turtle's pace. Things changed the moment one of the guides worked his way from the back of the line towards the front. Still three horse lengths back Gunter felt the animal beneath him push her hindquarters further under her body propelling her forward in an awkward manner. When the guide's horse was within touching distance the palomino was sidestepping to the left working to place Old Joe between herself and the other horse. Gunter assured Esme everything was good and told the guide to drop back a few lengths and release the press once he had the horse back in line. Over the course of the next several miles the guide alternated sides of the string of riders moving up on Gunter's horse either from the left or right. By the time they covered six of the ten-mile ride out into the Wenatchee National Forest the stocky mare was well lathered and still tightening her muscles but no longer side passing or threatening to bolt. As the string of riders reached the midway destination the mare had relaxed to the point where she made a chewing motion with her mouth and Gunter was confident she was well on the way to expanding her level of confidence.

The ride Gunter had selected was a twenty-mile trek with a twenty-minute rest at the halfway point. He realized that Esme would be sore from the ride but also knew if she was going to gain any understanding of horses and riding anything less wouldn't do. The rest spot was an old cabin used during fall roundup so it had the amenities of an outhouse and a hydrant for pumping water.

Climbing down from Old Joe Esme unexpectedly did a half squat with her knees pushing outward. Gunter caught her during her downward movement and returned her to an upright position. As she clung to Gunter's coat sleeve she reported, "Whoo, I understand why you see old cowboys so bull-legged. You should have told me this would be such an intense workout for my thighs."

Carefully rubbing her backside he inquired, "How's the butt?"

"You will be doing a lot more of that this evening, but right now, I gotta get in line to pee before I do something I haven't done since I was three years old."

Laughing Gunter teased her, "There's nothing like riding on a full bladder."

Waddling away like a penguin as fast as possible with legs pressed together she informed him, "I'm not listening."

Seated on an outcrop of a large rock enjoying the sunlight that filtered through the evergreens the two shared a ham and cheese sandwich and bag of potato chips that Gunter had purchased before leaving Seattle. As they chatted and replayed the trip thus far Gunter confessed that if this was some mushy romantic novel he would have also purchased a bottle of wine but since he wanted all her senses at one hundred percent he would save the wine for later that evening. Plus, it would dull the protest her bottom would unleash. After informing Esme about the importance of staying hydrated for the return trip Gunter wandered off to speak to the head trail guide.

Gunter lent a hand to Esme as she swung a leg over Old Joe's back and instructed her to stay put when the guides asked people to line up for the return trip. "We are going to bring up the rear and they don't have a problem with you and me riding side by side."

Esme was the first to break the silence after riding the better part of a mile simply inhaling the entire venue. "I understand why you love this animal, its gentleness, its smell. Everything about a horse is so relaxing, so soothing."

Reaching out and taking her hand in his as their horses pressed close together on the narrow trail Gunter said, "They are caretakers."

After recovering from ducking to avoid a low hanging branch Esme continued, "I could have used a horse this past year. It would have been money well spent."

Giving her the space to direct the conversation Gunter acknowledged her comment by sharing, "That's my dream, to develop a program that employs horses to assist people in healing."

"Has that ever been done?"

"It has. In fact, I was surprised to discover just how long. As a nurse you'll appreciate this. Hippocrates, in 460 BC, spoke of the value of horses and their movement. Following WWI a British woman, Sands something or other, offered the use of her horses to Oxford Hospital to be used with patients and the results were positive. But, it wasn't until fifteen – twenty years ago when the Germans developed a model that Equine Therapy became legitimate."

"That German thing again." Esme laughed as she spoke and Gunter joined her.

"So, this dream of yours and healing people, is it for physical conditions or something different?"

"There are programs like that, but I am leaning towards something different. More, if you will, of emotional and mental healing."

Squeezing Gunter's hand just before releasing it Esme focused her attention straight ahead as she spoke quietly. "That's exactly what I needed and probably still do. The year started last fall when I started the final year of the graduate program, which I passed."

"Congratulations, why didn't you say something sooner?"

"Graduation was two weeks ago. I guess I was conditioned to down play the event since only my children attended the ceremony."

"Oh Essy, I'm so proud of you. Your Masters."

"I wanted to share with you that my return to academics gave me a new appreciation for the work a professor actually does. During my undergraduate years I viewed the professor as a step up from a high school teacher. I didn't understand the depth of knowledge and experience one has to share with their students. I can only imagine the relationship you have with your students and how you enrich their lives beyond the classroom."

"Thank you, Essy, you are too kind, but there's more to your story which you are avoiding, now is the time to share it. If you can't tell me, tell Old Joe, I promise, he will listen."

After a bend to the right the trail narrowed to the point where Esme and Gunter had no choice but to ride single file. With both horses stopped Esme inquired, "Do you think your horse can handle taking the lead?"

"I believe so, but there is always one way to find out."

Before Gunter nudged the palomino forward Esme added, "If you are ahead of us you can listen as I tell Old Joe the rest of the story."

Without offering a comment Gunter squeezed his legs and the palomino stepped out and took the lead and Old Joe fell into place.

Esme started by providing a context to the story she was about to share. "The second weekend in October my Friday evening class ended earlier than usual. Since the kids were both staying overnight at friend's houses I decided to go straight home rather than put a couple of hours in at the library. Mark complained that I didn't make time for him so I thought I would surprise him and spend the rest of the evening with him. As I drove up to the house I thought it strange that the house was dark and Mark wasn't home. Passing through the foyer and into the living room I discovered pieces of clothing strewn about the room. I became concerned, Mark, a type A personality and obsessive compulsive about cleanliness, would never just leave clothing tossed about unless something was wrong. Working my way through the house I discovered more articles of clothing and dirty dishes and empty Chinese boxes. Now I knew something was seriously wrong. Halfway up the stairs I heard what sounded like muffled screams. My mind continued to race, I feared the worse. Had someone broken into our house? Was Mark being held captive and tortured? Over the years Mark had angered a few clients and created a small pool of enemies. At the top of the stairwell I was able to discern that what sounded like animalistic groans originated from our bedroom. I felt totally stupid that it took me that long to figure out what was transpiring on the other side of the door. The only question left to answer was, what bimbo was my husband nailing?"

"With my hand on the doorknob ready to burst into the room and embarrass the hell out of them, I paused for a moment and considered, what if I know the woman his naked body is rubbing against? What if it's my best friend? What if it's…does it really matter who it is? Releasing the doorknob and backing away I found myself wondering, of all things, would it be better if the woman having sex with my husband is someone I didn't know? Would it be easier if I never knew who it was? Leaning against the wall I questioned, why am I trying to make sense of this?"

The altitude combined with the evergreen and mossy scent freed Esme from her earlier reluctance to share and enabled her to recall in profound and precise detail the events from the evening.

"I worked my way back downstairs, not sure why or where I was headed. I ended up at the kitchen table with a glass of wine and there I simply waited. Fifteen minutes before I normally would arrive home on a Friday evening I heard voices laughing in the dining room and then the living room and then there was silence. It was only a matter of another thirty seconds before the kitchen door swung inward and Mark pranced in like a King returning from pillaging the countryside. My presence stopped him abruptly but the skilled orator that he had become he was able to compose himself at a moment's notice and he spit his words into my face. 'Oh, Esme, you're home, did you just get in?'"

"Sarcastically I answered, 'Seriously, you are going to stand there totally naked and ask me if I just got in?'"

"Grabbing a dishtowel from the oven handle he attempted to conceal his shrinking manhood before he spoke a second time, 'When did you get home?"

"'First off, remind me to burn that towel when you are done with it, or perhaps we should burn it now. Second, I arrived home in time to hear your bimbo pretend to scream out as though you were satisfying her every sexual need, which of course, I know from personal experience is totally impossible.'"

"Esme, I…"

"Before he could possibly finish a blatant lie I stopped him, 'Don't, don't even attempt to say something stupid like, I am sorry, because we both know you are not!'"

"As he pulled a chair away from the kitchen table in order to sit down, I screamed, 'Don't even think about putting your ass on that chair.' I wanted him to be as uncomfortable as possible. It was my only line of defense and offense at that moment.

Holding the towel with one hand while he held the back of the chair with the other he asked, 'What can I say?' I think he meant, what can I say to make this right?"

"Swallowing hard I answered, 'You can say, Esme, I am going upstairs to pack a few things and I will be leaving. We need some time apart to think about what the future holds for us.'"

"What about the kids?"

"Too late. You should have thought about them before you decided to sleep with the fifteenth different person."

"Esme, you know I lo…"

"You finish that sentence and you may be a permanent soprano. You have five minutes to get out of the house."

"But, Es…"

"Now you have four minutes and 45 seconds."

"Of course, Scott blamed me. He sided with his father who told him that I had become a little over emotional. Although I fully expected him to support Mark and even parrot his father, it still hurt. And Emily, well Emily being Emily, was grief stricken and became physically ill. Her efforts were not focused on finding blame but how to restore the brokenness. How to make everything okay again, even if that included turning a blind eye. Of course neither of the kids heard of their father's infidelity from me yet I think they knew or at least had suspensions."

Gunter noticed as he sneaked a peek over his shoulder that Esme no longer gripped the saddle horn but was running her fingers through Old Joe's mane just ahead of the saddle. It wasn't simply that her confidence related to riding grew but that the soothing rhythm of riding transported her to a place of peace and a willingness to be vulnerable.

"And just in case you are wondering. I think the woman stretching her vocal cords that night was our next-door neighbor. There was no car parked in the driveway or on the street and she was not able to look me in the eye for the next six months. I am pretty sure she was silently waiting for a knock at the door and my request to speak with her husband. As much as I fantasied about how such a conversation might unfold I had to question my motive. How would such an encounter help or alter my situation? What would I gain?"

She thanked Gunter endlessly for making the arrangements for the trail ride from the moment her foot hit the stubbly weeds that had no chance of survival and sealed it with a wet kiss at the side of the car. Playfully Gunter inquired if she thanked Old Joe in a similar manner for delivering her safely back at the ranch.

"Of course, why do you think it was so wet?"

The drive back to the Vance Hotel afforded Gunter time to probe for clarity regarding the events Esme detailed on the return trip, yet it was Esme who spoke first.

"Cowboy, it probably sounded as though I had it all together, but the truth was, I was a total wreck, sad to say, a basket case at times. If I had had your phone number or a means of contacting you I would have. Numerous times during the following several months I longed for your arms to hold me and tell me I had done the right thing by kicking him out."

"Do you still think it was the right decision?"

"Yes, I think so. And before you say anything, I know I am straddling the fence. You have to understand it felt like I was fighting against the entire world. His parents showed up at the house on Sunday. They didn't condone his behavior, in fact, they were mad as hell at him, but they also worked to convince me why I should give him another chance."

"Another chance?" Gunter nearly swerved off the road. "Good grief, even God in all his graciousness got tired of the faithlessness displayed by the people of Sodom and Gomorrah and set limits."

"I love Mark's parents, they have become my parents. I think I am closer to them than Mark is."

"Is Mark close to anyone?"

"That's a good question." She knew her answer immediately yet waited before sharing. "Probably not."

"So what happened?"

"Christmas was crippling. His parents, with whom we always spent the holidays, along with his siblings and their families, invited me to come. But I had to decline. I encouraged the kids to go with their father. It was a very lonely time. I felt sorry for myself. I questioned not only my decision to separate from Mark but the purpose and value of my very existence. In January, Mark started coming to the house more to see the kids and he hung around longer. We talked and he offered counseling to move this forward. I agreed."

"This?"

"Our relationship."

"Which lead to him moving back into the house?"

"Yeah, but not immediately. It wasn't until the fourteenth of February."

"Valentine's Day, how sweet."

"I can do without your sarcasm."

"You probably can, but I can't." Without giving her an opportunity to respond he continued, "Before I ask why you let him move back in, I need to ask, why did you marry him?"

"Why does anyone get married?"

"I don't know, but I am not asking everyone, I am asking you. Why Mark? Seriously, Essy, and yes, I know this is an overused saying, but it's true for you, you could have married anyone."

Staring out the passenger's window without comprehending the specifics of the scenery they sped past she whispered, "That's not necessarily true, Cowboy. The person you see, the person I am able to be around you, the person I am at work, is not the person other people ever see."

"And why is that?"

"I don't know. It's just so easy to be me with you. To laugh, to cry, to question, to challenge, to let life happen."

"We have been here before with this conversation, is it because it's safe, it's only four days out of the year and you, we, don't need to worry about day five or day one hundred and twenty five and being bored or worse yet irritated?"

"Surely, that is part of it, I would be foolish to suggest otherwise, but it's more. It's more because I love you! I want to share those things with you and have you share those things with me."

"So why did you marry him, Essy?"

The rhythm of the tires hummed their own melody as the car passed mile marker seventy-four on Interstate 90. It wasn't until marker sixty-eight that Esme finally spoke over the rubber orchestra. "I was tired of being lonely."

"And you took him back because...you were lonely?"

"I guess so."

"And the next time he is unfaithful..."

"I don't think he ever stopped."

"Essy,..." Gunter stopped and didn't say anything more.

The final forty-eight miles back to Seattle were completed in silence as they stared out the front window.

The weight of the conversation, Esme's suspicion that her husband never stopped hopping from bedmate to bedmate, and Gunter's refrain from stating what he thought about Esme's decision pressed upon them like a seventy pound backpack. It blanketed them as they made love on their final evening together. Both felt it but neither said a word. Secretly each hoped that the other was not buried beneath the question, what did this mean for their relationship? Yet, that was precisely what filled the core of their existence the last few hours spent in the company of the other.

Unable to sleep, Gunter's thoughts drifted aimlessly sifting through a host of topics. Esme's sporadic snoring brought Gunter's hand to her shoulder with the hope that his touch might startle her enough that she would stop. The supple feel of her skin yielded an image of Marcie from *Oliver's Story*. In the darkness Gunter feared that perhaps he too quickly aligned his story with Oliver's.

Esme's flight departed five hours ahead of Gunter's as she was unable to book an afternoon departure. The early arrival at the airport lessened the stress of avoiding the monkey lodged on their backs at the hotel. Seated in the gate area Gunter finally climbed the barrier and spoke the difficult words, the very words Esme was thinking.

"Essy, I have been thinking, maybe we shouldn't meet next year." The moment the words left his mouth tears were streaming down Esme's cheeks.

"Is that what you want?"

"It's not about what I want. It's about you and your marriage."

"Stop being a martyr and answer the damn question. Do you not want to meet next year?"

Before he spoke the gate attendant announced Flight 452 would start boarding shortly. Reaching for his hand and pulling it to her lap she asked again. "Tell me, Cowboy, what do you want?"

"We will start loading with first class passengers."

"Essy, I love you."

"I know you do. And I love you. But you have not answered the question."

"Anyone with small children or anyone in need of assistance may come forward to board the plane."

"I am not sure that it is fair to you that we meet."

"Thank you, but you let me worry about what is fair to me."

"I would, but your track recorded is not so good."

He saw her lift her left hand and he could have stopped her but he didn't. Her hand struck his right cheek and the edging from the band of her wedding ring tore his flesh leaving behind a two-inch gash.

"I guess I deserved that."

"Oh Cowboy, what's happening to us? We love each other, is that not enough?"

With blood seeping between his fingers as he applied pressure in hopes of controlling the bleeding he said, "I'm not sure."

Pulling several Kleenex from her purse and attempting to doctor his cut she spoke as she worked. "As much as I don't want this to be the end, maybe it is."

"This is the final call for passengers for Flight 452."

As Gunter walked to his gate he wondered if Segel might possibly have a third book in the works that would lend him direction.

CHAPTER 18
JUNE 12, 1978

The Versace black handbag, with its three star imprint, positioned on her lap to protect the contents from possible shoplifters served as a perfect book rest. The book, with its multi-colored cover nestled in the crease between her billfold and her checkbook, couldn't possibly slide downward as her fingers firmly held it. A glancing observation by any passerby revealed that two thirds of the book was crisp and clean, filled with virgin pages while the first third of the pages were worn and tattered as though the reader consumed every word several times over. The reader's eyes rose past the top edge of the book upon completion of every two pages. As her moist finger, recently licked, peeled the page she scanned the crowd that consisted of mostly new faces since the last time she looked. She wasn't interested in people watching, her eyes and her heart yearned for the presence of only one special person whose arrival wasn't guaranteed.

When her eyes, aided for the first time in her life by glasses, dropped back to the newly turned page she froze. The chapter title, *"Sometimes There Is No Reason,"* consisted of words she hadn't expected to find in the book. A friend of a friend had recommended the book and for that reason she agreed, reluctantly, to give it a try. Not ready for the argument that might follow her mind took a journey of its own. Friends were important. Each in their own way they had offered support but she discovered first hand that they just didn't understand. She wasn't critical of them she merely had to remind herself, again and again, as they offered hallow words of comfort and mindless platitudes that they couldn't comprehend the depth of pain, the suffering, and the emptiness without having experienced it themselves.

She read the title a second and third time and after each reading she sneaked a peek at the crowd. Being subtle seemed less threatening if the person she longed to see was not present than totally committing herself to scanning the crowd. She did not want to appear desperate but the truth was, she was desperate on so many levels and that angered her. She despised the idea that she felt weak, vulnerable, and discombobulated. It frustrated her that she feared she might fall apart at any moment. She was annoyed with herself that she displayed all the negative components of being a woman. She had never identified herself as a feminist, as though the label carried poisonous venom, yet she fully recognized the second-class citizenship cast upon women. Helen Reddy's lyric, *"I am woman; hear me roar,"* was the inner voice she strove to communicate but was muted. Although she didn't smoke and certainly had no desire to start, the newly released Virginia Slim's ad had struck a cord, *"You've come a long way baby."*

However, from the moment her world turned upside down she needed clarity, she needed answers, she needed him to be there for her. The idea that sometimes there is no reason was unbearable and she feared that she might never progress past page 63. She had reached this point in the book numerous times before and was unable to read the opening paragraph. She had convinced herself that in his presence and with his support she could digest the chapter but he wasn't there and she was beginning to accept the fact that he wasn't about to arrive.

He couldn't explain why, he just knew he wasn't ready. From a safe distance he inhaled her beauty, her innocence as though he was a coal miner returning to the earth's surface. The sweat from the beer glass in front of him soiled the napkin as the once ice- cold beverage was near room temperature. The waitress had given up coming to check on his progress as he ignored her inquiry, "Everything okay?" She wrote him off as a first time flier terrified to enter the gate area. She had convinced herself there would be no tip from this guy despite his expensive boots. As a waitress she paid close attention to a customer's footwear to determine the amount of the tip that would be left behind. She was within fifty cents to a dollar 92 percent of the time.

He sat quietly on the wooden stool in the bar and questioned why she had come. He knew why he was there, but why was she? Had he not made it clear that this was not in her best interest? Didn't she care about herself? With his sleeve damp from touching the napkin he contemplated not boarding the plane, but returning to the counter and scheduling the next flight back home. As his boots struck the floor and echoed through the make shift bar he stopped. What was he doing, he loved this woman why was it so difficult for him to walk to her, take her in his arms and hold her? Without moving he felt the fullness of her body, the strands of hair between his fingers, and he smelled the sweet scent of her perfume. Tossing a ten on the tabletop he grabbed his bags.

She didn't need to look up to feel him. His presence warmed her soul. She wept uncontrollably and he had no idea the depth of her pain. Overwhelmed by her tears his cheeks were moist and for one of the few times in his life he wasn't embarrassed or driven to explain.

The entire flight from Denver to Seattle they held one another. Not even nature's call could separate them as they squeezed together into the compact space labeled lavatory. Their departure from the tiny cubicle invoked smiles from the passengers seated in the aisle as though they knew what transpired behind closed doors. What didn't happen behind the closed door was an initiation into the growing phenomena called The Mile High Club.

Few words were exchanged. The presence of the other was enough to satisfy both of them. The shapely blond haired stewardess, who placed her ample breasts inches from his face while she offered a beverage and a bag of peanuts, was dismissed as quickly as possible. When unexpected turbulence tossed them against the side of the plane her handbag fell from her lap and the contents lay strewn on the floor. Even though the book rested upside down he recognized the title, *When Bad Things Happen to Good People.* He had read the book a few weeks earlier and he wondered if she was reading the book, as he had, because everyone else was, or because life's predicaments motivated her? The answer arrived shortly after they entered room 816, their room in the Vance Hotel.

Her shoes kicked off one stride past the door, her sweater in a heap at the foot of the bed; she held the bouquet of dahlias as she dropped into the overstuffed chair. His right boot, kicked free of his foot, leaned against the chair while the left partially concealed his tube sock when his ears bled with her announcement. "Scotty hung himself."

"Oh, Essy. What? How? Why?" Wrapping his body about her as though she was a caterpillar and he was her cocoon of security he dismissed the fact that his second boot never left his foot. "When?" All he could muster was one-word questions.

Far from transforming into a butterfly her body squirmed without offering a single detail. She pleaded for Gunter's theological position related to the afterlife. Unlike some who use such theological conversations as a smokescreen to avoid the real questions that was not the case with her. "Are you a religious person?"

"Are you asking, do I believe in God? The answer is, yes. Do I attend church regularly? Again, the answer is, yes."

She couldn't bring herself to look at him as she continued this line of questions. "Do you believe there's a heaven where good people go?"

As the words spilled forth from his mouth he realized it was not the conversation she desired, she probably needed him to just answer the question, but he couldn't help himself. "Good people? Who are the good people? Who defines and determines who are the *good* people? Are there levels or degrees of being good?"

She slowly lifted her head and looked directly into his soul and he could see, actually, he felt that she stopped listening to his theological / philosophical bullshit. She pressed, "Scotty committed suicide. Some say such an act is an unforgivable sin."

Grammatically speaking, there was not a question posed and yet Gunter heard the question.

"There's a saying among horse folk, at least among some horse people, 'If Heaven don't have horses, I'm not going."

Esme looked totally bewildered. She didn't need to say a word for Gunter to recognize he needed to explain the comment.

"For some people this is nothing more than a cute saying, for others the phrase is about God's grace. It suggests that salvation is a gift, a gift freely given out of love. Surely, a horse doesn't earn salvation and yet if they are saved, if there are horses in Heaven then certainly there is hope for me. The emphasis is not on me, am I good enough to be saved, but on God, is God forgiving and gracious enough to save even me?"

Esme cleared her face of any and all tears and forcefully asked, "So, is Scotty in Heaven?"

"Essy, I am not avoiding your question, I am being honest with you. I am not God, it is not for me to say who is not, all I can share with you is that God has gone to extraordinary lengths to present Himself as gracious, forgiving, and loving. My reply stays the same, if there are no horses in Heaven there is no hope for me."

"So you believe there are horses?"

"I am planning on riding for eternity."

She threw herself from the chair into his arms. Together they fell back onto the floor and with her arms wrapped about him she squeezed until he nearly passed out. She whispered, "Let's ride together and you can teach Scotty about riding."

Gunter saw the butterfly of the resurrection leave her cocoon and take flight. Such a flight didn't mean she wouldn't suffer additional pain, questions and doubts, but it meant she heard about God's goodness and how it challenges and breaks all the laws of nature and the laws constructed by humans to narrow their freedom.

The words, "Scotty hung himself" continued to echo in the room – but not in the same manner or with the same force.

"You never did share when this happened, if you're able I really want to hear."

A half-a-laugh snuck out prior to her response. "It's funny in a very sad sort of way that Mark's family, who surrounded us in efforts to support us, couldn't bring themselves to ask for details. Even Mark refused to listen, but that's a whole other story. Yet, here you are wanting to know."

He shrugged his shoulders but didn't comment.

"I found him March 26th, Easter morning. He had made a noose out of his bed sheets. He tied the end to the door handle inside the closet and draped it over the top of the door. He was totally naked which lead the police to conclude that it was some sex act that went terribly wrong as a chair laid overturned just out of the reach of his feet."

"Is it possible they were right and that it wasn't a suicide?"

"Based on the evidence they had to work with, yes, it's possible."

"But they didn't have all the evidence because you took it."

"How did you know?" As though a balloon had been popped behind her she looked totally surprised.

"Because I assume he left a note and you didn't mention any note. What did it say?"

Without giving it a thought she began, "I am sorry, mom…" She choked on her grief as she rocked back and forth. Gunter embraced her and together they rocked until the motion subsided. Pushing the strands of hair pasted to her cheeks she continued as if she was holding the note and read aloud. "I am sorry, mom. And tell dad I am sorry I couldn't live up to his expectat…" The sentence remained unfinished as she closed her eyes to remove herself from the printed word.

Granting her space to escape he sat without speaking. When her eyes fluttered open he asked, "Did you ever share the note with Mark?"

"You're joking, right?"

"No, I am very serious."

"What would that have accomplished?"

"Scott was his son too, doesn't he have a right to know the truth?"

"You don't understand. In Mark's mind and with the comments he shared both in private and publically, I am the cause of Scotty's death."

"So that means you don't share the truth with him."

"It means his mind was made up. He would only accuse me of writing the note. You need to understand, I didn't, and I still don't need any more stress."

"How did Emily handle the news?"

"Emily? Oh Emily is a rock. She grieved but she was the first to work to assure me that I didn't cause this. It was Emily who encouraged me to make this trip."

"Do you think she knows?"

"Knows about us?"

"Yes."

"I don't know. She has commented at various times throughout the year that I am always so happy when I come home from these trips. But that doesn't mean she has any awareness of what transpires during these four days."

"She's twelve, correct?"

"Yes."

"Well, if she's anything like my daughter, don't be surprised."

Sensing that she was ready to discuss Scott again he swayed the conversation in that direction. He made sure that each time he spoke her son's name he said, Scott,

Scotty, was reserved for her and her alone. "How had Scott become a disappointment to his father?"

"It was shortly after the first of the year that Scotty started talking about no longer wanting to be a lawyer. His chosen profession now was a doctor. His preoccupation with being a lawyer evaporated. When questioned by his father concerning this apparent sudden change Scotty would say something to the effect that he wanted to help people in a similar manner to the way I did. Mark was stung and devastated by Scotty's answer to the question, 'Don't you think lawyers help people?' Scotty said, 'No, they only take people's money.' Needless to say, that didn't sit well with Mark who blamed me for the change in Scotty. The more I thought about it, I recognized there were signs already in the fall of Scotty warming up to me, but I guess I was too delighted with the change to ask why."

"A mother shouldn't have to ask such questions."

"According to Mark, I was turning his son against him. Unfortunately, rather than working to restore the relationship Mark began to shun him. I knew it hurt Scotty, I just never knew how much."

"Has Kushner's book been helpful?"

"I suppose to a point. I have connected with Kushner though the pages of the book as someone who understands what it means to lose a child and the suffering that accompanies such a tragedy. But honestly, I'm stuck. I just can't read any more."

"Any ideas why?"

"I think I am experiencing a disconnect with what he is writing about."

"Essy, if you are searching for answers your journey may never reach its destination."

With her face flush and her neck covered with bright

red blotches she shouted at him. "Of course I want answers, wouldn't you? And don't say you wouldn't because you know you would. You can't just live in a world of questions forever! I don't care how good you are at asking questions, at pondering the unanswerable, at some point, when you wake in the middle of the night in a cold sweat, you will want answers."

He said nothing. He merely sat there and waited. She needed to vent, she needed to be angry, and she needed to be able to shout, swear if necessary. What she didn't need at that moment was a response.

While her lips didn't move her hands never stopped. The movement was a wringing action as though if she worked long enough or hard enough the answers might spill forth from her hands. She caught him staring at her hands and immediately they became still and her lips moved. "What?"

"I can't help but notice how agitated you appear."

"Dammit, my chest is so tight, the muscles in my neck and shoulders are tense, I am so angry and to make matters worse, I don't know who I am angry at." Her head dropped forward as she informed him that she was not angry with him even though it sounded that way.

"Are you angry with Mark?

"Yes. For all the reasons I have already shared, plus, and this is going to sound really bad, simply because he is Mark."

"Are you angry with yourself?"

"Oh God, where do I begin? The 'should've' statements never end. I should've been more aware of his mood. I should've pressed to explain his desire to spend more time with me. I should've checked on him before I went to bed. I should've ..."

Interrupting her before she finished the statement he asked, "Are you angry with Scott?"

"Yes…" Her eyes expanded, her breathing intensified, "I mean, no…"

The walls leaned in as though listening to hear what she would say next. How would she explain away her initial answer? It was Gunter who spoke and not Esme.

"I'm not a shrink and I won't pretend to be one, but I do have two things I want to say. First, for some things in life there just are no answers. It's called, living by faith and hope. I believe the things I can't see and I hope for horses in Heaven but I'll never know until I die. Second, promise me that when you get home that you will schedule an appointment with a professional, if you have not already."

"Really, I am not mad with…"

"I'm not going to argue with you, Essy, just promise me. I mean it."

Staring into his eyes she finally said, "Okay, I promise."

Silence engulfed them while a soft purple color was projected over their heads as the sunset increased the intensity of the single watt bulb bleeding through the dahlias. Both were lost in their own thoughts. Both were lost in each other. When lovers are in the presence of one another time is never a consideration and therefore neither Gunter nor Esme could report how long they sat holding each other.

Stepping out of her clothes and standing naked before him she shared her thoughts. "If it's okay with you, I really don't feel much like being out and about this trip. Do you mind if we just stay here?"

"I don't mind, but I would like to have one meal at 13 Coins."

"Oh gosh, Cowboy, that's a given."

At the airport Gunter promised that he would never again attempt to push her away or decide what was in her best interest. It was up to her to make those choices.

When Esme passed the first large garbage container she pulled the multi-colored book from her expensive black purse and effortlessly dropped the book in the garbage. When asked what she was doing she simply said, "I would rather meet face to face to discuss these issues. Plus, just so you know, I would rather lean on you than some book because, I love you." Smiling she added, "You are much softer and sexier and honestly, sometimes there is no reason."

Gunter smiled the entire flight home.

CHAPTER 19
JUNE 12, 1985

The yearly trip to Seattle had developed into a routine. Not that either Gunter or Esme complained, or viewed the habitual act as evil. It was strange, for both of them, to think that four days out of a year could merge into a habit, an act of voluntary participation. After ten years of meeting it was impossible to consider how it could be anything but. The days 12, 13, 14, and 15 of June had become sacred.

Meeting in Denver and using the connecting flight as an opportunity to flirt, to make small talk, to safely reconnect was critical for the physical rump, the passionate rekindling of love that occurred in room 816 of the Vance Hotel.

Sex, strangely enough, was one of the few things that changed over the course of the ten years. It became less of the focal point of their four days. Without pausing to think, Gunter and Esme would acknowledge that the sex was great, it was pleasing and exhausting, it was freeing, and mind-blowing. It also was the vehicle for expressing and sharing their love for one another. It just no longer lasted for hours at a time nor did it occur with the same frequency. The sex had been replaced with sharing the latest news from the home front, discussing work that included joys and frustrations and of course, promotions, and an investigation of the current book being read, those things became the new routine.

What was not routine and therefore challenged the norm was the heat experienced on the twelfth of June. The mercury pushed past 80 degrees making their room steamy even before the friction between their bodies elevated the heat index.

The card attached to the bouquet of purple dahlias perfectly positioned, as always, on the end table next to the lamp read, "Happy Anniversary, it has been a blessed ten years." After reading the card Esme shed her Chemise black dress accented with a gray neckline that rested elegantly upon her ample breasts as though the dress was designed for just such a figure. The entire act of disrobing took less than ten seconds as she reached gracefully behind her shoulder, pulled the zipper downward and the dress followed. Wearing the latest Simone Perele sheer bra that offered a teasing peek at half her nipples and G-string panties that left nothing to the imagination, Gunter wasted no time in tossing his clothes towards the chair. The clothes never quite reached the chair, as he was more interested in the body behind the undergarments than perfecting his tossing abilities.

Melting ice cubes across her body in an effort to lower her body temperature only minutes after he covered her with his sweat as they made love, created more excitement than Gunter ever imagined. He discovered that, unlike his body, which was settling into his midsection, nature had been extremely kind to hers. In spite of the size of her breasts they were still firm and had not yielded to the forces of gravity. Forty-five years removed from the moment she took her first breath her skin remained soft and taut. Consequently, wrinkles, the initial mark of aging, had yet to attack the outer layers of her skin with any consistency. He became more self-conscious than usual that he was aging more quickly than she. Her beauty caused the pulsating blood to return more quickly than he expected and her beauty also drained the blood from his manhood, as he feared she was too divine for him.

As the trail of melted ice framed her birthmark nearly to perfection her moment of relaxed ecstasy came to an end. The shock produced by the ice gliding across such a sensitive portion of her body made her pubic area shiver with excitement and caused her legs instinctively to pull together and her nipples to harden. Unexpectedly, her body was transformed from extreme heat and exhaustion to quivering wonderment.

Esme commented on what she identified as ironic. "Record heat and record cold."

Bewildered by her first words after having scratched the back of her throat by screaming the same two words over and over, "Oh god," his hand stopped pushing the sliver of ice and he asked for clarity.

Reaching for his hand she consumed the remainder of ice to sooth her sore throat before she answered his question. "On January 20th I found myself in Chicago where the conditions were brutal. The air temperature was minus twenty-seven degrees with a twenty-five mile an hour wind that produced a wind chill of minus seventy-seven degrees. Record cold in January and today, record…"

He interrupted her husky vibrato, "Chicago? If you were anywhere on the twentieth of January I would have thought Washington D.C."

"Actually, that's where Mark was. I was supposed to be there also, we had tickets to attend Ronald Reagan's second inauguration but my presence was requested in Chicago. I thought of you following the election wondering if you recovered from the humiliating loss for Mondale and Ferrero."

Not sure if she was sincere or leveling the playing field from last year's debate concerning the stupidity of Reagan he ignored that final thought and kept the focus on the weather. "Weren't those events cancelled due to cold temps?"

"Yes, at least the outdoor activities."

"So, what drew you to Chicago?"

"Junior, or I should say, Junior's death."

Squeezing her hand he offered his condolence. "Essy, I'm sorry."

"Thank you."

As the location and Junior's presence found union in his mind he questioned, "Junior was in Chicago? Were you aware that he was living there?"

"No, it came as quite a surprise."

"How long had he been in Chicago?"

"Your guess is as good as mine. I never was able to find out. The details surrounding his death, including the final days of his life, were all very vague. For all I know he may have arrived and died on the same day."

"This may sound harsh but I realize that the homeless are not a high priority when it comes to investigations yet wasn't there some signs or evidence? An autopsy?"

"There was no autopsy."

"Why not?"

"The honest response would have been, it was determined to be a waste of time and money. The answer provided was an attempt to conceal the truth. It's as though it happened yesterday, the coroner's assistant with his back to me said, 'the extremely cold weather would skew any results.' Therefore, the death certificate read, 'froze to death.'"

"Again, I am so sorry, that must have been frustrating. Have you been able to have any sense of closure?"

"Closure?" As though the word reminded her that both of them were naked and resting atop of the sheets she gracefully pulled her legs to her chest until she found an opening to dive beneath. "How does one put closure on a relationship that barely existed? On a relationship that was primarily one sided? A relationship..." She stopped herself and the word hung suspended as though the air was pregnant with endless possibilities.

Aware that she may be struggling with something other than Junior's death he attempted to make meaning of the conversation to that point. "Record heat and record cold, no doubt you experienced both during your time in Chicago. The heat of frustration, the absence of cooperation, the unanswered question of why Chicago, and the icy immobilizing sting of death striking your core to say nothing of the frigid bite numbing your skin, I get it."

Her head slid to a far edge of the pillow as she stared at him. When she spoke the words dripped with emotion. "Do you? Do you really get it?"

Joining her under the sheet as her words stripped him of any bodily warmth he responded. "I thought I did, but based on your response, I guess not. Enlighten me, what am I missing?"

"It just occurred to me that this relationship mirrors very closely my relationship with Junior."

His head shook, without his awareness, before he spoke. "What do you mean?"

She didn't let a second escape before she spoke. "I need more of you and from you. It has been ten years and your story is still vague."

He did not interrupt her or attempt to contradict her observation but the distance between their bodies expanded as his body moved towards the edge of the mattress.

"Talk to me, Cowboy. What is the deep dark secret that you labor to keep from seeing the light of day? What scares you? What drives you? You use your intellect to push people away and to maintain a distance and you do it with me."

As she turned and reached towards the nightstand he took the opportunity to pull the sheet higher in order to cover his shoulders. The only part of his body exposed was his head.

Rolling back she continued. "The greatest anniversary gift you could give me would be to hear what it means to you that the past ten years have been a blessing." After she handed him the card previously attached to the dahlias she put closure to her thoughts. "The heat and the cold are also about us. I don't want to spend another ten years feeling the extremes."

Having read and reread the card fifteen, maybe twenty times, he finally spoke. "It is difficult to know where to start. I could…"

Without waiting to hear what he proposed she stopped him. "I would be willing to bet that you talk to your horses all the time and you share with them things you have never shared with any one."

The bed bounced slightly as he nodded in agreement, and then she continued, "You let them in, I am asking that you let me in too."

Without hesitating he delivered. "The deep dark secret is that I have a low sperm count."

She nearly laughed until she realized he was not joking. She even said it, "You're not joking are you?"

"No, I am not joking."

As she spoke, her thoughts questioned why he would identify this as a deep dark secret. "I guess that's why birth control has never been a burning issue for you, I just thought it was a guy thing."

"Yeah, it was probably a little of both."

"So, when you say, 'low', just how low are we talking?" Slowly the pieces of the puzzle were starting to fit, but the picture lacked clarity, too many whites spaces continued to exist.

"I am not sterile, but…" The sentence went unfinished.

Esme found his hand and without saying a word held it tight.

Startled by the realization of what this meant for his marriage, his family, she blurted out, "Wow, it's a miracle, no, it's two miracles." As quickly as the volume of her voice erupted it disappeared. She faced him and whispered, "Did you and Emily have the sperm implanted?"

"No."

"I was right, it was two miracles."

"It was a miracle all right, but not the type you may be thinking."

Her eyes gazed past his face as she contemplated his words and tried to complete the puzzle and make sense of the picture being pieced together. She stuttered as she spoke. "I, I, I don't understand."

His response sounded judgmental. "Seriously, you don't get it? Think about it!"

Her eyes widened as though she saw the entire picture for the first time. Shifting her focus back to his eyes her words wept from her. "Oh God, no." Nothing followed for several minutes as she pulled forth memories of past conversations. "But, but that doesn't make sense, why a vasectomy, wait, you said you didn't think she had or was having an affair…"

"I didn't, remember how I only questioned her desire to

have an empty house to herself. It wasn't until four years ago that I became the holder of the secret."

The nonverbal cues imprinted across her face displayed total confusion. Unable to formulate a reply or ask a question she rested her head in the middle of the pillow and stared at the ceiling. The pieces of the puzzle she thought she wedged together correctly to form an accurate picture were precisely that, wedged together. Slowly Gunter pulled the pieces apart and aligned them so she might also become a holder of the secret.

"You remember I told you three years ago what happened when I returned home the year prior?"

"Yeah, 1981, right? I think it was the coldest weather we have experienced here."

"Yes. If you remember, Evelyn was not feeling well when I arrived home. Initially, we all thought it was a flu bug or possibly even food poisoning but as the week progressed she continued to get worse. The pain reached a point where she could no longer stand and we realized it was her appendix. Due to complications she experienced an extended stay in the hospital and received a blood transfusion."

"Blood transfusions are common occurrences during surgical procedures but not generally during an appendectomy. Is she a bleeder?"

"Yes, something we were unaware of prior to the surgery. Anyway, with this bit of new knowledge I decided it would be good to be tested, should another situation arise that demanded a blood transfusion, in order to be prepared to donate blood. Our family physician, while reviewing the results of my blood test, encountered what she considered an abnormality. Rather than alarm the entire family, as a friend, she contacted me and scheduled a meeting. She explained that the purpose of the initial test was to determine a blood match and not paternity. Yet there were red flags and she proceeded to share that she questioned if I was Evelyn's biological father. If I was interested she could request a genetic test that would be more accurate. After I picked my jaw up from the floor and recovered from what felt like a kick to the balls I said, 'Let's do it.'"

"Did you consider not having the second test?"

"Oh yeah, in fact, based on my hesitation the doctor suggested I take some time and think about it, but my words were, 'let's do it.' Two months later I was informed that I was not the biological father to either Evelyn or Elizabeth."

"Oh Cowboy." The room grew as dark as the hole Junior's casket had been lowered into. After ten minutes of silence she asked, "Did you confront Emily?"

"I told no one."

"What?! Why?" Esme, unable to control her response, sat upright allowing the sheet to crumble in her lap. She cradled his chin in her hand and lifted slightly so he would be distracted.

Staring into her eyes he asked, "What would it accomplish and what would it change?" With his hands positioned directly in front of his face as though framing each phrase he continued, "I have been, I am, and I will continue to be their father."

Finding her place at his side she continued, "I couldn't agree more, you are their father. But, Emily is a totally different matter is it not? What are you afraid of?"

He rolled his head to the left to face her even though she didn't move. "What has been done is done. It can't be undone so what is the benefit?"

"Come on, you expect me to buy that line of crap? You're scared, but scared of what, her leaving you? You confronting the truth that she had been unfaithful, that someone else impregnated her? What is it? You could have this conversation without your daughters ever needing to find out. Why have you been the sole bearer of this secret?" As she spoke it occurred that perhaps there was more at work here. "Does Emily know – do you think she knows that you are not their father? Talk to me Cowboy."

"I have no idea what she knows. All I know is, it's comfortable and it's safe."

Brow wrinkled she responded before thinking. "You're not serious."

"I have an older horse that I love to ride, but I would never let anyone else ride this horse because she's not safe. She has this habit of wanting to buck but not all the time. What makes her dangerous for others to ride is that they can't predict when the buck will happen. For me however, I know precisely when she will buck and I can prepare for the moment. It happens and then we move on. Knowing what to expect makes it comfortable and safe for me. I don't expect anyone observing us to be able to understand."

"Newsflash there Cowboy. Someone, maybe even several people, have been riding this horse you call your wife. Maybe you haven't been bucked off, but that doesn't mean you haven't been hurt."

A puff of air preceded his response. "I never suggested I wasn't hurt. I wouldn't be human if this hasn't been extremely painful – but…" He chewed back the remaining words. With his eyes closed his fingers moved in a circular motion on the bridge of his nose. When he opened his eyes tears escaped. "I am afraid for my daughters and I am scared who I will see in the mirror if the secret becomes public."

"I don't understand, I'm sorry, who will you see in the mirror?"

"That's just it, I don't know who will be looking back at him. Do you understand what it means that another man has fathered my daughters? What does that suggest about me? This person, or perhaps, two different men have done what I couldn't, can't…" He stopped himself to gather his emotions. "You need to understand Essy, a father's role is already at a position of disconnect and this situation only compounds it."

"Are you saying that this is about your manhood?"

"I am not sure what I am saying and for that reason I have kept the secret to myself. That being said, it feels right to have shared it with you."

"Because you know the secret is safe with me? I don't have access to Emily or your daughters."

"No, because I trust and love you."

"I remember you once said to me that you are not my shrink. I am not yours either but I do believe that we should be able to share with each other what bothers us, what surprises us, what brings joy to us. Love is about being invited to journey with one another without knowing where the trail may lead. That's what I want, no, that's what I need Cowboy, I need you to invite me to join you on the trail."

"Glad to hear you say that, because I planned a trip to Winthrop for a trail ride tomorrow."

"You do know that, as much as I enjoy the idea of riding a horse, this is not about riding a horse down a trail, right?"

"Yes, but when I made the reservations I never imagined our first hours together would unfold in this manner."

Nuzzling up against him she whispered, "Well, Cowboy, maybe you should give me a riding lesson, one that includes preparation for the unexpected buck."

Causally strolling the sidewalk under the moonlight, assisted by city streetlights, both commented on the disappointment of not seeing Todd. The evening manager at 13 Coins checked the work schedule and reported that Todd would not work until the evening of the fifteenth. Having not missed a year of connecting with Todd, Esme asked their waiter, who was a nice enough gentlemen, just not Todd, if he could find her a piece of white paper. Ten minutes later he returned with a single sheet of thin typing paper explaining that was all he could locate in the restaurant. Requesting the use of his felt tip pen she started her masterpiece. Throughout the meal, and two additional glasses of Chardonnay, she drew.

Gunter was amazed, first by her artistic ability, and second that never during the course of any conversations over a ten-year period had she shared that she had a gift for drawing.

As the waiter collected the money for the evening meal Esme asked if he could make sure that Todd received the picture. The waiter informed her that would not be a problem and asked if he might unfold the page and view the picture. He marveled at her artistic ability and commented that she not only drew the restaurant well by capturing the spirit of the environment but she also drew Todd to perfection at their tableside.

Reaching the halfway point between 13 Coins and the hotel they decided to sit on the curb, watch the traffic sail by and enjoy the warmth of the evening. The conversation eventually turned to the details concerning the next day's outing. Where, when, what, and how flew from Esme's mouth. Gunter stopped her, "Whoa, whoa, slow down for a second. Does it matter when we are going?"

Beneath the gushing wind created by a semi that accelerated to beat the yellow light and the lingering diesel vapors she shouted, "Of course it matters…"

Teasing her he delivered the question with a bit of edge and without looking directly at her. "Because you need to know how early to rise in order to select your clothes for the day and primp yourself?"

"Yes. Is that a bad thing? You have never complained in the past..."

Aware that what was intended to be playful banter had the potential to become explosive banter he pulled back and offered the details she requested. "The ride is scheduled for one o'clock. Since the trip will take at least four hours we probably should be on the road no later than eight thirty."

The Sun Mountain Lodge tucked on the face of the North Cascade Mountain Range was breathtakingly beautiful and became the first place that the two of them slept together other than the Vance Hotel. As the lodge became the obvious point of destination Esme, unaware of Gunter's reservations for the night, said, "Let's see if they will allow us to see one of the rooms."

Gunter, wanting the surprise to remain a surprise until after the trail ride, responded nonchalantly, "That sounds like a good idea, maybe after the ride we can swing up to the lodge and stop for a drink and check out the place."

Gunter was proud of his efforts to convince Esme to pack additional clothes for what she thought was a daylong trip. Beyond packing for mountain conditions he persuaded her to bring a more formal outfit in case they found an eloquent restaurant as well as something causal to change into after riding.

Gunter stood in front of the massive wooden reception desk of the lodge having completed the three-hour trail ride through the Methow Valley that was just beginning to germinate to life. He stood alone at the desk having informed Esme that he would ask if they might be afforded the opportunity to view a room. Esme was more than happy to recline in an oversized leather chair near the entrance as her throbbing thighs reminded her how much work riding demanded. Several minutes passed before Gunter returned with a key in hand. He shared how the manager agreed only after he promised that they would be out of the room in less than five minutes. Making sure that Esme bought the story he added, "If a Bible was available I think he would have made me swear on it."

Upon entering the room Gunter performed a belly flop on the center of the queen size bed that brought forth a squeal from Esme. "Cowboy, what are you doing? You will mess up the bed." Gunter proceeded to attempt a somersault that was awkward at best but placed him at the minibar where he pulled out a Coke and popped it open. Setting the half empty can on the mantel of the fireplace he noticed Esme had taken a seat on the edge of the bed and was smiling. "Ok, what gives? I'm not buying your story anymore, care to tell me what is really up?"

"Happy Anniversary."

"You mean, we are staying here tonight?" She stood and took several steps towards him as she spoke. "You were able to get us this room?"

"I called five months ago to make the reservation. By the way, we also have reservations at seven for dinner in the dining room."

Standing next to him at the hearth she performed her best Marilyn Moore imitation. "Enough time for a long lingering bath."

"Wonderful idea, wish I had thought of it."

"You should have because this bath is for me, myself, and I." She winked at him and then fell into his arms.

The fireplace beckoned their presence, as they felt a bit lethargic following the evening meal. The door to the balcony propped open invited the mountain air to mingle with the burning wood while offering an unobstructed view of the mountains lit by the moonlight. With his arms wrapped around her and her head resting peacefully on his chest he shared a quote he encountered several months earlier.

"Have you ever heard of Robert Bly?"

"No, I don't believe so. Can you give me a context?"

"Robert is a poet, among other things, who lives not far from me. Over the course of several years we have become acquaintances, one might even say friends. Robert writes what I would call, earthly poems. His images are from daily life, from the earth itself and he invites the reader into the poem and then challenges the reader to make meaning, to see life."

As he tucked his arms up under her breast she said, "This must be the weekend for surprises. I never saw you as a reader of poetry."

Savoring a sip of Merlot Gunter watched the burgundy liquid slowly return to a state of calmness before he spoke. "With the exception of Bly's work you would be correct. Poetry is not my thing. But with Bly there is something that draws me into the text. Listen to these words from his newly published book, *Loving a Woman in Two Worlds*, I mean, the title alone captured my attention." From memory he began to recite:

"Every breath taken in by the man
Who loves, and the woman who loves,
Goes to fill the water tank
Where the spirit horses drink"

Before he added his own words to the poem he waited for the words to soak into her pores. He intended for his words to give meaning to what he heard and felt. "Every breath I take says, 'I love you, Essy and this love is bigger, it is greater than just you and me. The horses drink from it. It gives life to others.'"

"I know what you mean because I have felt it from the first time I said, 'I love you'." Melting into his body that they might become one she asked him to share more. "Tell me more about how the title captured your attention."

"It's me, it's us. I love you in two worlds. In this world, where we are together for four days every year and in the world where we are not physically together, yet together in spirit, in thought, in heart. Two worlds, not what Bly meant, but our two worlds. And everyday, everyday I watch the horses drink from the tank and I know our love is strong."

"I love you, Cowboy. I can't wait to see where the next ten years takes us. Happy Anniversary."

CHAPTER 20
JUNE 12, 1990

Each individual, with his or her unique and colorful persona, flooded his thoughts as though these fictional individuals actually existed – and in many ways they did exist. It was not necessarily Sherman, Maria, Peter, Albert, Abe, Larry, Tommy, or Judge White who existed but the profile that each of these characters represented. And of course, that was the attraction, the enticing factor behind *Bonfire of the Vanities*.

The book had been published in 1987 and Gunter's students, some three years later, still referenced the characters and the plot in class as it related to a topic under critical analysis. In spite of that Gunter never took the time to actually read the book. However, as the movie based on the book was set to open in theaters later that year, he decided it was time to crack the binding.

He was hooked by the title assigned to the first chapter, "Master of the Universe." The Prologue pulled him in, as though he was a fish, hungry and defenseless, swimming to catch the bait but it wasn't until he bit on the title that the words that followed would reel him in. Therefore, the more he read the more he saw life unfolding before him.

In the community where he lived, a town not a city, and the small liberal arts college campus where he taught, he personally knew people who were the Shermans of the community, who considered themselves "masters of the universe." The chair of his department was one such character. The elder academician thought his moral character was somehow above others and therefore it was acceptable for him to "advise" female students all hours of the day and night in his office behind closed doors. He had met more Marias than he cared to acknowledge both in his professional career and volunteer work in the community. He rubbed shoulders with the Peters of the world waiting for the one big story, discovery, or event in their life to propel them over the top. He sipped coffee with the Alberts and Abes, the Larrys and Tommys all hoping to use their job or the people below them to climb the ladder of social and political success. He even dined with the Judge Whites who had social responsibility placed at their fingertips and took the burden seriously, yet somehow never was successful at making a difference. As his flight took him westward he realized he didn't need to travel to New York City to understand that the plot of the book was all around him on a daily basis.

Turning each page and moving towards Wolfe's final page he asked himself, does it have to be this way? Is this the end result of human nature? He couldn't wait to ask Esme if she had read the book and inquire if she thought this was the norm. But the question was never asked.

The airliner had yet to land in Seattle and Gunter bust forth with the news. He told himself that he wouldn't act foolish, he even prepped on how he could weave the announcement into the conversation. But seated next to her, holding her hand and feeling the warmth and acceptance of her presence, his game plan was sucked out the window at some 30,000 feet. "What do you think it would be like to sleep with a grandpa?"

"I don't know, I have never slept with one."

"Well, that's about to change."

Knowing what he actually meant, but attempting to turn the tables on him once and tease him as he did so consistently with her, she calmly responded, "What, rather than a bouquet of dahlias have you invited some old grandpa to join us for a ménage a trois?"

"Very funny, you know perfectly well what I mean."

Leaning in to give him a kiss she said, "Yes, I know what you meant. Congratulations, Cowboy, or should I say, Grandpa?"

"Cowboy will do just fine, thank you."

"Details and of course, pictures."

"Pictures?" It was his turn to take back the teasing. "I'm not sure I have any pictures with me."

"Yes, pictures! If you are a grandpa you have pictures. It wouldn't surprise me if you rushed out and purchased a new 35 mm camera."

Reaching into his briefcase he said, "I may have one or two with me."

"Yeah right. What, one or two from every day of the child's life? So, I'm still waiting for the details? Boy? Girl? Name? Date? Size? You know all the important stuff."

"Katie Marie. Six pounds nine ounces, born on the twenty-second of April. She is healthy with all ten fingers, ten toes, and is a very happy and content little girl. I might add, happy and content when she is resting in Papa's arms."

"And this is Elizabeth's baby who was married two years ago?"

"Yep" "And is she still pursuing her masters?"

"Oh yeah. Don't ask me how she does it, or I should

say, how she and Shawn do it, but they seem to make it work."

"Starting a family today doesn't mean that mom has to put her life on hold. In fact, in most cases mom can't afford to be a stay at home mom."

"I'm not suggesting they should give up their career goals or put life on hold, but I do wonder what it means for the children that they may be spending more time with someone other than their parents, or parent for that matter, during the critical years when learning grows expeditiously."

"My, my, grandpa, how old you sound. How would you have responded to that statement twenty years ago?"

"Probably the same way my daughter would if she heard me pondering such. But, that makes me feel as though I was successful in my job of being a parent."

As the wheels bounced on the tarmac at the Seattle/ Tacoma Airport the two had discussed and resolved the problems, or so they told themselves, of the current generation about to enter the world as young adults.

Fifteen years doesn't have meaning until placed in relationship to something, or placed in a specific context, only then does the measure of time in years have meaning. At least that was how Gunter perceived it. For example, one would never expect a child of two and a child of seventeen to perform a task with the same precision, yet that same fifteen year difference may not alter expectations in the work force between one worker who is twenty five and another who is forty. However, performance expectations on a football field between a twenty two year old running back and a thirty seven year old running back are enormous. Gunter could only conclude, as the thoughts rolled through his brain, that context defined the significances of fifteen years. Therefore, as he and Esme panted like two dogs on the verge of heat stroke he pondered, what did fifteen years means in the context of sex? Was there a difference between sex at thirty-five and sex at fifty? For that matter, was there a difference between a thirty-five year old and a fifty year old having sex with one another? That thought emerged because when he closed his eyes he saw Esme as the thirty-five year old he met for the first time in the Denver airport. When his hands scaled her body it felt like the firm, well-rounded thirty-five year old body he explored the very first time with uncontrollable excitement. He concluded that when it came to sex fifteen years made a tremendous difference even though he wasn't sure what that difference was. As he turned to share the silent musings with Esme his words were muted as she spoke over him.

The sex was as good as ever, her entire body trembled as she reached the heights of nirvana yet her mind, the strongest sexual tool, was distracted. She was distracted because her mind was cluttered with things that disgusted her and things over which she had little control and these things she needed to share with Gunter. One more time, even though she was 3,000 miles away from home and told herself she was emotionally disconnected from Mark, Mark was in bed with them. She was distracted because she had to inform Gunter of Mark's plans for the future.

"I'm sorry to cut you off but if I don't share this now I may eat the words and our time together will evaporate without telling you what the future may hold. And it has the potential to affect you."

"Don't worry about it, obviously whatever you need to share is burdening you."

Her words were laced with a strange mixture of anger and sadness. The delivery of each word caused her voice to crack and waiver while the flush coloring of her cheeks became dense. "Mark is considering a run for the US Senate seat. The entrance to his law office and our home has become a revolving door with a steady stream of people from all sectors encouraging him to run in '92. The Republican party, at the state and the national level, is convinced that Senator Fowler is vulnerable."

"And you don't want him to run?"

"Cowboy, you don't understand who some of these people are that have come calling. The pockets of these people are deep, money is not an issue."

"Okay, money isn't an issue."

"Do you remember me telling you how Mark has walked a fine line when it comes to upholding justice? He has defended and worked for some shady characters. They have paid him well to represent them and now they see an opportunity for him to represent them at another level."

"You're telling me there may be a mob connection?"

"Possibly."

"Have you asked Mark? Have you questioned him on this?"

"Oh yes, it started long before this topic of running for political office arose. We have argued about this issue many times and he assures me that this is not the case and accuses me of being overly paranoid."

"I understand your anxiety but I don't see what this has to do with me."

"Before I left this morning Mark informed me that he knows about us."

"Specifically about us or assumes what you are doing when you leave for four days?"

"A thorough investigation has been underway for the past several years. These people are not going to invest without knowing exactly what they are purchasing. Mark knows who you are. He knows that you are a Socialist, which made me laugh because I think that was more upsetting to him than the actual affair."

As Esme described Mark's aspirations to hold political office Gunter couldn't help but begin to place the cast of characters in Wolfe's novel. He wondered what peripheral character he would represent. The idea of casting himself in the novel made him laugh.

Confused Esme immediately questioned him. "Why are you laughing?"

"It reminds me of a book I have been reading."

"It's not funny Cowboy. Mark knows everything about you and he has promised to destroy you if we don't end this relationship. People will accept his wonderings, his lack of faithfulness, he is a man after all they will say, but they will not accept, they will not overlook the fact that his wife is not faithful to him."

"Everything?"

"Yes. I knew you were a grandpa before you told me."

The color drained from Gunter's face causing him to miss Esme's words about informing Emily and the College. But the moment she described the threat of telling his daughters the truth of their biological father his ears glowed fire red and like a raging bull his breathing grew heavy. As he spoke each word pounded the air as though it was the hoof of a buffalo striking the virgin prairie soil. "I am too old to start running now. My life is more than half over. Your husband doesn't know me if he thinks destroying my reputation matters to me. But my kids and you, Essy, that is another issue."

The bonfire of vanities had cast a shadow over the remainder of their days and nights. Gunter was angry as

Esme shared pictures someone had snapped of their trip to Leavenworth the previous year. The trip was meant to provide Esme an opportunity to gain a better understanding of Gunter's German heritage, possibly even offer a rationale for his stubbornness. Something Gunter persistently denied with a clarifying statement. "It is not stubbornness when one is right."

Esme and Gunter first become aware of Leavenworth in 1985 on the way to Sun Mountain. They commented that a day trip to the city would be worthwhile yet it took four years before a trip was completed. The itinerary included beer tasting, savoring a plate of cheese and bread, brats and sauerkraut and, of course, rich heavy desserts. They window-shopped the entire town. Esme couldn't control her laughter when she found a shirt with the words, "You can always tell a German, you just can't tell them anything." To see their smiling faces captured in photos, their embraces, their prost (toast) of beer steins, and their kisses increased the pressure of blood pounding in their chests.

Gunter felt violated that someone had invaded their intimate space at 13 Coins. Gunter wondered if, in the stack of photos, he would see himself making love to Esme. The photographer had access to their daily outings why not access to their room. The final picture was of Gunter and Esme sharing a kiss before she made her way to the gate to board the plane for her return flight home. There were no pictures of them naked but Gunter realized that did not mean they did not exist. He would not have been surprised to learn that Esme removed such photos. That was the sort of person she was, she never wanted to embarrass or humiliate another human being. That was one of the reasons he loved her.

It aggravated Gunter, as they slowly walked through the airport to find their respective gates, that fifteen years could not withstand the pressures of a husband who only cared about their relationship when he wanted to pursue his political desires. As they sat on elevated chairs next to a tall table Gunter realized that he was scanning the crowd, both those in the bar and those passing by to find anyone with a camera. At that moment he confessed to Esme that he too was allowing her husband to control his actions. He reached across the small table, brushed her hair from her chapped cheeks, the results of three plus days of crying, and whispered, "Fifteen years ago I made a promise to you that I would return – I will be here next year." He then got off his chair came round the table, kissed her passionately and walked away without ever looking back.

As he stepped through the doorway of the plane he wondered what would have happened to Sherman if he had never looked back…but then he quickly realized that life isn't about looking back.

CHAPTER 21
June 12, 1998

There are moments in life when everything feels as though life is going to hell in a hand basket. The second the alliteration wormed through Gunter's consciousness he was obsessed with its origin. Seated on the plane with no access to resources he eased his inquisitive mind by identifying a clearer definition. "...everything feels as though life is moving towards an inevitable disaster."

Whatever the definition, Gunter was confident there were events and situations that overwhelm a person and may cause one to consider giving up on life. Gunter also believed that there were encounters in life, by chance or by happenstance that changed everything. Some identified such encounters as luck, others as fate, and others as God's hand intervening, Gunter didn't care what label was attached he was simply thankful they existed.

The binding had not yet bore the marks of repeated fanning of the pages yet Mitch Albom had already defined how he was reunited with Morrie Schwartz, a mentor from his distant past. When Mitch learned of Morrie's condition, a death sentence of Lou Gehrig's disease, he altered his life in order to visit Morrie on Tuesdays. Subsequently the recording of these encounters were compiled and published under the title, *Tuesdays with Morrie*.

The Tuesday visits with his former college professor challenged Mitch to confront the cultural indoctrination he had experienced his entire life. Morrie invited Mitch to develop his own value system rather than act like a thirsty dog and lap up whatever was placed before him. Even on his deathbed, a bed he literally avoided until the very end, Morrie was teaching his mentee how to accept and ready oneself for death. Similar to how a knock on the door, or in Mitch's case watching Nightline, resulted in an encounter with an old friend that changed Mitch's life.

As the small, simply clad, brown covered book was carefully stored in the leather briefcase, a queasy feeling germinated in the pit of Gunter's stomach and spread like wildfire consuming dry kindling. His efforts to stand were rewarded with waves of nausea. For the first time in twenty two years he was about to pass through the airplane door without savoring the fragrance of Chanel No. 5, or having the tip of his nose tickled by a strand or two of her hair, or feeling her shoulder press against his chest as she leaned back to whisper an enticing, alluring comment.

He was planted in seat F, the window seat he hoped would afford him the opportunity to disconnect from those next to him in order to pursue possible reasons for her absence. The persistence of an older couple traveling to Seattle interrupted Gunter's solitude the moment he mistakenly shared that he traveled yearly to the city. Gunter learned from the woman seated next him, beaming with pride, that the purpose of their trip was to celebrate her husband's retirement from forty six years of working at the same place of employment. The woman, bathed in the overly sweet scent of Tabu, reminded him of his grandma when he desired to inhale the sultry taste of Esme. When the gray haired woman spoke of the place her husband had been employed she formed the words with great precision as though referring to one of the Seven Wonders of the World. Each word was delivered with confidence and clarity. "Cripple Creek Silver Mine."

Any other time Gunter would have relished the opportunity of sitting next to such a couple in order to hear of their experiences and the tales associated with such labor. To question what it was like to work at the same job for forty-six years and how his wife supported him throughout that time. Even though he had no idea what task the gentlemen actually performed at Cripple Creek the notion of working at a silver mine created an air of nostalgia sprinkled with rugged romanticism.

Rather than succumb to the temptation of conversing with the couple the entire trip Gunter carefully pulled Mitch Albom's book from his bag and directed his attention to the words on the page. If the husband or the wife had monitored his behavior they would have discovered that Gunter was not actually reading; the pages of the book were never turned. Instead, staring at the page Gunter created and analyzed every conceivable reason for Esme's absence.

The most obvious and easiest to grasp and accept was, she missed the plane. Or, better yet, the plane was delayed and the connecting flight out of Denver was given the green light to depart. He liked this latter option because it wasn't Esme's fault for not being seated next to him, that burden belonged to another. A small patch of turbulence bounced him back to reality and he explored other explanations. Perhaps she was ill and couldn't make it to the airport. The word "rocking chair" leaped from the page before him and forced him to recall twenty-three years of stories. He realized that in twenty-three years he never once heard Esme speak of being sick. Which meant she never got sick or she was a martyr and never spoke of it. The captain's instructions to the stewardess elevated his head from the book and from the labors of creating a convincing explanation.

Unwrapping a stick of Juicy Fruit for the landing he acknowledged that the explanations were all about removing responsibility from Esme. He simply was not about to admit that she was responsible for her absence. As the tires squealed and a thin layer of fresh rubber lied on the tarmac as the brakes were applied Gunter's body pressed forward and another possible option for Esme's absence moved through his thoughts. She was waiting for him at the hotel.

Racing north on I-5 towards downtown Seattle in a Toyota Camry Gunter clung to the idea that Esme, for whatever reason, took an earlier flight and was held up in the Vance Hotel. At the reception desk, winded from running the block from the parking garage he didn't inquire if Esme had arrived. He decided he would learn soon enough once the elevator stopped on the eighth floor and he turned the handle to room 816.

Expecting to see her seductively spread atop the comforter his heart throbbed once and ceased to pump and his throat closed making it difficult for him to swallow and eventually to breathe. Moving slowly to the entrance of the bathroom he swung the door open praying that she would leap from behind the shower curtain and surprise him. The only thing to greet him was a gush of air responding to the door swing and it whispered, "fool." His knees buckled as though he had just been thrown from a horse. Instinctively he stepped back until he fell onto the bed. His body landed at the very spot he had expected Esme to be.

Over the course of his professional career he had spent many nights in a hotel room when attending a conference.

On each excursion he elected to pay the extra cost in order to not have a roommate. He knew what it was like to be by himself but this was the first time he felt alone. TV did not console him nor did the radio offer any comfort. In fact, songs like *You Make Me Wanna* by Usher and *Candle In The Wind* by Elton John heightened the stress and drove him deeper into despair. Even though it was a Friday evening the only thing left was for Gunter to travel with Mitch and to sit beside Morrie and feast upon the wisdom he offered.

Rising before the city came to life the next morning Gunter stood outside Starbucks a block from the hotel waiting for the twenty something employee to complete her duties inside and unlock the front door. The only other people on the city streets at such an early hour were the homeless who took advantage of the morning light to find crumbs along the sidewalk and half smoked cigarettes tossed in the gutter. With the Venti size coffee of the day and a slice of banana bread, the only food Gunter had purchased since his arrival in Seattle, he returned to the hotel room.

Seated in the chair he stared at the bed envisioning Esme fast asleep. Many a mornings over the course of two decades he sipped his coffee and munched on banana bread as he watched her sleep. Her beauty was captivating. The sound of her breathing was life giving. With his eyes shut he saw her, he heard her, he even felt her, but disappointment struck when he opened his eyes to discover she wasn't present. As the final sip of coffee spilled from the cup he entertained the idea that Esme wasn't coming.

He had not considered such a thought since the spring of 1991 when he feared Mark's campaign for Senate office might keep Esme from making the journey to Seattle. But he discovered on the twelfth day of June that it was a meaningless fear as she greeted him the moment he stepped into the waiting area. It was meaningless because Mark's political dreams became a nightmare when his largest financial backer was jailed for tax evasion. To make matters worse, the individual was a client of Mark's.

A wine glass replaced the coffee cup and Gunter told himself he would not allow himself to waste his energy worrying if Esme was going to arrive. At that point he could not alter the outcome of the weekend, either Esme would arrive or she would not. The internal discourse was focused on moving forward.

Sipping the Merlot the pages of *Tuesdays with Morrie* practically turned themselves as Gunter was seated next to Morrie who was driven to a bed with his bodily fluids extracted through a catheter. His limbs failed to respond to his requests to move yet, as a teacher, he continued to teach. Gunter, like Mitch, absorbed every word, every expression, every…until…

The book, like blades of a helicopter, turned revolutions as it sailed over the bed and struck the wall. "Alive in the memory of those who loved him." The words played again and again, 'those who loved him." Mitch had just asked Morrie if he feared being forgotten and his answer provided the same response for Gunter as Usher and Elton John. He knew he would never forget her, Esme was the love of his life, even though, even though they only spent four days a year together. Not a single day passed without him thinking of her, whispering to her. But the most powerful tool of the devil wormed it's way into his thoughts, doubt. He questioned if Esme would remember him. As much as he worked not to worry the empty bottle of Merlot only returned him to a state of worry and doubt.

The combination of 12.5% alcohol and not sleeping the previous night kept Gunter from retrieving the book and increased the weight of his eyelids. He drifted off to visit another world. A world that was not restricted with such laws as gravity or time, or even logic and rational thought. Yet the one consistent presence that seemingly sailed from scene to scene was Esme. At times she spoke, at times she was clothed and at other times she was naked. No matter the state of her appearance or what she did or did not do she was beautiful. Watching his own hand reach out to touch her breast the action was interrupted by a pounding, the force and weight of which halted his arm from moving forward. He tried a second and third time and the same force, pounding, pounding, greeted each attempt. Before he could attempt a fourth try Esme faded from his sight and Gunter awoke to a knock on the door.

Groggy and stumbling toward the door, still a bit frustrated that someone would dare to remove Esme from his dreams he slid the deadbolt and pulled open the door. Having forgotten to undo the chain the door handle slipped through his fingers as it refused to open more than six inches. The figure peering through the narrow opening resembled someone whom he thought he should recognize but he didn't. The person spoke, "Hello Cowboy" and for the third time in less than twenty-four hours he became nauseous.

His fingers fumbled to unhook the chain and expand the entrance that his visitor might cross the threshold. Unfortunately for Gunter the more quickly he tackled the shiny gold chain in hopes of sliding it free from the track the less successful he was. It wasn't until he realized that he needed to completely shut the door in the face of the person standing in the hall that he was able to free the chain and swing the door wide open.

The flowing hair, the voluptuous figure, the wrinkle free complexion of the woman he remembered from twelve months previous was gone. The woman who stood in the hall and stepped forth as though it hurt to move resembled his mother only hours before she took her final breath. "Essy?" The name emerged and hung in the air as a question but that was not what he intended.

He wrapped his arms around her to pull her further into the room and he felt resistance, a writhing in pain beneath his touch. He released his grip and started to step back when she, with her eyes still closed, asked him to not back away. "Please, just hold me. It has been months since anyone has attempted to touch me for purposes other than to poke and prod my body."

Together, bodies melting like snow to form an inseparable union, they stood just inside the door. Gunter lost track of time for all he knew time stood still as well it should, his Esme had arrived. She was resting against his chest as she had so many times before and yet this was different. Things were different. He didn't know what it was, but it was.

Out of nowhere she offered up, "I love you, Cowboy."

Without hesitation, without needing to analyze the words, he spoke, "I love you too, Essy."

"No, I mean, I love you."

Realizing his shirt was damp from her tears he drifted back, lifted her head with his hand under her chin, and spoke softly, "Talk to me, Essy. What's wrong?"

"I need to sit down. I am totally spent."

He picked her up as he did twenty-three years earlier and carried her to the bed, but rather than tossing her he slowly lowered her body to the comforter. As he pulled the sides of the quilt up to cover her she was asleep. Carefully he placed his body next to hers as his mind raced, what has happened to my Essy?

Two hours passed before she awoke. Embarrassed that she fell asleep. Embarrassed for how she looked. Embarrassed for how she felt. Embarrassed that before she could explain she needed to pee. She needed to pee all the time. How do you tell someone who worshipped your body that your body has become the enemy?

As she pushed open the bathroom door she discovered Gunter had moved from the bed to the oversized chair and was nursing a full glass of wine. The scene of him seated with a glass in hand and a bouquet of dahlias peeking over his shoulder brought a smile to her face. Running her fingers through her Winona Ryder pixie cut made it appear as though the absence of hair was by design rather than an attempt to salvage a few strands. Crossing the narrow passage between the foot of the bed and the armoire holding the TV she realized that what she wanted was not to talk but to fall into Gunter's lap and feel his arms draped about her body. It required energy to talk and it was exhausting to revisit the journey she had traveled since the last time she rested peacefully in his arms. Her feet came together and she stopped when it occurred to her that the last time she felt at peace was one year ago in that very room. Before she took another step she told herself Gunter needed to know, he had a right to know and so after nestling in and feeling safe and protected she took him back to August 8, a day she would revisit again and again.

"It was a Friday, hot and humid, I remember I wore a sleeveless blouse, it was light blue and rather sheer." As though she forgot she was talking to him she added, "I have never pulled that blouse from the hanger since." Remembering where she was she lightly patted the back of his hand that was resting at her waist and then continued. "I didn't wear that outfit for that long, in fact, I wasn't wearing much of anything. The garment I was directed to wear felt like paper, a paper towel robe held closed by a thin string that kept coming untied. My butt was cool as I was seated on an examination table waiting for the physician to return. Have you ever sat in the doctor's examination room and listened to the conversations that occur in the hallway? I heard everything from weekend plans, last night's meal, the desire to get lucky, having gotten lucky the previous night with the new hot intern, and the depressing news that so and so was on their last leg. Whatever a last leg is." She knew Gunter would question the phrase so she beat him to it.

"Anyway, eventually it was my turn. There was a knock on the door followed by the turning of the door handle and in he walked. Chart in hand, still reading as he entered. It was the specialist, who I discovered are doctors who don't specialize in bedside manners."

"After tossing my file, which was becoming a small encyclopedia, onto the small desk he instructed me to lower the robe and his hand proceeded to feel me up. Well, not really, he was checking to feel for a lump, but there was no lump to be felt. What he was able to discern was that my left breast was slightly swollen and extremely tender. Any touching of the nipple was painful. When he stepped back and instructed me to pull the robe up I noticed that a nurse had followed him into the room and was present during the examination. He said he would be back shortly and that I should get dressed and the nurse should wait with me in the room. I remember thinking, why do I need a nurse to stay in the room?"

"It was probably another twenty minutes before the Specialist returned and he brought with him my General

Physician. The four of us formed a circle of sorts and my General Physician, a woman who I trusted with my life, pulled out the mammogram I had completed earlier and started to explain the conclusions they, as a team, had reached. I held up my hand to stop them and simply said, 'invasive lobular carcinoma.' The two doctors nodded and the Specialist took over. He said that because there was no family to create a family history profile it was difficult to know what path would be best to follow. Again, I stopped them and said that I wanted to tackle this cancer aggressively. I had watched too many women die because they were not assertive in their treatment."

Cautiously, as though attempting not to be noticed, similar to teenage boy on a first date working to get a feel of the girl's breast without being overly aggressive, Gunter's left hand moved upward. Using the same direct approach Esme used with her medical team she said "It's gone, the entire breast, in fact, they are both gone." To assure him she was not joking she took both of his hands and placed them where her breasts once were.

Neither one moved for several minutes. It was Esme who spoke first. "Do you want to see what it looks like?"

At that moment he realized it was not about what he wanted but what she needed. Motivated to say the right thing he said "umm" several times before actually delivering a recognizable word. It was not until he admitted to himself that it wasn't about being right it was about being honest that he made sense. He wanted to see not because he was necessarily curious but because she offered.

Responding to his "yes" she stood and pulled him to the bed while undressing.

He realized over the course of the past three hours that Esme's body was fragile and he needed to be careful. The last thing he wanted was to inflict more discomfort. But as he slowly lowered his body next to her she pushed him back and rolled on top of him and informed him, "I will not break. I want you to make love to me."

Initially it was strange and awkward for both of them. But they managed, they relaxed, and they found pleasure in pleasing one another with foreplay in slightly different ways. Esme's birthmark offered Gunter a place to begin after they kissed passionately and he began to move down her body. Without forethought he extended his arm and reached to fondle a breast that no longer existed as he remembered. She caught his wrist before his hand returned to her waist and she guided him across the smooth skin that had been reconstructed to her nipple. He lifted his gaze to follow his hand and to view what remained of her breast for the first time. Their eyes met and she whispered in the sultry voice that always made his body respond, "The nipples survived the surgery and they are still as sensitive as before." The invitation was clear and Gunter positioned himself on top of her and fondled her smooth skin and teased the dark amber nipples as he had always done.

When she was ready and demanded that he enter her it felt right. Without thinking they found the rhythm that had become a part of their sex life. It was pleasing, it was exiting, and rewarding for them.

Resting on his elbow at her side rather than on her chest he spoke, "Essy, I love you."

"I know."

"I mean, it doesn't matter what…"

She pressed her finger against his lips to stop him from attempting to explain. "I know. I just want you to rest your head on me."

With his head on her chest they fell asleep.

As usual Gunter awoke first but he remained as still as possible and listened to her breathing. He discovered that her flesh was growing wet and the beads of water originated from his tears. He was overcome with emotion. The thought of losing the woman he loved was unimaginable. How does one go on? He wondered how Mitch did not become a blubbering mess of tears every Tuesday he sat with Morrie. Unaware that Esme awoke he was startled when he heard, "It's okay Cowboy, it's okay."

"I didn't know what to think when you were not at the airport or here waiting at the hotel. I tried not to envision the worst, but it's…"

"I know, but I just couldn't meet you in the airport. I didn't want you to see me for the first time in that space. I want you to always have the memory of that first encounter. Plus, I didn't know if I would physically have the strength to endure the entire trip in one day."

"Is the cancer still active?"

"No, they think it is in remission. The prognosis is very positive. I still get tired very easily, I need a lot of sleep for my body to heal, and I need to pee all the time. Like right NOW."

When she emerged from the bathroom Gunter met her with a hug. "Essy, I trust you will always be honest with me, that you will tell me what you need and when you need it. Therefore I will move forward making suggestions and expect you to accept or reject based on what you need. So, are you up to dinner at 13 Coins? We will drive not walk this year, next year, well that's another story."

"I would love it."

A bit of disappointment registered on their faces when they discovered Todd was not working the evening shift but during the course of the meal and evening it actually was a good thing. They had the privacy needed to discuss any topic freely without fear of being interrupted.

Between the appetizers and the salad, while sipping wine, out of nowhere Esme interjected Mark into the conversation. It was Esme's first glass of alcohol since August 9th, on the eighth of August, after returning home from the hospital, her body still feeling the imprint of human hands and cold sterile machines, she opened a bottle of Chardonnay and savored the entire white substance throughout the course of the evening. Feeling confident, or perhaps, a chemically induced bravery, she directed the conversation to Mark. "During this ordeal Mark has refused to touch me. I'm not even sure he has taken in or absorbed my physical appearance. My nakedness drives him away. Even when I am completely clothed he can't look at me."

"I'm sorry."

"Why? You didn't do anything." Gunter would acknowledge within that she was not requesting answers but someone to just listen. So he sat and said nothing.

"He journeyed about three steps behind throughout everything. When he did show up at the hospital or for an appointment, or took a day off here or there to stay home, it was to support Emily. Emily." She smiled the moment her daughter's name was uttered but it was clear she was about to cry. Her body fell away from the table's edge and the glass of Chardonnay followed and she consumed nearly half the contents before she spoke again.

"It's because of Emily that I was able to make the trip. About midway through May, I can't recall the exact day, she asked if I was going to leave on the twelfth of June. It caught me totally by surprise. We had never discussed these four days even though we have openly talked about every other difficult and challenging issue in our lives. After choking back my surprise, pretending to have something caught in my throat, I shared that I wanted to travel but I just didn't know if I could manage it. Without a moment's hesitation she looked directly at me and said 'Mom, you're going. You need to spend the time away. You always returned so happy and full of life. If you need me, I will travel with you and stay in another hotel.'"

Unable to keep the words, he spoke. "Your daughter takes after her mother, always thinking about others."

"Well, that wasn't my first thought. I wondered what or how much she knew and then I realized, it didn't matter to her. What mattered was what this relationship has done for me."

"Have you ever wondered if Mark was as sensitive to your needs as your daughter and was able to share his desires with you, if you would be sitting here?"

"Yes, this past year I have wondered that more than any other time in the past twenty some years."

"And?"

"I don't know, Cowboy, I really don't know." The impregnated silence was disrupted as the waiter arrived with their salads and two more bottles of wine, a gift from the manager for their patronage to the restaurant.

Gunter poured the final drops of Merlot from the first bottle completely aware that at some point Esme would place the same question in his lap. Its arrival came more quickly than he anticipated.

Pushing the salad plate aside and setting down the wine glass in its place Esme leaned forward and asked, "So what about you?"

The sound of the question had a bite and he wondered if he irritated her with his question. He took a drink and considered how best to answer. "I honestly can say, yes.

I love YOU, Essy. I love you not because my relationship with my wife is unfulfilling, but because I love you. And no matter what happens between us, or God forbid, to you or me, our story will carry on."

"Our story? I don't understand."

He smiled and ended that part of their conversation by simply saying, "I have a book I want you to read and I promise, when you reach the end of the book, you will understand."

During the next two days she repeatedly asked for the book. She wanted to start reading that she might discern what he meant by "our story." Playfully he continued to put it off with the promise to place the book in her hands before they departed.

Streaming through the airport surrounded by hundreds of strangers he directed her to the wall out of the path of people scurrying to catch their flight when they reached her departing gate. He pulled the small book from his briefcase and placed it in her hands. The title struck her as odd. Quickly scanning the back jacket she commented, "This is about two guys, a student and a teacher, this is not us. I am not your student." The inflection in her voice rose, she was done being patient with him. She was angry. She desperately wanted him to just explain, to tell her the importance of their story.

With as much passion as he could express with his lips he kissed her and then he pulled back and reminded her again, "I love you Essy. I will always love YOU." He turned and walked away.

CHAPTER 22
JUNE 12, 2002

He sipped his coffee from a Styrofoam cup while his eyes never drifted from the woman across the aisle. Her beverage of choice was a diet soda, specifically a Diet Coke with no ice. A smart directive as more pop was placed in the cup. Apparently the middle-aged man dressed in professional attire had no problem staring at the twenty-something woman sporting a tube top that lacked adequate material to contain her boobs. The woman never returned the gentleman's gaze, there was no acknowledgement that she knew him, she merely worked her gum so that it snapped and cracked with consistency. The person seated next to her wore a St. Louis Cardinal's baseball cap pulled low on his forehead and covered his ears with huge earphones so that he was oblivious to both of them. He would never see or hear anything even if he desired. The guy pushing the cart smiled pleasantly but the moment the order had been filed his facial expression was anything but pleasant. As he worked to complete the request his eyes shifted right and then left. He scanned the faces, especially the eyes of everyone even though he pretended to focus all his attention on one individual at a time. But who would blame him, only nine months had passed since his place of work became a tool of murder.

Her eyes were tired, strained, and in need of a break from reading, so she took the opportunity to observe the other passengers on the plane to determine if they resembled any of the characters in the book.

She loved the cover design of the book. It was the reason why she selected it from the display rack at Barnes and Noble. Of course, the cover also displayed the Oprah's Book Club stamp. The woman on the cover, apparently in a café, could easily have been her. In spite of there being a gentleman seated directly across the small wooden table, the woman, with a heavy ceramic white coffee cup in hand, stared out the window. The man, equally distracted or, perhaps disinterested, stared at the table top, also with a cup in hand. She concluded that whether looking out or looking in through the windows of life no one really knows what the true story may be.

Esme opened the book again; it was the start of chapter thirty. She hoped this chapter would connect all the characters. The pages were dwindling, only two chapters remained, and there were so many loose ends, so many things lacking conclusion, so many people in search of meaning and purpose to life. So many…

The captain announced that Denver International Airport was only twenty minutes out and the crew should complete final preparations for landing. Esme had just reached the decisive point in the chapter, if not for the entire book. Tick, a high school student and a part-time employee at the café, pictured on the cover, conveniently managed by her father, speculated whether or not things happen quickly or slowly. She concluded slowly, but they may climax suddenly. Dropping in altitude and seated directly above the hydraulics that roared as the wheels were pushed from the belly of the plane, Esme contemplated perhaps that's how life was – in the absence of a clear linear plot - life moved in a slow lumbering, sometimes forward, sometimes sideways, and sometimes backwards motion until, quite unexpectedly, there was a climatic event or moment that resulted in the conclusion that life was a race speeding forward. Humans, Esme surmised, reached such an erroneous conclusion because they, herself included, fail to see, to comprehend the scope and sequence, humans don't grasp the full picture they merely search for the next climax.

As the aircraft slowly taxied toward the terminal she smiled devilishly. If she were honest she'd have to admit that she never would have imagined that, at the age of sixty-two, the word climax would carry sexual connotations. Yet, the warmth flooding through her body assured her she too was searching for, or rather, anticipating the next climax.

Heading north on I-5 after a comfortable and relaxing flight from Denver to Seattle, Gunter suggested that rather than heading directly to the Vance Hotel they stop for drinks and appetizers at a placed called, Zig Zag Café. The venue had been recommended by a colleague of Gunter's who was in Seattle for a conference after the first of the year. "Jim spoke more about Zig Zag than he did about the entire conference and he was one of the main presenters. Supposedly the place specializes in classic cocktails. Jim said their signature drink is something called 'Aviation.' If you like gin, it's to kill for."

Esme readily agreed acknowledging to herself that at sixty-two there were several ways to warm the flesh. Besides, a cocktail or two might just increase the intensity of the climax.

Spotting the café located along Pike Hill Climb was an adventure in and of itself. How they missed the place on their descent they had no idea. It wasn't until they started the climb toward Western Street that Esme noticed the place tucked under and next to the steps. Happy hour prices had been in place for the better part of half an hour and yet the bar/ restaurant was not bustling with over stressed workers in need of a cocktail. Although the host assured them, "Give it twenty minutes and there won't be a seat available. Especially since the sun made an appearance late this afternoon enhancing the attraction of the outdoor seating." Which was precisely where Gunter and Esme chose to sit. Sure enough, by the time their deep fried potato chips arrived colorfully complimented by a pair of thinly sliced beet pickles, the patio was filled.

Gunter knew it was not wise to mix different types of alcohol but a single "Aviation" was all his taste buds could endure. It wasn't that the drink was necessarily bad or mixed improperly he just was not a fan of gin. Jim's comment about gin now made sense, "it's an acquired taste." Gunter wasn't so sure he would ever be patient enough to acquire the taste, especially when there were bottles of Merlot just waiting to be uncorked. He ordered a glass of Merlot and Esme followed with a glass of Chardonnay.

A second plate of potato chips arrived as Gunter and Esme sat back and listened to the young crowd of professionals replay the stress of the day. A table of four, what sounded like computer programmers, lamented about the absence of technology to keep up with their visions. At another much smaller table, three women spoke in hushed tones about how their bosses were making subtle sexual advances toward them and how it was disgusting and demeaning and sadly how each one realized that was part of the game if they wished to move up the corporate ladder. Several tables had been pushed together to accommodate a dozen employees from the same office. The first two rounds of drinks yielded laughter but when the third appeared it was as though it signaled the start of a therapy session.

One by one each person spoke as the others listened. Each monologue was a laundry list of complaints directed towards "the man." Away from the restrictions of office life Gunter wondered if some from this group might have been secret followers of the band Rage Against the Machine, a band some of his nonconformist students rallied towards. No one offered a response, or a word of advice, or a rebuttal, there was only an occasional nod of the head and the raising of glasses to sip the brain numbing liquid. When the last person finished speaking a fourth round appeared on cue and the volume from the group erupted as a volcano spewing forth laughter and lewd comments that drowned out all other voices.

Esme leaned forward to share a comment, recognizing that the little café named Empire Grill, had been transported to Seattle. The characters from the book she sought to find on the jumbo jet had made their way to Zig Zag's. Even their waiter fit the script. "You are not going to believe this, but," she twirled her finger as she worked to include the entire crowd into her sentence, "every single person in this place walked right out of the book I am reading."

"What are you reading?"

"*Empire Falls*, it's actually the name of a small town in Maine on the verge of bankruptcy. Miles Roby, the central character, reflects on the dire situation in which both the town and the town's people find themselves. Russo, the author, creatively brings a host of people, all with their own unique stories, together."

"Sounds like the author has successfully pulled you into the story so that you find yourself writing the script for the characters before he does."

"Yes, it is very well written, but even more than simply being a good story, the book sheds light on life itself."

"How so?"

"Have you ever noticed how we drift towards the chaos in other people's lives when our own existence, or own life is chaotic, if not hell itself?"

Gunter was about to stand up and tell everyone in the restaurant to shut up and listen to this wisdom, but instead he waved for the waiter and ordered another Merlot. He was so close to admitting that his life had become hell, but he decided this was not the place or the time.

Esme, hearing herself pontificate such wisdom considered sharing the hell she sunk into seven months earlier, but was distracted as Gunter waved the waiter to the table and ordered another round. She didn't need another drink, she needed a sudden and unexpected climax. She needed to speak the truth. As the waiter handed her the glass of Chardonnay she found herself staring off into the window of life just like the woman on the cover of the book. She knew this was not the place or the time.

Even in their sixties, the headboard banged the wall, their voices became hoarse from screaming out in delight, and the climax came without warning. Recovery from the physical climax was about the only difference between sex for a person in their thirties and sixties. And of course, sometimes one needed to be more patient as the final ecstasy was slow in arriving. It was also not uncommon to require the assistance of outside help, extra lubricant, a toy or two, and for some males a little blue pill. Esme was surprised that Gunter didn't need any assistance in getting hard and staying hard. He did however remind her that it wouldn't happen again until morning.

Seated in the tub facing one another surrounded by bubbles it was time for another climax. Two, in fact, both of which arrived quite suddenly and very unexpectedly.

With his hands cupped holding a foamy layer of bubbles he blew them toward Esme. "You do realize that the only time I take a bubble bath is when I am with you."

"What's the matter, your manhood threatened by a few bubbles?" The smirk penetrated deeper than the words.

"Yes." He returned her smirk with a simple smile. "There is something mystical about the bubbles that weakens my ability to remain stoic and a bit aloof." With a toss of his hands into the air above the bubbles he finished his thought. "Or, maybe it's that we always consume a fair amount of alcohol before we…"

"Mark is dead."

The bubbles settled downward beneath the weight of Esme's revelation. In a similar manner the weight drove the air from Gunter's diaphragm and he was speechless. As his lungs filled with air he recited her words to make sure he heard correctly. Initially all he could push forth was, "What?"

With her legs crossed she remained lifeless. Her thoughts were flooded with images and words flashing like a neon light, but what distracted her most, in that moment, was that this was not how she had rehearsed this disclosure. She surprised herself that she had not, or could not share the news sooner. She wanted to tell him the moment she fell into his arms at the airport but that would not have been fair to him or her. Then it was Zig Zag's and that local was as inappropriate as the airport. The only other time was when they arrived at the hotel and she wasn't about to interrupt their lovemaking. So, naked, sitting in a tub of bubbles the announcement just sort of spewed forth. She too wondered if the bubbles had a similar effect on her.

More confident that he had heard her correctly Gunter pressed for details. "When, where, how?"

With her hand she cleared a path free of bubbles between herself and Gunter and then she answered. "Last November, while driving home late at night, Mark lost control of his Corvette and hit an embankment that launched the car and it struck a tree."

"Suicide?"

"Mark?" She nearly laughed. She caught herself realizing that Gunter had no way of knowing. "Good heavens no! The last thing Mark would ever do is kill himself. No matter how bad things got, he would never take his life. Mark was afraid of death. He couldn't understand how I could work in a place where people died. And of course, Scotty's death made him even more fearful."

"Was alcohol involved?"

"Oh yeah. He was both drunk and high, but not so far out of bounds that he could not drive. I know that sounds ridiculous but you had to know Mark. I don't have proof but I am quite sure he put on a sexual performance before embarking on the journey home. That had become his routine. He left the office sometime after nine and headed to one of the expensive restaurants in town for a late dinner. From there he would find himself a young lady for an hour or two of relaxation and five minutes of sex. He would sleep for an hour or two and then head home at three in the morning. The effects of alcohol and drugs by that time were minimal especially for someone who did that six out of seven nights a week. Plus, he loved his Corvette, it was a 1970 LT-1, he would never risk driving that car if he was not in control of his fatalities."

"Essy, what are you saying?" Gunter's wrinkled brow revealed that he didn't like the possibilities of where this was headed.

"I am saying, it has been a chaotic seven months." As

she spoke her hands worked the water away from her body as though she was symbolically creating space between herself and Gunter.

He reached out and took her hand in his. "Come on, don't shut down now. Talk to me." His eyes, combined with the words he spoke, invited her to trust him and to continue speaking.

The water was getting cool and the last of the bubbles had popped. Gunter suggested they return to the bed where it would be more comfortable and Esme could fill in all the missing pieces.

Resting in the crook of his arm with the sheet covering their nakedness Esme began. "I wish I could fill in all the missing pieces, but I can't. I can only speculate and in part, that's good because it keeps me safe and it gives me a healthy life insurance policy. Emily and my grandkids will never need to worry about money."

"Life insurance agents love to meet potential policy holders who have a fear of dying."

"OH yeah! Mark had more than one policy, each one larger than the pervious. In fact, he had several which initially raised the question of suicide. But once that was put to rest I was paid in full."

"But that's not the end of the story, is it? Perhaps, I need to steal the line from Paul Harvey, 'now, the *rest* of the story.'"

For several minutes Esme was silent and Gunter feared that the story was going to end there. He reached to the end table and plucked a dahlia and carefully stroked her cheek and neck down to the point where he met the sheet. Lifting the white cotton fabric just enough to place the flower beneath he traced the length of her arm until he dropped the purple blossom between her fingers. He kissed her cheek, her neck, and her shoulder and whispered, "When you're ready to tell me the rest of the story, I am ready to listen."

At that moment she just couldn't go on. Cowboy was right there was more to the story. There were so many more things to share, but at that moment she was exhausted. The climax of this story had drained every ounce of her energy. She needed life, if for only a few hours, to return to the slow course. She trusted him and knew he would not offer to wait if he didn't mean it. She also trusted that tomorrow would bring another climax or maybe two. And so for now she told herself...

The words jumped in and out of focus. It took a moment to collect herself and remember where she was and with whom. Although only the lower half of his body was visible the Seattle Times hid the upper portion. As sleep left her eyes and she adapted to the morning sunlight streaming through the window the headline from the sport's page became clear. "Lakers win another championship, O'Neal MVP." She shook her head to test that she wasn't dreaming. It was Thursday morning, she slept the entire night, she couldn't remember the last time that happened.

Sensing that she was awake, Gunter lowered the paper and welcomed her to another day. "Good morning my love."

"Good morning. Have you been up long?'

"It rather depends on your definition of long. Now if..."

"Oh will you stop it, you know perfectly well what I mean." She tried to sound irritated but her white teeth sparkling as she spoke gave her away.

"I know. I just couldn't resist."

"I am not going to rephrase the question, so answer it."

"Yeah, awhile."

Rolling out of bed directly in his line of vision she knew that he wanted her to question the word *awhile*, but instead she stopped in front of the chair, wiggled her butt and marched off to the bathroom. As she stepped through the doorway she heard him comment, "That's going to get you in trouble, you know." Leaning back so only her head was visible she answered him. "I certainly hope it does."

The morning was filled with light-hearted banter and joking with each other. Both realized they had not been this carefree and relaxed with each other in years. And although neither one said it they both understood that a milestone had been removed from this relationship.

The unusually warm weather pushed the couple to travel to Bainbridge Island. It had been years since they biked about the island. The changes were subtle yet profound. What captured their attention most and brought a smile was the development of a vineyard across from the island, and not just vineyards and small production wineries but a tasting venue. Bainbridge Vineyard offered a sampling of their wines. As they sampled, savored the full aroma (bouquet) by swirling the shot of wine in the glass and sipping half the shot and rinsing the liquid about their mouth before swallowing, their ears also were treated to the tails of more tasting venues set to open in the very near future. The tease offered was to return to Bainbridge Island in four or five years and enjoy a host of tasting rooms.

Armed with two bottles of Bainbridge Vineyard wine, one dry red and one semi-sweet white, the couple leaned against one another as they walked the commerce street of Bainbridge Island before returning to the ferry. Gunter confessed he needed fresh air to clear his thoughts before sailing back to Seattle.

Less than a block from the tasting room Esme dragged Gunter towards a wooden bench placed strategically between the sidewalk and the street. Before Gunter was comfortably seated Esme erupted, "You remember how I told you that Mark frequently represented clients who were connected with less than respectable individuals?"

"I remember." Gunter positioned himself so he could face Esme. "Wasn't his main financial backer for the senate run found guilty of tax evasion?"

"Yep. That one was small stuff as it turns out. When I started going through the records I discovered there were links to various crime organizations. The first few shovels of dirt barely hit his casket and I started receiving phone calls and uninvited guests knocking on the door wanting to make sure that all of Mark's records were destroyed."

"So how does all this relate to Mark's death, which I assume you are suggesting was no accident?"

"I am convinced it wasn't. On the day of September 11th Mark said, 'That's small potatoes compared to what people in this country could unleash if provoked.' I didn't understand what he was telling me and when I questioned him he merely said, 'Better you don't know.'"

"I'm not sure I am connecting all the pieces."

"A year ago in July Mark lost a criminal case that sent his client to prison for life. The case was under appeal but I guess the client decided Mark wasn't his lawyer anymore."

"You're serious, aren't you?"

"Yes."

"Essy, how have you survived? Why didn't you call?" Gunter stopped for a moment before he finished his thought. "I know you have the ability to track me down. In fact, I don't doubt you have my number."

"If you only knew, Cowboy, if you only kn…" Before she finished the sentence she turned away, reflective of her actions the previous seven months.

With his hand resting gently on her shoulder he directed her back towards the street and him. "What is it I don't know but should?"

Her hands folded in her lap as though praying for strength to continue she eventually spoke. "I punched the number into the phone several hundred times and then I would quickly flip the phone shut before hitting send. The one time I did press send the number dialed was to your office. I got your mailbox. You will never know how good it was to hear your voice asking me to leave my name and number and a brief message."

"But you didn't do either."

"I took it as a sign that I wasn't supposed to call."

"Essy." Her name dangled from the limbs of the tree above them. His heart ached, it had not hurt like this since the day he buried his beloved Skippy. No one but a cowboy would understand the bond between a cowboy and his horse. It would sound foolish to most people that a grown man should weep for the passing of an animal, a beast defined by some. But for Gunter, the golden palomino was his connection to life. That horse taught him how to understand a horse, how to be patient, how to be a better rider, how to be a better father, and how to respect life itself. As his tears wet the freshly packed soil that now held his Skippy he vowed to God, that if horses, if Skippy was not in Heaven, he didn't want to go. That same pain, that same sense of loss ripped at his chest. A second time he spoke her name, "Essy."

She saw the pain written across his face as she answered, "It's okay, Cowboy."

'No, Essy, it's not. It's not okay. You needed me and because of some stupid rule put in place twenty plus years ago, you couldn't call me."

"It's more than that Cowboy. You couldn't just drop everything and come galloping to my rescue. You have your life."

"You are so wrong. I would have been on the next plane."

Her head fell back and she stared up at the limbs of the tree. "Easy to say now."

"No. I mean it. What was the date of Mark's accident?"

"November 7th, why?"

"It was a Thursday."

"Excuse me, but how do you remember that. Since when did you develop hyperthymesia?"

"I haven't. But let me explain. The first semester I taught an evening class on Thursdays. As a part of the course the students were working on a rather large group project that, during the final weeks of the semester, they would present. On November 7th we met for roughly an hour in order to discuss the reading material for the week and to check in on the progress of their project. Realizing that they needed time to meet with their group members I sent them on their way to use the remainder of the evening for that very purpose. I arrived home earlier than normal to discover Emily and one of her thirty-something assistants in bed. You want to know what was totally strange about that encounter?"

She never spoke, she only nodded.

"My first thought, as I stepped back into the hallway and closed the door was, I remembered the story of how you walked in on Mark after an early dismissal from class." He laughed, not because it was humorous or funny, but because it was sad. His laugh was laughter of sadness. And then he continued, "I don't dismiss class early anymore."

Esme took his hand in hers and kissed the back of it softly. "Sounds like chaos to me."

"Yeah, that's a fair statement."

"And, where is Emily today?"

"She is in the house."

"Did either of you ever leave? Ever separate?"

"I moved into the guest room. I moved my office into that space. The girls, when they came home for Thanksgiving and Christmas, accepted the explanation of convenience. The grandkids were a different story. They lined up and spit forth questions."

"Of course they did, chaos doesn't make sense to kids. They have not been conditioned to accept it as a normal part of life."

"You understand now why I said I would have come?"

"Yes, I understand that in your mind, you think you would have come. But no, I don't believe you would have made the trip. I can see your bags packed, I can see you walking out the front door of the house, and I can see you sitting in the vehicle unable to drive away."

"Essy, listen to me, we are free."

"Are we? Could you really move and leave the college, your horses, your daughters and grandkids?"

"I was thinking you would move to join me."

"Really?" The sarcasm dripped like sap from a newly tapped maple tree, the word just hung in midair. And then she made it ever more biting. "What, were you thinking I would move into the guest room with you?"

"Come on. That's not fair."

"Why not?" The moment the question was delivered, whether Gunter attempted to reply or not, she knew she just delivered the climax. Those two words exposed so many more facets to their relationship than just fairness.

The ferry ride back to Seattle was quiet. Neither spoke aloud even though the internal voices never ceased. Both were thankful that Friday did not start in the manner Thursday ended. The four hour long trip to Olympic National Park, and specifically to Ruby Beach, would have been deadly under the shadow of silence.

The rental car pointed south on I-5 and sped along at speeds greater than seventy miles an hour until the road intersected with Hwy 101 and the car then traveled in a northwestern direction. Fueled with caffeine from a Venti portion of coffee and a Grande size hot chocolate delivered in cups labeled Starbucks, they had energy to burn. Confined to the car the only release for the caffeine was talking. They talked virtually the entire four and half hour trip to Ruby Beach. Nearly every topic was covered except for one. The vinyl car seats did not absorb any discussion directed towards answering Esme's question from the previous day, "why not?" Instead the focus was what's next? And that conversation, carefully crafted, avoided addressing "what's next?" in the context of their relationship.

Consumed by the contradicting scenery, snowcapped mountains and wild flowers blooming along a raging stream, Esme, newly retired from work, described how she desired to focus on painting. She wanted to try watercolors and oils. "Could you imagine what an artist could do on a canvas with this as their motivation?" She spoke of her frustration of how she allowed Mark to convince her that she was not an artist and painting was a waste of time and money. Weaved into the conversation was how the intentionality of painting could serve as a form of therapy, a way to express her feelings.

"Perhaps, that's what Mark feared. That you would express your feelings and that might cause you to question him, challenge him, or even worse yet, leave him."

"You are probably right. The past few months I have

come to realize, or admit to myself, how he was such a manipulator, how he needed to control things and, in fact, he was very good at it. I mean, think how he kept the crime bosses at bay, how he got their money, how he convinced them they needed him and how he kept it from me and how he survived for such a long period of time. And he used the same skills on me."

Gunter's inquiry about the possibility of creating an art studio offered the perfect transition for Esme to describe her adventures in searching for a new house. "Initially the excuse for moving was because the current house has too big of a yard, too many rooms to clean, and too many memories. But over time I was able to admit that it was about burying the past. It was about having a fresh start and that was okay."

Sensing that Esme was searching for an affirming word, Gunter said, "If nothing else, you deserve it. Have you found anything? Have you sold your place?"

"Yes and no."

"Yes, you have found something and no you haven't sold your place?"

"Yes and no to the first question, 'have I found anything?'"

Fortunately the stretch of interstate was straight because Gunter gave Esme a long look of total confusion.

"Let me start from the beginning. Realtors. Have you ever worked with realtors?"

"Can't say I ever have."

"My experience started off horribly. I called the top realtor in the area and I was transferred from one office to another, and each time I gave an account of what type of house I was seeking. Finally, I was directed to the office of the man whose name was associated with the business.

Rather than attempt to discuss my situation over the phone he scheduled an appointment for us to meet face to face. I was fully aware of ageism and sexism, I just never associated these concepts with my life, that was until I started working with male realtors. I was shown homes that I had no interest in, I was directed to the kitchen as though that was the place I would be most interested in seeing. I was told a single woman should live in this neighborhood, or this neighborhood has a lot of children and it would probably be too noisy. The list of assumptions projected onto me never seemed to end.

"Do you think they always were projected onto you and you could ignore them or did something change in how others viewed you because you are single and financially secure?"

"Great question. I really don't have an answer. I can only speak about what I know I experienced. Fortunately, many of those things went away when, by accident, I met a woman realtor."

"Accident?"

"Yeah." She stopped speaking for a moment as she laughed recalling the memory. "I was standing in the checkout line at the grocery store and I was reading the bold print headlines of *The Star* tabloid. The picture and bold print caption was something about a star selling a mansion and out loud I commented, 'Good luck with that adventure.' The woman standing behind me said, 'Excuse me, were you asking me a question?'"

"I quickly apologized and explained that I was merely commenting on the frustration of buying and selling a house. Without pausing she offered, 'I am sorry to hear that, perhaps I can be of some assistance, I am a realtor.' Three days later she was showing me houses that interested me and had lined up two families interested in viewing my house."

"Have you seen anything that is of interest?"

"Yes. When I get back I plan to submit an offer on a three bedroom, two bath home in the suburbs. One of the bedrooms would make a great painting room. It's more house than an old lady like me needs."

"You're no old lady, Essy."

"Right, and I am that same attractive, curvy woman whose breasts you fondled for hours, with the long hair you loved to stream your fingers through as we made love!"

"Just because you don't look as though you stepped out of a magazine complete with all the latest airbrush techniques, does not mean you're old. And it certainly doesn't mean I love you any less."

"Well, thank you, Cowboy."

"I mean it. As horses age, some of them become more seasoned. They are able to offer the rider more opportunities for growth. There is a maturity that is shared with the other horses in the herd and with the rider. I think what separates these animals from others are a sense of peace, an awareness and acceptance of who they are. Unfortunately, some of these horses are labeled as "dead broke" horses, but it's quite the opposite. The spirit has never been more alive. They are neither dead nor broke, they are at peace and they are one with all of creation. That's you Essy. That's the woman I feel sitting next to me. That's the woman I make love to. That's the woman who is not old but at peace."

She slid to the center of the front seat, reached out and stroked the back of his neck and playfully bumped the rim of his white straw hat threatening to push it down over his eyes. "I suppose I should be offended that you have compared me to a horse. It's something that has been done frequently throughout history, 'the old nag, war horse, broken down old mare,' and if anyone other than you tried to make that analogy, I would be upset. But I know precisely what you mean. To compare me to a horse, for you, is the greatest complement. Thank you."

"It's not something I have come up with, oh, the horse image yes, but it's really nothing more than Erikson's stages of life. If I recall correctly he associated the language of wisdom with this stage and said something about an identity being strong enough to withstand anything."

Her hand dropped into her lap and she turned away and stared out the window mindlessly. The beauty of the landscape couldn't penetrate the iris because she was a thousand miles away and the pictures firing in her brain were more than seven months into the past. Some were more than twenty years old. As though she spoke to the wilderness scene she said, "I have not always been at this stage. I was anything but wise or strong or…"

"I don't know what it is you see in the past, but I do know, you can't change it. Especially things that might include Mark."

"I know, but it is easier said than done."

For the next twenty miles they drove in silence.

It was Esme who brought voice back into the car. "What's on the horizon for you?"

Gunter described how he planned to start one more young colt. He acknowledged how, in all likelihood, the newly purchased six-month old colt would be the last horse he taught through all the stages of training. He was confident that he would continue to train two and three year old horses for clients, but it was different starting with a weanling. He also admitted that this horse would probably out live him or at least his serious riding days.

With her hand held up Esme waited for Gunter to call upon her. The moment he did she asked, "How did you determine this was the horse you wanted?" She stared at a picture of the colt as she asked the question.

"It's really a two part story."

"I think we have plenty of time."

"Let me begin with the second part of the story, which I think is what you meant with your question. I made lots of phone calls, several trips across the five state area, and then late last fall, into the month of December, just as I decided to wait until spring, I noticed an ad posted by a retired lady who was selling her last two colts. The price was reasonable, actually it was cheap, so I called. I visited and I came home with Nevada."

"You bought him because he was cheap?"

"No that was just icing on the cake. I bought him because I liked his disposition, I admired his conformation for a six month old, and because he was black."

"But, I remember you telling me once the color of a horse doesn't make the horse good or bad."

"It doesn't, but that's the result of the first half of the story. Early in September I noticed one morning when I went to feed that Skippy, the golden palomino, wasn't interested in rising. From the very first day I brought him home as a six-month old colt, also in the month of December, he would lie down every night, an unusual characteristic for most horses. So, initially I wasn't too concerned. When I fed in the evening he was standing but away from the other horses and he showed no interest in eating. His age was catching up with him. I hadn't ridden him much during the summer. He always had the freedom to roam the farm at will and when I rode others he could follow if he desired. Two weeks prior to that September morning he no longer fell into step behind the other horses. The vet confirmed that his heart was weak and it would only be a matter of time."

When Skippy didn't move two days later I called the neighbor who dug me a hole with his backhoe and I broke the law. It's against the law to bury a horse but I didn't care. If caught, I'd pay the fine. As the first few shoves of dirt covered his body I reminded God that if Skippy wasn't in Heaven I don't plan on going either. He was part of the family…"

As Gunter talked about his beloved Skippy Esme wondered what was more painful, his losing Skippy or the loss of his marriage? She was pretty sure she knew the answer, but wasn't about to ask.

"That horse taught me everything I know about horsemanship. He taught me how to be patient, how to be accepting, how to be consistent, and how to practice empathy. He taught me and every person that got close to him these things. Nevada is my new Skippy, but you never replace such a horse and therefore I couldn't purchase a palomino, I needed a color furthest away."

"Black."

"Yep. And the really funny thing is, Nevada is a paint horse, but other than his two white socks and narrow white strip down his forehead, he doesn't have any color. He is as black as night and Skippy was as golden as the sun."

Appreciating that talking about horses was a form of therapy for Cowboy she informed him that she was curious how working with a weanling was different than working with a two year old or a ten-year old horse. The remainder of the trip to Ruby Beach was filled with Gunter enthusiastically leading Esme step by step through the process of working with a horse at different ages.

The bed molded to their bodies as they dropped like bowling balls lofted into the air. Both were exhausted. Both thought about their desire for sex but agreed it would be more enjoyable in the morning. Both expressed how wonderful the day had been. Both were excited for what the future held for the other. Both silently mourned that the future for them would only be four days a year. And that was the climax, the chaos in an otherwise slow life.

Boarding the plane Esme stared at the picture on the cover of the book, *Empire Falls*, and she considered that maybe she had it all wrong. Maybe the couple was not ignoring one another. Maybe it wasn't that they were disinterested in each other, but the truth was they were comfortable. They were comfortable with themselves as human beings and therefore comfortable with each other. Esme allowed herself to consider that the couple didn't need to look at each other every minute to trust and respect each other. To be a couple was about more than holding hands and making googly eyes, or having sex every day. Being a couple in love was just that, being a couple. Being patient and waiting for the arrival of the climax, which arrives in a variety of ways. And that was the true story. She smiled, she wanted to shout, "I got it!" but no one on the plane would understand and it would probably scare some and get her kicked off the plane. So she just sat quietly and smiled. She smiled because she finally understood what Gunter meant so many years earlier, she was the keeper of his story and he was the keeper of hers. Their relationship had evolved into the telling of their story.

CHAPTER 23
JUNE 12, 2009

"That the world in all its shades of black and white is wonderfully interesting. That sorrow can be managed: it can be banished to a minor place within. And that even the most seemingly moribund life is open to the possibility of change – in youth, in middle age, and always." Nuala O'Faolain, 14, January, 2008.

Prior to reading from the introduction of *"Best Love, Rosie"* Esme shared how she came to possess a copy of the book published in Ireland on May 9, 2009, the one year anniversary of Ms. O'Faolain's death. Emily was aware of the enjoyment Esme received from reading the first four books penned by Nuala O'Faolain so on the day it was announced that a posthumous book would be released she ordered a copy. It had arrived the day before she left for Seattle.

Naked and reclining like a King and Queen supported by pillows and surrounded by artwork fit for royalty, Esme pulled the book from her oversized handbag and read aloud. Even though it was the fourth year since the Vance Hotel was renamed Hotel Max and had become an art focused boutique hotel they both marveled how everything changed. Similar to the seventies and early eighties the hotel once again was steaming with life and character. It was popular and a place to be seen. Unlike the final years of the Vance Hotel when, upon arrival they were greeted by a new manager each year, they were now recognized as returning guests. The first year sleeping under the new neon lit sign, Hotel Max, Esme commented that with the hotel filled to capacity she would need to harness the volume during their love making for fear of disturbing the other guests, to which Gunter immediately questioned, "Did you ever?"

Chapter 1 began, "I was in bed with Leo on Christmas morning in a chilly *penstone* near the docks in Ancona. It took courage to unpeel from his back and slide an arm out from under the duvet to ring…" Esme stop reading abruptly, as the book tumbled towards the comforter she turned to Gunter and commented, "In thirty four years not once have we ever discussed how we spend Christmas."

Retrieving the hard covered book that resembled a tent as it rested next to his leg, he handed it to her and said, "Maybe because for the past thirty four years it is always June and not December when we see each other."

She spoke as she turned the opening pages to locate the spot where she left off reading. "I am curious."

"Honestly, it has changed drastically over that time period."

"Are you avoiding the topic?"

"No, no, merely making an observation and I suppose seeking clarification, Christmas thirty years ago or last year?"

"I'm not asking for a detailed account year by year, but rather, are there specific customs or traditions that occur each Christmas?"

"Before I describe Christmas would you mind if I went and got a cup of coffee from the Starbucks on the corner?"

"I guess not if you really need coffee at this moment."

Gunter placed the coffee with caramel carefully on the nightstand and quickly stripped and crawled back under the covers next to Esme.

"Are you better now that you have your coffee?"

"Yes. But it's not about the coffee."

Totally confused Esme frowned as she rolled onto her side that she might look directly at him when she spoke. "Was that supposed to be some kind of a joke? Because if it was, I don't see anything funny, especially since you went and left without your key, forcing me to open the door naked."

"No joke. But it is related to Christmas. The tradition started when the girls were two and four years old. Old enough to become impatient but not mature enough to discern that I was attempting to make a point. The tradition on one level has nothing to do with Christmas and yet on another level it captures the very essence of Christmas. On Christmas Eve, after returning home from the candle light service, we prepared and ate a Christmas meal. The girls, in anticipation of opening their Christmas gifts, would rush through the meal. As the table was cleared and dishes washed they would begin to pester if it was time to open the presents. Making a fresh pot of coffee I would say, 'As soon as I have finished my cup of coffee.' Nervously they would wait, at times racing between me and the tree to make sure the gifts remained. The more they prodded me to drink the coffee the slower I would drink. At about the time they gave up any hope that I would finish the coffee I would announce, "I'm done."

Running her fingers across his chest and with an apologetic tone she confessed, "I'm sorry, I don't see the connection to Christmas other than teasing your kids."

"It has nothing to do with teasing, but everything to do with learning to wait. Advent, the preparation for Christmas, is a time of waiting, of anticipation. The arrival comes at an unexpected moment. Sort of like a climax. I wanted the girls to learn that God's arrival in the form of his Son occurred at the most unexpected moment. I also wanted them to discover that Santa Clause was just as silly as associating coffee with Christmas."

"Wait!" Esme, in her surprise, raised up letting the covers fall to her lap. "Your kids never believed in Santa?"

"Nope, and surprisingly, they turned out just fine." Gunter could not resist Esme's nakedness, he leaned forward and took her left nipple into his mouth and began to suck.

Playfully she pushed him away reprimanding him, "That's not fair, you can't use sex to change the subject."

Moving closer he said, "You want to bet?"

"No I don't because I know I will lose. But seriously, I want to talk about this…"

Looking up at her as he used his nose to caress the underside of her nipple he interrupted her. "I bet, what was his name, Leo, didn't want the woman peeling herself away from him either. He probably was ready for a little Christmas cheer. We can talk the rest of the evening, right now I am ready to hear you make the people next door uncomfortable."

Two hours later Gunter sipped cold coffee and Esme stepped from the bathroom refreshed from a quick shower. "I gotta tell ya Essy, I never grow tired of seeing you naked."

"Cowboy, you are just a horny old man."

"That I am, that…I…am." he delivered the words a second time very slowly and then added, "But only when you are next to me."

"Really?" The final comment surprised her.

"Essy, the last time I had sex was the afternoon before I boarded the plane to fly home one year ago."

"The same is true for me."

"Well then, is it any surprise that we are horny?"

"Guess not, Cowboy. I guess not."

Neither spoke for several minutes. Gunter nursed his cold coffee and watched the actors on TV make fools of themselves as Esme nestled next to him with her eyes shut. Sensing his cup was nearly empty Esme spoke. "Do you mind if I take a short nap before we have something to eat this evening?"

"Go ahead. My muscles could use another twenty or thirty minutes of relaxation."

She interrupted his channel surfing. "Don't think we are done talking about Christmas either, I want to hear more and I don't think you have it within you to keep putting it off with sex either."

Laughing he said, "Hey, but it will be fun trying." She never heard his reply, she was already asleep.

Todd sashayed up to the table and directed his initial question to Esme. "How is the lady of my dreams?"

"Very cute, Todd, thank you for that, but I have to tell you, if I am the lady in your dreams you are worse off than Cowboy here." Her hand took hold of Gunter's forearm and squeezed letting him know she was only teasing. Gunter never minded the teasing. She had a sexy air about her whenever she did.

"Are the two of you staying in the room with the picture on the door where the guy's hand is lightly stroking the woman's upper arm as though he is about to hook his thumb under her spaghetti strap and carefully guide it downward so that the lace top might follow?"

Gunter couldn't hold back the smile. "Yep, room 816. For the past thirty-four years we have stayed in the same room."

Sensing that Gunter was enjoying this banter and ceasing the opportunity to tease Esme a second time, Todd leaned across the table so he was closer to Esme than Gunter when he whispered, "Do you think they purposely selected that picture because of the two of you?"

The idea that Gunter and she might be the reason for the artwork selected for the door was more than Esme could fathom. Her cheeks grew rosy and red blotches surfaced on her neckline. "Todd, I'm ready for my Chardonnay now." The dismissal of Todd was to allow fresh air to filter across their table. Unfortunately, Gunter picked up the notion.

"Wouldn't that be something if we were the root cause for the selection of the picture on our door?"

"First, it's not our door. Second, the entire floor contains photos by Amy Mullen. And third,…"

Todd arrived at the table delivering their drinks cutting Esme short of being able to silence Gunter.

"Say, Todd, we were just discussing your idea about the picture on our door and Esme tends to agree…"

"I said no such thing!" Even though it was a Friday evening and 13 Coins was nearly packed everyone heard Esme.

Todd took a single step back and pivoted in order to make a quick exit, but before he was out of ear shot, he heard both of them laughing. He knew he should have pestered the bartender to pour the drinks more quickly. He left them too much time to plan their revenge. That's what he enjoyed about the couple, they always made his job enjoyable.

Before the cup of French onion soup was consumed Todd was summoned to bring a bottle of Merlot and a bottle of Chardonnay.

Discussing the options for dessert Esme was reminded of a Chocolate store she had read about that could possibly serve as a destination spot for tomorrow – as Todd stood patiently waiting for the couple to decide if dessert would serve as a bookend to the dining adventure he decided to make a suggestion for a possible destination outing. "If the two of you are planning to visit *Intrigues Chocolate Co.*, I would suggest you first do the Bill Speidel's Underground Tour, if you haven't already."

Returning the wine glass to the table Gunter said, "For the past ten years we have said we are going to do the tour and each year, as the final day of our stay in Seattle rolls around, we say, 'next year.'"

"*Intrigues* is only five or six blocks from the underground tour. It makes for a nice afternoon."

Esme thanked Todd for the advice and sadly informed him that if she was eating chocolate tomorrow she didn't need any dessert tonight.

Sunday evening, reclining next to one another, Esme continued to read aloud unfolding the adventures of Rosie and her aunt, Min. Gunter wondered, as he listened to Esme's voice become one with Rosie's, if they might be one and the same. Not in having lived the same lives, Rosie never married or had children, but as soul sisters. Both of them, perhaps, mourning the "what ifs" of life. Both of them struck by the reality that in the end, life is black and white. In spite of their efforts to color the world, to paint broad brush strokes, the truth was that black and white are at the base of each color and eventually as time wears on the colors fade and the scenes captured on canvas become more black and more white.

Laughter erupted as Rosie declared that making love

was the only worthwhile use of time. Esme and Gunter's kiss was an acknowledgement of agreement even though Sunday was about to pass without making love. As Esme prepared to pick up reading Gunter placed his hand across the page and pressed the book down. Esme assumed she knew what was going to happen next, her body began to tingle with the excitement of anticipating Gunter's touch. But instead of her erotic zones being touched her ear was poked. "Essy, if you could change something what would it be?"

Her assumption led to a moment of frustration and then disappointment but she eventually delivered the two-word sentence. "Change something?"

"Let me rephrase the question, do you have any regrets? Many years ago I inquired about changes you might make, but this is more about regrets."

The O'Faolain book was closed and tossed to the edge of the bed where it teetered for a moment, balancing like a gymnast attempting to stick a landing, before it fell from the bed, flipped once and landed next to Gunter's lone cowboy boot. The noise went unnoticed by Esme and Gunter as he listened for her answer and she listened to her inner voice telling her to speak the truth.

"Why didn't we ever extend our time together?"

"I suppose it's sort of like the architects of Seattle we heard about yesterday. Rather than challenge or change the paradigm we just went with it. Rather than address the flooding as the tide rose or the sewage threatening to drop down from those who lived above the city, they built a wall and eventually elevated the city. The walls constructed by us were the twelfth and the fifteenth and we packed as much as possible into those few short days. Do you even remember why it ended on the fifteenth?"

"It was the day you left after attending your friend's funeral. We set those dates because we were not sure the other would return the following year."

"That was the case the first two years, but after that I think I convinced myself this affair was less evil, less sinful, less threatening to my marriage if it wasn't longer than a few days and it only happened once a year with no additional contact."

It was the first time Esme ever heard Gunter speak of their relationship in this manner. As was her custom when she wanted to be taken serious she sat tall and straight and delivered each word with clarity. Gunter had seen this many times prior, the sheet in her lap and her chest bare. "Do you still think of us as an affair, something that is evil and sinful? I would ask about threatening your marriage but I know that is in name only."

Without repositioning his body he looked directly into her eyes, her lovely eyes and spoke, "I am surprised that you need to ask such a question. As I said, in the early years, yes, I thought that, but as my love and commitment grew, no."

Dropping back to the bed she apologized. "I'm sorry, I just never heard you refer to us as an affair. It caught me so off guard…"

He kissed her lips with his finger letting her know it was okay without ever having to say it. With his hand, again under the covers, weaved between her fingers Gunter picked up the issue. "Essy, we have lived a long life, nearly seventy years, is there anything else you regret?"

"Nearly every aspect of my marriage was less than satisfying or rewarding, yet I cannot say I regret it. That would be to only focus on the small picture, the larger picture tells another story. If there was no Mark there would be no Emily and no grandchildren, and there would have been no Scotty. Scotty," she sucked the words back into her body and waited. With her free hand she wiped away the tears before she permitted herself to continue. "Scotty could be a book by itself entitled, *Coulda, Woulda, Shoulda*. Not a single day passes that I don't think about him. A very wise person once told me, 'A life shouldn't be measured in years.' Do you remember sharing those words?"

"I do, and I still believe it, but I don't know about the tag, wise person."

She already decided how she would put closure to this topic and shift the focus off herself before he completed his thought. "I do not regret marrying Mark, but I do regret that I never left him. And you? Any regrets?"

His silence led her to fill the space. "I realize the book is about women, and even more specifically, a single woman, but men can have regrets too."

"Yes of course. I was simply trying to figure a way to share this one in a fresh manner. We hear it all the time, but it is a regret of mine. I wish I had spent more time with my daughters. When I was young I would listen to Harry Chapin sing, *Cat's in the Cradle and the Silver Spoon* and I would think that will never be me. And now, that's me! My daughters have grown up just like me. It sounds like a cliché, but it's the truth."

In silence they lie next to one another. Gunter was the first to move as he carefully scooted out from beneath the covers and retrieved two bottles of wine. One from the mini fridge and the other from the small table. Hoisting the cork from the bottle of Chardonnay with the dollar ninety-nine plastic handled corkscrew, Gunter theorized, "Perhaps that's what O'Faolain meant by, 'The world in all its shades of black and white is wonderfully interesting.' Each one of us want our lives to be something unique and special, different and colorful, but in the end, its black and white and my daughters have grown up just like me. And, here is the real kicker, maybe that's not so bad."

Each holding a glass of wine, Esme in her left hand and Gunter in his right, the couple used their free hand to hold the book so that Esme might continue to read to discover if Rosie reached the same conclusion. As the ink of each word bled into the words above and below so that Esme could no longer discern her place on the page and Gunter's fingers tumbled from the book they decided it was time to put Rosie to bed and allow themselves the same privilege.

Best Love, Rosie sat prominently displayed on the coffee shop table as Esme and Gunter strolled out the door of Starbucks hand in hand. While Gunter sipped his coffee and Esme her hot chocolate, they decided that they did not need to finish the book. They were more interested in finishing their own stories rather than having Rosie or O'Faolain finish it for them.

The Seattle air was damp and cool but neither cared, quite honestly, neither one noticed as they walked and talked and took time to stop and watch and simply let life wash over them. With her head on his shoulder Esme said, "I had forgotten just how much I like to people watch."

Smiling, Gunter added, "I had forgotten just how much I like to watch you watching people."

CHAPTER 24
JUNE 12, 2014

"Excuse me. Are you sure it is okay for the two of you to take this ride? It can be stressful. It's not uncommon for the wheel to stop and have people swinging at the top for several minutes as I unload and load passengers."

"There is an extra five for you if you make sure we stop at the top." The tan colored leather wallet was open and a five-dollar bill was partially lifted proving its existence.

"You want to see the city? The two of you want to snap a few pictures to add to your photo album?"

"No, I want to make out in front of the city."

"Cowboy!? You promise?"

The twilight was casting shadows and the Great Wheel's colored lights shimmered off the surface of Puget Sound and Esme's cheeks as she stood staring upward. The Great Wheel, a ferris wheel in its second year of operation was a wonderful addition to the waterfront. Unfortunately for Gunter and Esme it was only the first week of employment for the college age kid instructed to make sure all riders met the proper qualifications. He could not afford to lose the job and, as he tried to explain, he was only being cautious because the ride could be stressful.

Gunter's comment concerning his true intentions embarrassed the kid and he quickly opened the door to the ride and ushered the couple into the carriage that awaited them. The couple that stood behind Gunter and Esme should have been seated in the same carriage, to add balance and stability, but…the kid wanted to clear the mental picture of grandpa and grandma making out any way possible, and that meant out of sight out of mind, or so he hoped.

The glass enclosed carriage protected the couple from the breeze that blew off the water and the tiny particles in the less than perfect glass refracted the rays of light adding to the romantic setting. Hormones raging as though he was twenty once again, Gunter pulled Esme close to his body and wildly kissed her soft lips. As her body melted next to his, his tongue explored her mouth and he worked his hands beneath the layers of clothing. With a jolt the Ferris wheel stopped after the third revolution with them directly at the top. The car swung freely but neither of them noticed as their attention was focused on each other.

Their carriage, after another half dozen trips past the attendant, stopped abruptly and the door swung open. The kid's hand appeared inside the doorway to offer assistance to Esme as she carefully stepped back to earth. She was thankful for his presence, as she felt a bit weak. When Gunter reached for the kid's hand to offer stability he made sure the five bucks greased the kid's hand. As the kid thanked the couple for riding the Great Wheel he thought about mentioning to Esme that the buttons of her blouse didn't align, but the image of grandpa and grandma making out reappeared and he didn't need them lingering.

Confident that Gunter would want to head back to Hotel Max Esme suggested, "The Zig Zag is just up the street, you want to walk over for a drink and an appetizer?"

Somber, almost in a grim mood he answered. "Yeah, I suppose since we are already down here we could stop for a drink." Before she could say anything he added, "But you do remember it is quite a climb up from here."

Smiling she leaned into him as they stopped at the crosswalk waiting for the light to change. "You're a good sport, Cowboy. I promise, when we get back all your needs will be satisfied. But, really, I need something to eat. I have to watch my blood sugar."

"Are you diabetic?"

"So far I am able to control it with diet. I just need to be careful."

"Doesn't alcohol throw-off the blood sugar?"

"Oh yeah, I need to watch what and how much I drink. I now order Merlot, less sugar."

Seated in Zig Zag's, nursing a Merlot, Gunter sought clarification for a comment Esme made earlier. "I am curious, just what needs were you suggesting need satisfying?"

"Why Cowboy, I am surprised, are you suggesting that a few kisses and light petting satisfied all your manly desires?"

"Now wait a minute, Essy, I am not suggesting any such thing. I merely am questioning how you can conclude without asking me what my needs are and if they need attention."

"Well, I suppose I could be wrong, but based on the past thirty eight years I can say that once you get started you generally don't like to stop. Am I right?"

"It's not that I can't, it's just that with you being so beautiful and all, well…"

"So, was I wrong in suggesting there are needs waiting to be satisfied?"

"Well, no, it's just…"

"Stop the presses, did you hear that? You just admitted that I am right!!! Let's see, what is that, twice now in nearly forty years that you have acknowledge that I am right!!! That calls for another drink!'"

Friday morning came and went, at least in Gunter's mind. By the time Esme's feet hit the floor it was 10:30. Gunter had consumed the complimentary coffee from the mini-four cup coffee maker, enjoyed a Grande dark roast from Starbucks, and read every article in the newspaper. He was beginning to think that he should check to make sure she was still breathing. The night after all, had been filled with strenuous activities. To the untrained eye or young child it may have appeared as though they were wrestling. He didn't care what it looked like or for that matter if his shoulders were penned to the mattress for a ten count, he considered himself the winner. For that reason, even though his boredom had lead him to examine his calluses in great detail, the TV remained dark for fear it would disturb her slumber.

Waltzing back from the bathroom, her nakedness captured Gunter's attention. He was embarrassed to admit to himself that it took seventy plus years to comprehend that it was one thing to behold the beauty of a naked woman walking away; it was quite another thing to feast one's eyes on a woman as she gracefully strides towards you. His gaze slowly drifted down her body until he spotted the pulsating of her heart. The expanding and contracting movement of her heart shaped birthmark mesmerized him. As her left leg reached out the birthmark folded inward and partially disappeared and as her right leg stepped forth the birthmark reappeared in all its beauty. When she was within a foot of his chair he tossed the newspaper from his lap to the floor and, as though touching a wild colt for the first time his movement forward was slow, cautious, and the weight of his finger on her skin was extremely light and soft. Starting at the top he carefully traced the mounds of the heart and with great patience his finger slid downward like a rusty sled in snow. When he reached the tip of the heart her body tightened and her voice uttered excitement. He was tempted to move his finger down and across the neatly trimmed silver mound of hair that matched the color of her newest hairstyle of short layers with longer bangs. Instead, he slipped both hands behind her body, momentarily caressing her butt, and then pulling her down into his lap. "Essy, you are going to give me a heart attack one of these years."

"I thought you maybe needed a little excitement after reading all that depressing news."

Staring directly at her nipple he said, "As usual, it worked." Circling the dark brown nipple several times, careful not to touch it with his tongue, he leaned back and added, "But let's wait until this evening for round two of the wrestling match."

"Sure. Get me all hot and bothered and then just like a typical man, stop! You might be sorry later on."

"Oh, I doubt it. There has never been a time you…"

Pulling his head forward so his cheek was touching her nipple she stopped him in mid-sentence. "You have heard the saying, 'bake while the oven is hot'?"

Moving his hand between her legs he titled his head back so he could look directly into her eyes and he added, "I think I can get the oven hot again tonight. Besides, anticipation is half the fun."

"I sure hope so Cowboy."

She squirmed as he slowly removed his hand from between her legs. "I am pretty confident I know just how to get the fire burning. Since we have that settled, what would you like to do today?"

Esme reached for the blanket behind her and pulled it off the bed to cover her nakedness. "Something different. Something we have not done together."

"Do you have anything in mind?"

"I don't know. What can we do in the city that we haven't done to this point?"

"I was just reading in the sport section of the paper that the Mariners are playing in town."

"Playing what? Who are the Mariners?"

"The baseball team. They just finished a series with the Yankees and the Texas Rangers are in town for a three game series."

"Baseball, ha? I have never been to a professional baseball game. I would love to go. Can we still get tickets at this late date?"

"The way the Mariners are playing right now, I am sure we can."

Safeco Field offered a bevy of activities and it was a good thing since every inning offered a goose egg for a score. For a follower of baseball who enjoyed defense and good pitching, the Friday afternoon game was a dream come true. However, for a first time spectator who needed action to provide interest and purpose to the game the event left something to be desired. Fortunately, mild weather conditions coupled with the slowness of the game offered an ideal backdrop for people watching. Gunter's ribs were getting sore from Esme's elbow directing his attention away from the diamond and into the stands that he might witness another couple making out or a young child demanding a third hotdog.

As the Mariner players took the field in the top of the ninth inning Esme inquired, as she had done periodically throughout the game whenever something happened she didn't understand, "If neither team scores a point this inning does the game end in a tie?"

Dipping his shoulder in order to lean closer without losing sight of the batter Gunter responded. "They don't score points, but runs. And no, the game doesn't end in a tie. If each team fails to push a run across they play another inning and do so until a team scores."

"First team to score wins? That doesn't seem fair."

"No, the Mariners, as the home team always..."

Cowboy's explanation was interrupted as Andrus drove a single into center field and the surprisingly healthy crowd of forty thousand plus loyal Mariner fans groaned in disappointment. The level of frustration in the stands increased as Andrus successfully stole second and eventually third base. Gunter informed Esme that in spite of being an American League team, the Texas Rangers were playing what was called "small ball." Unfortunately for the Mariners, the strategy worked, a throwing error on a routine double play that would have ended the inning without the Rangers scoring, allowed Andrus to cross the plate. The Rangers went up one to nothing. In the bottom of the ninth the Mariners put up another goose egg and lost the game one to nothing.

Remaining seated in order to avoid fighting the crowd on the stairs and in the parking lot Esme confessed that this was probably her first and last ballgame. She enjoyed watching the people but said she could accomplish the same thing in the mall. As for the game itself, it was boring. "Watching paint dry is more exciting."

"Yeah, Essy, baseball is meant to be a game where spectators can relax, kick back, enjoy the outdoors, be surrounded by friends while being entertained by athletes playing a kid's game."

"If we are going to sit and watch people I would rather have a glass of wine in my hand and a comfortable seat. I say tomorrow we cross over to Bainbridge Island and see if the wine bars are up and running."

"Fine by me, you know I will never turn down a good glass of wine, or two."

Seated in *Suzanne Maurice Wine Bar,* the third wine bar of the afternoon, Gunter whisked Esme away to the wilderness of Montana. Separated by the tiny table that held two glasses, one filled with Saviah "The Jack" Cabernet and the other with Tait "Ball Buster," a bold, full-bodied red from Australia, the air was filled with adventures of Gunter's last summer's horseback trip.

"My youngest granddaughter graduated last spring from high school and requested that she and I take a horseback trip."

"Yes, I remember you mentioning something about the trip you were going to take in July, but I don't remember the details."

"Ella graduated from an innovative charter school that invites kids to take ownership of their learning through projects. Her senior project was an investigation of the events surrounding the Nez Perce trip from eastern Oregon to northern Montana. In an attempt to secure peace for the people Chief Joseph, among other leaders, determined Canada as their last hope for sanctuary. Unfortunately, after months of weary travel covering nearly twelve hundred miles, the seven hundred and fifty plus men, women and children surrendered at Chinook, Montana just miles short of the international border. Their story is another sad and painful chapter in U.S. history of the holocaust inflicted upon Native Americans. As a result of empathy Ella developed she decided that together we should follow the trail through Yellowstone and northward towards Chinook."

"I can only imagine the beauty you saw."

"Quite an understatement. The journey was about more than the viewing of nature that Ella read about from journals and reports that had been uncovered over the years. She became the teacher that I might experience in a minute manner that which our ancestors endured a hundred and thirty-five years earlier. We did our best, even for an old man of seventy-three, to live day by day as they might. We did not have a schedule so we took our time. Some days we traveled five miles due to the terrain and scenery and the next we covered thirty miles."

"Most memorable experience, besides time with your granddaughter?"

"I think it was our third day out. The horses had been nervous and overly cautious for the better part of forty-five minutes. I assumed there was a pack of wolves off in the distance that captured their attention. Anyway, we were on the final leg of having crossed this vast meadow, a full day's ride across when the grass as high as the horses' shoulders was mowed flat. Since it was less strenuous for the horses we proceeded to follow the path even though at times it meandered worse than a drunken soldier. It was probably another fifteen maybe twenty minutes when the tall grass of the meadow gave way to the forest. The moment we stepped clear of the dense grass there he stood, facing us. The horses had been aware of his presence the better part of an hour but I pressed them to continue forward, and at the moment, I wished I had listened to Nevada." Gunter stopped speaking and took a sip of his "Ball Buster."

Esme leaned forward, taken in by the story, and asked, "What was it, a wolf?"

"If only. If only." After delivering the chorus more slowly and with added emphasis Gunter placed his elbows on the edge of the table and rested his chin on top of his fingers before he continued. "There, less than fifty yards away, stood a moose. I am guessing, I didn't pull out a tape measure, but I am guessing his antlers were five feet from tip to tip. Fortunately our horses trusted us enough not to take flight. They merely stood still and stared at the moose. After a few minutes of sniffing and a bit of huffing the old guy turned and sauntered off into the meadow. We rode another half mile in the opposite direction to put some distance between the moose and us before we dismounted and tried to stand still even though our legs were shaking."

Esme initially thought Gunter was actually back on the horse coming face to face with the moose as he recounted the experience. He skin tone darkened and tiny beads of sweat appeared on his forehead, but when he dropped back against the chair and the red "Ball Buster" dribbled down his pants leg she became concerned. "Cowboy, Cowboy, you okay?" Dropping to her knees she knelt behind him and continued to ask, "What's wrong?"

His eyes closed and his jaw clinched, his lips parted as he informed her, "Inside my pants pocket - a small tin –…" His breathing was labored.

Panic controlled Esme's hand causing her to fumble her way into his right front pocket. Feeling nothing but the thickness of his thigh she muttered, "There is nothing here!" Even though she whispered others at a nearby table heard every word.

"The other pocket." His eyes remained closed and his body grew rigid revealing the intense discomfort Gunter was experiencing.

Esme pulled a small square tin from his left front pocket that contained a dozen small, off white pills. Following Gunter's directions she placed one pill under his tongue. Noticing his cowboy hat was about to fall from his head as the back of chair pushed it forward she removed his hat. Holding his hand as only a lover might, she inquired if she should call for an ambulance.

"No, just give the pill a minute or two to work."

"That was a nitro pill, wasn't' it? You are having chest pain, maybe even a heart attack."

Opening his eyes for the first time he looked directly at her and said, "It's no heart attack, merely a bit of discomfort."

"And you would know the difference because…you're a doctor?"

"Do you want to give me a heart attack? Please, stop arguing and just let the pill do its thing."

Seven minutes passed, Esme knew the exact time as she eyed the clock on the wall directly above the bathroom door, when Gunter squeezed Esme's hand startling her. She shifted her attention back to her patient and was instructed to place a second tiny white pill under his tongue.

Before the pill had a chance to totally dissolve she announced, "I am going to call 911."

"No, just wait, if this one does not lessen the discomfort, you may call 911."

"You stubborn German. You better not die on me!"

After several more minutes Gunter spoke without opening his eyes, "What, you think I want to embarrass you here in *Suzanne Maurice Wine Bar* by dying on you?" His jaw relaxing and a smile appearing preceded the sarcastic comment.

"You are feeling better I take it?"

"I told you, you just needed to be patient."

"PATIENT!" She nearly shouted the word. "Oh, don't even go there. Just so you know, we are **not** walking back to the ferry. If I have to I will find a wheelchair and push you back. And once we are back at the hotel I want a full explanation."

He started to respond but she immediately cut him off. "Not a word from you. You just sit there and get your strength back." She was both angry and relieved.

Both of them feeling a sense of security and safety behind the door with the picture of a man attempting to assist the woman out of her clothes, Gunter tried to replicate the scene. The moment his hand stroked Esme's shoulder she responded. "Don't even think about it. You have some explaining to do so get started."

Taking his place in the chair he followed her command. "Three and half years ago I had some angina."

"People don't have 'some' angina." Her finger gesture of air quotes told him she wasn't buying his explanation.

"Well, I did. It felt as though a horse was sitting on my chest. Anyway, the doctors took it all pretty serious as my blood pressure was elevated and there is a family history of heart failure. In fact, I am the first in the family to make it to seventy without suffering a heart attack. Needless to say, I was put through a battery of tests. Long story short, I was placed on blood pressure pills."

"Wait a minute, why I am hearing about this now for the first time? Isn't this something you should have shared with me three years ago?"

"I suppose…"

"You suppose? What else are you not telling me? I have the feeling there is more to this story."

"The first year the blood pressure medication worked

well. Then a year ago, on Christmas Day, I was working with a feisty three year gelding and I had another bout of angina. The doctors decided I needed to add beta-blockers to my medication since I wasn't about to give up horses."

"The doctors concluded that adrenaline was increasing the risk of your angina."

"Exactly."

"Okay, and the story here is…what?"

"The side effects."

"Sorry, you will have to forgive me, I am rusty on the effects of medications, it has been awhile since I handed out drugs. What are the side effects?"

"Impotence."

With wrinkles on her forehead she spoke with a degree of skepticism. "I don't recall any inability to perform last year, in fact, if I recall you were a raging bull. Or maybe I should say, moose."

"Funny." Gunter pretended to smile but he was not smiling, it was a smirk.

"I'm not trying to be anything but honest. You were not impotent nor have you been…wait a minute, wait one minute." She moved to the edge of the bed and placed her hands on Gunter's knees, causing their faces to be only a few feet apart. "When was the last time you took your medication?"

Gunter stared at the carpeting as though the back of his earring was missing.

"I'm serious Cowboy, when did you last take your meds. It certainly hasn't been since we were together."

"Three weeks ago. I stopped taking the medication three weeks before coming here and I became fully functional again."

"Damn it Gunter, do you have a death wish!" As she

spoke she pushed herself away from him and sat upright on the bed.

"Gunter? What happened to Cowboy?" He couldn't remember the last time he heard her call him anything but Cowboy.

"I am mad at you, but even more, I am disappointed." Her head dropped and she stopped herself before she said something she would regret.

Selecting each word carefully he attempted to respond. "Look, Essy, I didn't want to disappoint you…"

"Do you really think that the only reason I show up every year is for the sex? Well, you need to know I have many gentlemen callers who would like nothing more than to have sex with me, but I tell them that dinner and a movie doesn't earn them sex, in fact nothing will. The sex with you is wonderful, don't get me wrong, but it is wonderful because it is an expression of our love. I have allowed myself to feel things and do things with you I would never have imagined or allowed with anyone else, but Cowboy, if we couldn't have sex ever again I would still be here year after year." She again leaned forward, rested her hands on his knees and lightly kissed him on the lips. Still softly touching his lips she spoke, "Now, do you have your meds with you?"

"Yes, but…"

"There is only one butt here and it belongs to me, which you may admire anytime your heart desires, except for tonight. Tonight you are going to rest.

Swallowing the medication Gunter took a second sip of water that he gurgled in the back of his throat as he teased Esme. "But tomorrow is a new day and I plan to stake claim to that butt."

Turning and walking towards the bathroom with his glass of water in hand she exaggerated her steps so her hips pressed higher and dropped lower. At the doorway she stopped, leaned back and as sultry as possible said, "We'll see, Cowboy. We'll see."

Under his breath he muttered, "That's all I am asking, just let me see."

It didn't matter if it was year one, year twenty, or year thirty-nine, departing never got easier. In spite of trying a variety of strategies to diminish the stress of leaving one another it all boiled down to the same thing. They were going their separate ways and would not see or speak to each other for another three hundred and sixty one days. Gunter, in his loneliness of watching Esme walk away one year, calculated the hours, eight thousand six hundred and sixty-four and then the minutes, five hundred and nineteen thousand eight hundred and forty, of their separation. Those numbers made him even more depressed so he decided to focus only on the number of days.

Fortunately, the anxiety withered slightly once the plane left the ground. Gone was the opportunity to cast all reason and logic aside and remain in Seattle indefinitely. Unlike most years, their flights departed within minutes of each other and both Gunter and Esme sipped Starbuck's coffee and tea respectively and replayed each moment of the past seventy-five hours.

Without remorse both were able to recognize that they didn't know how many more years they had left together. Both were able to recognize that in a new and different way they cherished their time together more fully. It was the little things that gave depth and meaning. It was a look, it was the way a word was delivered, it was a playful tease, it was a naked dance, or it was a simple kiss. Both were able to recognize that they wanted to be together 24/7, a phrase Esme's granddaughter taught her, yet each realized that was not their story. Their story of love was but four days a year. Their story wasn't about days but commitment, fortitude, persistence, and the making of a relationship in spite of barriers, of everything that said, "No." They simply said, "Yes."

The relationship that started as a physical attraction became love, the unexplainable commitment of loyalty.

The moment their respective flights reached cruising altitude they reclined their seats slightly and whispered softly, "I love you, Cowboy." "I love you, Essy." And they closed their eyes and dreamt of what the year might bring.

CHAPTER 25
JUNE 12, 2015

A strange feeling overwhelmed Esme's entire body thirty minutes into the flight from Atlanta to Denver. Her muscles tightened, her skin tingled with the eerie combination of being chilled and flush, and her head began to ache. Her first thought was, "am I having a heart attack?" She was fully aware that the signs of a heart attack for a woman were different than for a man. But it wasn't a heart attack. It wasn't a medical condition that prompted a bodily response. The throbbing in her head was a response to a flash of light that streaked before her eyes. In an effort to minimalize the movement of her head she methodically rolled her eyes first right and then left to scan the core of the plane for confirmation that others experienced the light. Yet none of the fellow passengers demonstrated any signs that they had witnessed the flash of light. Closing her eyes to eliminate external distractions Esme accepted the possibility that perhaps the flash had not occured before her eyes but rather behind her eyes, in her brain. Unfortunately, such an explanation offered few viable solutions to justify the muscle contractions and the warmth and cold that radiated through her body.

Her eyes remained closed and a blanket was draped across her body to ward off the chills as she continued to sweat and the pain in her head slowly began to subside. As the pain decreased clarity of thought emerged in addition to a process for an explanation. For some reason Mrs. Bakken's name popped into her thoughts. Mrs. Bakken was an older woman who belonged to the same book club that Esme had when she was much younger. Mrs. Bakken, Esme never had learned the woman's first name, at the time of the book club was probably younger than Esme was as she sat on the plane, and yet Esme could only envision her as an old woman.

Mrs. Bakken arrived at the weekly book club meeting, a meeting she never hosted, with her book in one hand and her crochet basket in the other. From the moment she started pulling yarn from the basket until lunch was served her comments had nothing to do with the book. On many occasions Esme wondered if Mrs. Bakken read the assigned chapters or if she could even read. What Esme never doubted was that at some point during the meeting Mrs. Bakken would wander off into the realm of the unbelievable. Mrs. Bakken loved to regale the women with strange stories of how she received premonitions of events as they unfolded. With the jet closer to Denver than Atlanta Esme realized that much of what Mrs. Bakken described fit with what she had experienced, except for one minor detail, there was no vision or premonition of events unfolding.

Although she never put much stock into the stories the old woman shared Esme began to reconsider. Maybe the woman wasn't an attention seeker like the rest of the book club members concluded but was someone who needed to share the unexplainable with others. Maybe she was desperate for affirmation that she was not crazy. Maybe she was a prophet sent to speak a word of warning and no one in the book club took the time to listen. Maybe... At that moment Esme decided that as soon as she landed in

Denver she would call her daughter to make sure everyone was safe.

After repeatedly assuring her mom that everyone was just fine Emily questioned Esme to make sure she was okay. "Mom, you don't sound very stable. You sound a bit rattled. Is everything okay?"

"That's why I am calling you, honey, to verify that everything is okay."

"No, Mom, I mean with you. Did something happen?"

"I'm fine. The flight from Atlanta to Denver was a bit rough and I guess I just got worried that maybe a storm was headed your way."

"No, Mom, everything and everyone are fine. There are no weather warnings of any type. Promise me when you land in Seattle that you will call, okay?"

"Oh honey, there is no need for that and besides I don't want you worrying if I forget to phone."

"But Mom…"

"My connecting flight departs in a few minutes and I need to use the restroom before boarding. I love you and I will be home in a few days."

She was the last passenger to board the plane and did so only after the attendant pestered her for the fourth time. "I am sorry madam, but if you wish to take this flight to Seattle you must board at this time. The pilot has ordered the door closed and the flight attendants to prepare for takeoff."

"Yes, yes, I apologize. You have been most patient with me. I am meeting a friend and I assume his flight has been delayed."

"I can assure you all connecting flights for this flight arrived on time and as of twenty minutes ago all flights scheduled to land here were on time. Perhaps your friend is taking a later flight?"

"Yes, perhaps."

The taxi ride from the airport to Hotel Max was lonely. Esme didn't realize how much she enjoyed sitting in the car with Gunter and commenting how little the scenery changed from year to year. The ride up the elevator was even more depressing as the hotel manager had informed her that Gunter had not checked in. As she unlocked the door and placed her hand atop the gentleman's hand in the picture she wondered if a bouquet of dahlias awaited her arrival. She also remembered how she stopped Gunter from undressing her the evening before their departure for fear his heart could not endure another love-making session.

As had existed for the previous thirty-nine years a bouquet of purple dahlias greeted Esme as she quietly stepped into the room. Without Gunter present the room felt cold, dark, and lifeless. Dropping her luggage on the bed she reach for the card, neatly tucked between the stems, that bore the same words it had for the past thirty-nine years, "I love you with all my heart and soul and strength and mind. Cowboy."

Positioned in the center of the queen-sized bed she was grateful that she adhered to Gunter's directive to always carry a book. Although he was able to transition into reading from a Kindle she preferred the old method of reading from a book. There was something soothing about turning the pages and feeling the weight of the book against ones' fingers, plus it was less stressful to her eyes. She had no idea why she grabbed, *Considering the Horse*, by Mark Rashid, from the bookshelf as she walked out of the house earlier that morning. She actually, upon Gunter's recommendation, had purchased the book several years earlier but never cracked the binding.

Every noise that sifted beneath the door resulted in

Rashid's book landing on the comforter as Esme anticipated that Gunter was about to enter the room. The sound would evaporate and she was left to the silence of the room and Rashid's story of how he encountered an old man who taught him how to love the horse. Even though the hour grew late she refused to contemplate the notion that he might not be coming. Even though the experience from earlier in the morning engulfed her body she continued to dismiss the "episode" to not having had breakfast. An empty stomach, she told herself, can be deadly.

She awoke with her cheek flush from the warmth of the sun shining into the room. Startled to discover that she was still clothed, since their first night together she slept in the nude, she pushed the vase aside to read the time displayed on the clock radio. 10:33. The warmth on her face spread down her neck and eventually her entire body was prickling with heat. Something was not right she told herself. He should be here by now.

For Christmas her grandchildren gave her an iPhone. "Grandma," they said, "it's time you catch up with the rest of the world and use something other than that old flip phone." Esme couldn't understand the need for such a contraption but since it was her grandkids the gift was graciously accepted. They schooled her on how to use the phone's features but until 10:35 on Saturday, June 13, she had never accessed the Internet via her phone.

As she tapped the face of the phone carefully in order to strike the proper key on the miniature keyboard her finger twitched. Her nervousness was compounded by what she feared might appear seconds after she hit send. Using the Google search engine she sent the following: *Gunter Rettmann, MN*. She was thankful that Mark had told her Gunter's last name and state in which he lived.

The phone slipped through her fingers before she completed reading the top item on Google. The phone rested on the bed, right side up, staring at her as though mocking her fear. Reluctantly she bent forward to read the entire phrase printed in bold blue letters.

Gunter Rettmann, died tragically...

A flash of light raced passed her eyes and her muscles tightened and she felt both flush and cold in the same moment. Luckily she was leaning over the bed so when she fell forward – the result of fainting – the landing was soft. She came to quickly but could not force herself to tap the screen and open the Mankato Free Press link to read the article.

With her arms crossed as though attempting to hold herself, as she once held her children when in need of comfort, she rocked atop the bed. The very bed in which Gunter held her tight and whispered in her ear and traced the outline of her heart and made love to her, she was forced to hold herself. The words dribbled from her mouth as if she was but a child speaking for the first time. "Cowboy, how could you? How could you leave me?"

The clock radio flashed 5:00 pm. She realized she could not postpone the inevitable, she needed to read the story.

Beloved college professor and horseman, Gunter Rettmann, died while doing what he did best, offering assistance to another in need. En route to the Minneapolis – St. Paul International Airport early Friday morning, Gunter stopped to assist a young woman with changing a flat tire. While at the side of the vehicle, Professor Rettmann was struck by a drunk driver attempting to flee the Highway Patrol. Dr. Rettmann was killed instantly. The drunk driver walked away without a scratch. Funeral arrangements are pending.

Todd carried to the table two bottles of the best wine 13 Coins had in stock. He uncorked the Chardonnay and waited for Esme to grant approval before he filled her glass. Before opening the bottle of Merlot he inquired, "Will Gunter be arriving soon? Shall I wait to open the wine?"

Without looking up Esme instructed him to open the wine and fill the second glass to the top and then to leave her alone until she signaled for him to return. Trusting she knew what she wanted and needed, Todd did as instructed and stepped away from the table.

Seated outdoors in the cool evening breeze she could smell the salt from Puget Sound making its way inland. It was amazing how when sorrow finds a resting place and it blinds the eyes with tears, how the other senses come alive. She heard things and smelled things she normally would have not noticed. Even in death, Gunter was offering her a gift. She smiled, clicked her glass against his and took a sip. She had forgotten how she enjoyed the sweet taste of Chardonnay. Staring out into the dimly lit night she noticed two lovers walking past the restaurant. Their arms swung in unison as they held hands. They stopped at the gate to the outdoor terrace as though trying to determine if they should stop for something to eat. Esme watched closely as the woman, in her early thirties, leaned in close and kissed his neck. He responded by pulling her close to his body and running his hand up the side of her body and stopping as it reached her breast. Another kiss from the woman replaced any notion of food and the couple turned and walked off into the darkness of the night.

Filling her glass a second time she admitted that she still enjoyed people watching and creating stories to fill in the missing pieces. But instead of crafting their story she simply wondered what story those two young lovers might be creating and where would they be in forty years from today?

Directing her attention to the empty chair she pondered the likelihood of her being able to tell her daughter about Cowboy. Emily knew that she traveled to Seattle to meet a man but that was all she knew. As she finished her second glass of wine she established that Emily was not the person to tell. Rather than listen to the story and appreciate Cowboy for who he was she could ask a steady stream of questions. Instead, she decided that her granddaughter would be the recipient of the story. She would learn of Cowboy and the love they shared.

Standing two strides from the table Todd interrupted her thoughts. "I am sorry, I know you said you would signal when you were ready, but I am worried about you. Are you sure everything is okay."

Looking at Todd for the first time she said, "I am fine, thank you, Todd."

"Will Gunter be joining you this evening?"

"Not this year."

Taking a step closer to the table he said, "I am saddened to hear that."

"This will also be my last visit as well."

"Oh." Todd was silent for a moment trying to digest the entire conversation. "Please know that the entire evening is on the house."

"That's not necessary."

"You and Gunter have been valued patrons of the restaurant. This is but a small token of our appreciation. If you don't mind, may I ask, is Gunter ill?"

Wearing a smile of sheer delight she answered him, "Actually, he is riding a horse named Skippy."

EPILOGUE
June 15, 2015

A bouquet of forty purple dahlias shipped from Pikes Market in Seattle, Washington was placed by the funeral director at the head of Gunter's casket. The arrangement created quite a stir as no one, especially family members, could explain the bouquet's presence. Even the pastor stopped to admire the flowers and read the card that said, *Yes, Cowboy, there are horses in Heaven. I love you with all my heart and soul and strength and mind.*

ACKNOWLEDGEMENTS

I wish to thank the following people without whom *Horses in Heaven* would never have seen the light of day. Shannon Ishizaki, owner of Ten16 Press, believed in the possibility of this book and supported me throughout the entire publishing process. Kaye Nemec, my editor at Ten16 Press, labored to enhance the quality of the writing. I am indebted to her skills and keen ability to assist me in becoming a better writer. Cover Photo by Shelley Paulson. The receptionist at the Hotel Max in Seattle permitted me to roam the halls of the hotel admiring the artwork and gaining a sense of the rich history contained within the walls. Michael, the waiter at Zig Zag Café, when he learned that I was doing research for an upcoming novel made time to share the story of the restaurant and entertain questions about Seattle. Todd, the waiter at 13 Coins, modeled the generosity and hospitality my wife and I experienced everywhere we went in the city. Finally, my wife, Tammie, assisted me in my research and never questioned as I hunkered down night after night pounding the keys of the computer. To these people I say, "thank you."

If you enjoyed *Horses in Heaven* I invite you to look forward to my next two novels. *Stars in Heaven* is a Christmas story that unfolds in a German town in Minnesota complete with a cast of lively characters. *Fingerprints of Noepe* is a story that develops on Martha's Vineyard as twin sisters attempt to reconcile sixty-eight years of jealousy and hatred. You can follow me on Facebook under Douglas Knick. I welcome your comments.